## FAMILY SLAUGHTER

Inside the house, Inspector Busch began his detailed examination of the first of the two bedrooms where the murders had taken place. He knelt beside Jolaine Lanman's body to study her injuries. The smell of blood was heavy as he came close to examine her neck. A man's shirt was wrapped around her throat and a pair of black-handled scissors were embedded deep into the front. The bloodstains on her sweatshirt across her breast indicated she'd also been stabbed in the chest.

As he looked at the blood-smeared face, he wondered why this woman and her three-year-old son were chosen as the victims of such savage fury.

**ORDINARY LIVES DESTROYED BY EXTRAORDINARY HORROR.**
**FACTS MORE DANGEROUS THAN FICTION.**
**CAPTURE A PINNACLE TRUE CRIME . . . IF YOU DARE.**

# DEADLY DECEPTION

## ALVA BUSCH

PINNACLE BOOKS
WINDSOR PUBLISHING CORP.

## ACKNOWLEDGMENTS

My deepest respect to those who lived the realities of this crime. As one of the investigators in the Lanman case I was presented with the worst and best in people: The human quality that man possesses that surfaced from this tragic occurrence was a display of courage by many. I am grateful to the scores of people that helped me complete this book. Special thanks goes to Rose Mandelsberg-Weiss, Editor-in-chief at *True Detective,* and to my literary agent, Susan Crawford for her support during the hard times. My appreciation to Paul Dinas, Executive Editor at Pinnacle Books, for his patience with me on my first book.

PINNACLE BOOKS are published by

Windsor Publishing Corp.
475 Park Avenue South
New York, NY 10016

Pinnacle and the P logo are trademarks of Windsor Publishing Corp.

First Printing: July, 1993

Printed in the United States of America

# One

Wednesday, September 27, 1989, started out a very ordinary day. The first signs of sunlight crested over the green stretch of fairway marking the perimeter of Villa Madero, a middle-class subdivision in the vicinity of Belleville. The tranquil neighborhood stirred to life. Encircled by both golf course and open farmlands, this four-hundred-home tract seemed far removed from both the pace and violence that define major urban centers like St. Louis, twenty miles west.

It was this very peacefulness that convinced John and Jolaine Lanman to select Villa Madero as the site for their dream home four years earlier. Beginning construction on the three-bedroom house in 1985, they looked upon the area as an ideal location for raising a family.

No one could have predicted the events that would shatter the idyllic community on this Wednesday morning in September.

At 7:30 A.M. John Lanman backed his silver 1984 Volkswagen out of the two-car garage and headed for work. Wednesdays were house cleaning and laundry days for Jolaine. The thirty-four-year-old housewife donned a grey sweat suit in which to perform her household chores.

Their son Kenneth was up bright and early, too. His dark hair swept to the side, and a smile ran from cheek to cheek. He was a boy that always seemed happy.

Jolaine picked out a blue sweater for the three year old to wear with his grey jeans, part of the routine that prepared him for nursery school. By the time 8:15 A.M. rolled around, Kenneth was ready. It was her next-door neighbor Brenda Nixon's turn to drive the children to school two miles away. Hugging him as they walked from the kitchen, through the garage which led to the driveway, Jolaine walked her son to the Nixons' house. She secured Kenneth safely in a seat belt before going back inside. She poured a cup of hot coffee for herself and then began loading her husband's shirts into the washing machine.

At 8:30 A.M. Jolaine called a woman friend who lived down the street and asked if she could pick up a gallon of carbonated water for her when she went to the store. The neighbor dropped off the bottle of water at 11:30 A.M. Within the next thirty minutes Kenneth returned home from preschool. Leaping out of the car, the young child waved the paper he clutched in his small hand. Beaming with pride, he displayed to his mother the yellow and green finger painting assignment he had completed. Jolaine chatted with the neighbor who brought Kenneth home. Plans were made for Brenda, Jolaine, and Sebastine Hope to meet at Jolaine's house later that afternoon for a walk around the neighborhood. Both Jolaine and Sebastine were expectant mothers.

The morning hours of Wednesday, September 27, 1989 were uneventful for Jan Conder, who worked as a special events director at a local hospital. Having given birth to a beautiful daughter earlier in the year, she had decided to convert the basement area of their home into her business office.

Jan's secretary, a nun from the hospital, had stopped by to have some papers signed. The two sat at the kitchen table discussing business, while Jan fed her infant daughter. Shortly after 2:00 P.M., Jan received a phone call from her mother, who lived around the corner from her on San Mateo. She asked her to look out her living room window at the blue car sitting on her street. Carrying the portable phone in her hand, Jan moved to the picture window.

The blue car turned onto her street and parked beside the vacant lot at the side of her house. Jan watched the man seated in the car. He seemed to be arranging something on the front seat. Standing at her glass storm door, she could see the rear of the blue Oldsmobile clearly. She saw the Illinois license plate and the 3-BBB on the left side of the trunk lid.

The driver opened the door and got out. He

placed the strap of the large black shoulder bag over his right shoulder and walked over to Chula Vista Street. After Jan lost sight of him, she walked back to the kitchen and talked with her mother about the stranger.

At 3:05 P.M., when Jan's secretary left, the car was still there. Later that afternoon, Jan saw the blue car backing down her street. It backed past the intersection and pulled forward onto San Mateo. The same man was driving. It was 4:45 P.M. when he drove away.

The temperature was in the low fifties at 4:00 P.M. as Sebastine arrived at Brenda's house pushing a stroller. Brenda called Jolaine on the phone but she got the answering machine. The two neighbors walked toward the Lanman residence, clad in sweat suits. Sebastine, with her eighteen-month-old son in the stroller, waited at the edge of the driveway as Brenda walked into the garage. She placed her hand on the knob of the kitchen door at the side of the garage. The knob would not turn. Jolaine had been her neighbor for the last three years, and Brenda could not remember the door being locked during the afternoon. Friends would walk into the two-car garage and come in to visit. She knocked and waited. There was no response. She called out to Jolaine. Still nothing. Walking out of the garage she stopped abruptly, thinking she heard a child scream.

"Did you hear anything strange?" asked Brenda.

"No, I don't think so," said Sebastine, tending to her young son in the stroller.

An uneasy feeling about the locked door and what she thought was a scream led Brenda to walk around to examine the front of the house. There were no lights on inside. The shades were down in Kenneth's room but that was normal. He usually took a nap in the afternoon. Rejoining her walking partner at the end of the driveway, she talked about the uneasy feeling she had.

It was probably just a yell from a child playing nearby. Jolaine's Aerostar van was parked in the garage. Maybe she was having a hard time getting Kenneth to take a nap. The two women began their walk around the neighborhood. Fifty-five minutes later as they finished their walk and stopped at Brenda's house, they saw John Lanman drive down the street toward his house. They waved and John returned the wave.

John pulled the Volkswagen into the garage and parked beside his wife's van. He walked up to the kitchen door and tried to open it. It was locked. *Strange,* he thought. *Maybe Jolaine had taken a nap with Kenneth and had locked the door.* Using his key, he opened it and walked down the hallway to the master bedroom. The door was closed. Opening it, he looked inside. They were not sleeping on the bed. He walked into Kenneth's bedroom. No one was there. Turning to leave, he noticed something on the carpet in front of the closet. A wet stain. Looking closer, he could see that it was blood.

The fear that parents have about harm coming to one of their children tore through his mind. His heart raced and from that point on he was in

9

the grip of a nightmare. Running back into the master bedroom, he stopped when his eyes caught something out of place. The afghan lying alongside the bed seemed to be covering something. He raised the afghan up. There under the bed was Jolaine. Her face was smeared with blood. Her eyes were wide open and fixed. A pair of scissors protruded from her throat.

He was devastated. His next thought was of fear and anxiety about his son. *Kenneth. Where was Kenneth?* He called out to him as he began to check the room. At the end of the bed, he saw a smear of blood on the blue carpet. The tan dustcover on the bed that hung to the floor had smudges of blood on it. Kneeling at the foot of the bed, he raised the dustcover. He could see the small socks that covered the feet of his son. Reaching under, he pulled out his son. It was too late, Kenneth had not been spared by the intruder.

Running into the kitchen, John picked up the portable phone on the desk. He punched at the phone buttons through tear-filled eyes. He dialed 911, then waited. A woman's voice answered and told him that there was no such number. His nightmare worsened. He needed to get help but the simple task of dialing the phone became a labored chore. His mind raced. He threw the portable phone down on the couch in the living room and tried the phone on the end table. Again punching the button on the phone, he dialed Zero and got no response. He hung up and ran next door to the Nixon's house, surprising

10

Brenda Nixon. Before she could speak, he blurted out the shocking news.

"Brenda, call the police. I think Kenneth and Jolaine have been killed."

# Two

Inspector Alva Busch returned home from the crime laboratory at 5:00 P.M. Taking off his gunbelt signaled the end of his duty day. He had completed his assigned duty week on Tuesday morning. It had been a long week. Twelve cases: six burglaries, two auto thefts, and four homicides. Looking forward to a Wednesday evening at home with his family, he took off his sports coat and tie. He had agreed to cover the ten-county area while the other three investigators in his unit were upstate at a funeral. They were expected back soon.

Busch sat behind the large desk in his den. His fingers moved rapidly over the keyboard of the word processor. He had started writing true-crime stories for publication in detective magazines in 1985. He found it relaxing even though it covered the everyday theme of what he did for a living. He investigated murders. His thirteen years with the Bureau of Crime Scene Services of the Illinois State Police had involved him in over four hundred murder cases.

The ringing of the phone on the desk beside him brought Busch's typing to a halt.

"Hello," he answered.

"Mr. Busch," said a female voice.

"Yeah."

"This is Crime Scene Service. We just received a call from St. Clair County Sheriff's Department. They have a double homicide and need a crime scene technician in Belleville. Do you have the duty?"

"Yeah, I'm covering for Dee Heil. I'll take care of it. I live in the west end of Belleville, the scene shouldn't be to hard to find," said Busch.

*Belleville,* thought Busch. *Belleville is like a town where Beaver Cleaver could live. Their homicide rate may be one a year.* East St. Louis, at the base of the bluffs west of Belleville, is where he usually spent most of his time. *The scene had to be outside of Belleville city limits for the county to be involved.*

Busch turned off the word processor and called the St. Clair County Sheriff's Department. Dispatcher Daniel Crockett answered the phone.

"Yeah, this is Busch. You got a double?" he asked.

"Al, I'm not sure on the details but they need you at Chula Vista over in the Villa Madero Subdivision."

"I'm not familiar with that area. Is that east of Belleville?"

"Yes, take 161 east about three miles. Villa Madero is on the south side of the road," said the dispatcher.

"Okay, I got it now. Tell them at the scene not to move the bodies."

"What's your ETA?"

"Twenty-five minutes."

Busch hung up the phone, picked up his jacket, and walked downstairs to the kitchen. The dining room table was set for supper. His wife would be upset that he was leaving without eating with the family. Linda looked up at him as she set the main dish on the table and noticed he was wearing his jacket.

"Where are you going? We're going to eat in a few minutes."

"I got a double on the east end of Belleville. I'll be gone all night probably. You and the kids go ahead without me," said Busch, kissing her on the lips before leaving. She just nodded sadly and went back to setting the table. After years of being a cop's wife, nothing surprised her anymore.

Backing out of his driveway, he radioed the state police dispatcher and advised of his activated status.


St. Clair County Deputies Steve Mathis and Steve Jones were already en route to the scene after receiving a radio message: "Units fifty-three and fifty-four respond to possible homicide scene on Chula Vista."

Dispatcher Crockett had taken the call from an

hysterical woman. She told him that her neighbor's wife and son had been murdered. Crockett remained calm as he spoke with the excited woman, got an address and dispatched an ambulance to the location, hoping that the victims were not dead.

Lanman waited in the driveway for the police. When Mathis and Jones arrived, Lanman was asked to wait outside the house while the officers searched. They wanted to be sure that the perpetrator was not hiding inside.

The two officers inched their way through the house. They paused and listened for sounds of movement. The silence of the house could be felt by them. At the end of the hallway, they entered the master bedroom. Viewing the bodies briefly, they walked outside. They had seen enough.

Additional police units arrived. Captain James Lay and Lieutenant Johnnie Davis of the Sheriff's Department assisted in securing the scene. Yellow crime scene tape was used to cordon off the area around the house.

Busch pulled his unmarked squad car into the Villa Madero Subdivision, and noticed the area was well kept. He wondered what kind of scene awaited him. He had worked just about every type of murder: those involving children and babies as victims, gang executions, love triangle slayings, and contract killings. He cleared his mind of personal matters. When he worked a murder scene, he concentrated on facts and physical evidence.

Walking up to the yellow tape that ran chest

high across the Lanmans' driveway, he spoke to Captain Lay.

"What have you got?" said Busch.

"Two dead inside. A young boy and his mother," said Lay.

"Who found them?"

"The husband, when he came home from work."

"Where is he now?"

Lay motioned. "He's the guy in the white shirt leaning against the squad car."

Busch turned and looked toward the squad car parked on the south side of the driveway. He studied the man briefly before approaching him. He looked dazed. Busch had seen the expression before. The look that people have when their world is crushed.

This was the part of his job that he hated. Lanman had just lost the two most important people in his life and now Busch had to get a detailed account of what he did after he returned home in order to process the crime scene. He also needed all of the information he could get about the victims.

He had to question John Lanman about many aspects of his family life to get a feel for the crime scene, and why the victims were killed. The timing was always bad for the bereaved. Valuable evidence could go undetected if the interview wasn't done as soon as possible. It was best to talk before the crime scene was entered by the crime scene investigator. This allowed him knowledge of what should and should not be there.

Something as simple as an object out of its normal place could be overlooked if the investigator didn't know what the norm was.

Busch knew that many of the questions would sound cold and heartless, but they needed to be asked. He would have to push to get the information to conduct a proper investigation.

"Mr. Lanman, my name is Al Busch. I'm with the Illinois State Police. I know this is a very hard time for you but I'll be processing the crime scene, and I need this information to help catch the person who did this."

The inspector watched the man that leaned against the squad car. Lanman fought back tears as he tried to speak. His words were slow in coming. His voice was soft and shaky.

"Okay, what do you need to know?"

Busch felt uncomfortable. He sensed the pain the man was enduring as Lanman labored with responses. The man was asked to describe step-by-step his action when he returned home: what items he moved inside the house and what movement of the bodies was done by him. Busch kept eye contact with him as they spoke. Lanman would stop talking momentarily to gain back his composure and wipe his bloodshot eyes. He was having a hard time coping with the simple questions at this point.

Waiting for the slain woman's husband to pull himself together, Busch looked for blood on the man's clothes. From the distance of three feet, he could not see any obvious bloodstains. He would get Lanman's clothes but would be tactful in ob-

17

taining them. Busch had worked enough homicide cases to know that there were no sacred areas in a murder case. None. All persons involved in the investigation must be screened. There would be no exceptions.

The next question was about the number of keys to the house. There were only two sets of keys. Jolaine had one set, and John had the other. Busch pushed further with the interview. He asked to see the soles on John Lanman's shoes. Lanman leaned against the car and raised one foot and then the other. No blood on the smooth soles of the brown loafers.

Lanman seemed to grow weaker while he leaned on the car. He crossed his left hand over his chest to support his right elbow. Then raised his right hand to his face and bowed his head. Busch signaled Captain Lay that he wanted to talk to him.

"This guy is out of it. He needs to go to the hospital and get medical attention," said Busch.

"What do you think?" asked Lay.

"I don't know yet. Gut feeling, I don't think he's good for the murders."

"I guess I'll send Miller to the hospital to get a statement if he decides to go there."

"Make damn sure Miller gets his clothing. I want Lanman's clothes."

It was suggested that Lanman go to the hospital to get checked out. He walked with unsteady legs to the ambulance parked nearby, the pain in his chest intensifying. His wife's and son's bodies still remained inside the house. He didn't want to leave them. Reporters shouted questions at him as he boarded the ambulance. Lying back on the stretcher, he closed his eyes. The door to the ambulance shut with a bang.

Busch took charge of the crime scene. From this point on, he was responsible for security. Standing in the center of the driveway, he requested a list of officers that had entered the house prior to his arrival. Within minutes he was surrounded by several men in brown county uniforms. The soles of each officer's shoes were studied in the event that shoe designs were developed at the crime scene by the inspector. He would be able to eliminate the officer's shoes.

Walking around the exterior of the house, he examined each window for signs of forced entry or shoe impression on the ground under the window. He noted in a sketch that the one-story, wooden-framed house had three doors: The front door at the west side, the kitchen door located inside the two-car garage, and the rear door located on the east side. A four-foot-high chain link fence enclosed the backyard. Inside the fenced-in yard were a swing set and children's toys. A large ditch separated the backyards of the neighborhood from the golf course that ran east of the subdivision. The crime scene would be studied from the exterior first, and slowly worked toward the center. There were no signs of forced entry. Busch's focal point would be the doors of the house.

Inside, Busch took detailed notes as he examined each room for clues. He began with the garage. He felt the engine of the van. The engine was cool. It had not been recently driven, which suggested that the victim had not transported someone to the house shortly before her death.

He examined the metal entry door that opened into the kitchen. Its gray paint was clean and promised to be a good surface for obtaining fingerprints. The door had two locks. A dead bolt lock was above the knob lock. On the interior side of the door, the dead bolt had a knob to lock and unlock the door. The exterior side of the dead bolt could only be turned by the use of a key. Busch found that interesting. The kitchen door was locked when the neighbor tried to enter at 4:00 P.M. and was still locked when Lanman returned home around 5:00 P.M. That suggested that the killer would have to have a key to lock the kitchen door dead bolt from the exterior side or would have to leave through another door. If both keys were accounted for by each spouse having one in their possession and the other two doors were locked, then the husband would have some explaining to do. He checked the rear door. It was locked from the inside. He headed for the front door. It had the same locking system as the kitchen. Busch found that the front door was unlocked. The killer had walked out the front after the brutal murders.

Years of experience had taught Busch to reenact the steps of the crime in his mind. This helped him focus on what areas the perpetrator had come in contact with. Standing in the carpeted hallway, he looked at the kitchen door. The locked kitchen door indicated that the killer had walked across the kitchen floor to lock the door from the inside. Looking down at the kitchen floor, Busch cursed. It had a vinyl surface with a raised pattern design that would not be conducive to obtaining shoe patterns. The kitchen floor would have to be dusted with a small fingerprint brush. For each phase of the crime scene processing, he weighed the different methods of evidence collection and which would be the most vital to the case. The entire crime scene would have to be photographed before any processing could be done. The floor would have to be processed first since any movement on it might destroy valuable footprint evidence.

After photographing the kitchen, Busch dusted the floor for shoe patterns. Forty-five minutes later, his efforts went unrewarded. No shoe patterns. The floors in the other rooms were carpeted. Standing up to stretch and to give his back and knees a rest, Busch noticed how immaculate the place was. Jolaine kept a clean house. There was a large package of ham in the drain-rack in the kitchen sink, probably placed there to thaw for supper.

The kitchen door was processed for latent fingerprints. Several were developed and lifted from both sides. The sliding door in the dining room that opened into the backyard was dusted for fingerprints with negative results. Now, the front door. The door the killer left by. With care, Busch applied the fingerprint powder. He developed a smudged fingerprint on the doorknob of the front door. It would be of no use. *There has to be something here that will link the killer to the scene,* thought Busch, *they always leave something or take something with them.*

# Three

John Lanman stared at the roof of the ambulance during the twenty-minute trip to St. Elizabeth Hospital in Belleville. He had no energy left. The pain in his chest seemed to subside as he was jostled from side to side during the ride. He thought about how trivial his other problems were. Two months earlier, he had visited a doctor about chest pains. It turned out not to be a heart problem, and now this.

The door of the ambulance opened, and John was wheeled into the emergency room. Detective Robert Miller of the St. Clair County Sheriff's Department parked his squad car in the parking space marked "Police" at the hospital lot. He quickened his steps as he headed for the glass doors of the emergency room. Inside, he found John Lanman seated on the bed resting his head in his cupped hands. Miller stepped into the treatment cubicle. Lanman raised his head and slid his feet over the side of the bed.

"Mr. Lanman. I'm Detective Miller from the

Sheriff's Department. I need to speak with you."

Lanman looked at the tall, thin man standing in front of him. *What did he want? Why was he here?* Lanman placed his hands on the side of the bed for support. His mind was foggy but he wanted to help.

"What do you need?" said Lanman.

"I need to get a statement regarding where you were today," said Miller.

The detective's words echoed in Lanman's mind, setting off an alarm of fear. *My God,* thought Lanman, *do they think I killed my family?* The nightmare seemed to be endless. He took a deep breath and tried to think.

"I left home about 7:30 A.M. I went to my office in Belleville. At 8:30 A.M., I left the office and was at the job site till 1:45 P.M. I returned to my office around 2:30 P.M. and left around 4:00 P.M. I stopped at the golf course where I putted for a while," said Lanman.

"Did you see or talk to anyone during the day?" asked Miller.

Lanman told the detective the names of people he had talked with while he was at his office. In a trembling voice, he named the people he had seen during that day. Lanman began to cry as he got closer to the time he was at the golf course.

"Take your time. What's the matter?" said Miller as he watched Lanman pace the cubicle.

"If I hadn't stopped to play golf, I might've been home and this might not've happened," said Lanman.

"It's one of those things that happen. You

24

can't blame yourself. It probably happened earlier, we don't know for sure yet what time it happened," said Miller.

Miller waited until Lanman sat down on the bed before he continued the questioning, jotting down Lanman's statements as they spoke.

"Did you see anyone that you know while you were at the golf course?"

"No," said Lanman.

"Was there anyone else there?"

"Yeah, there were some high school kids, but I didn't see anybody I knew."

"I'm going to have to collect the clothes you're wearing."

"My clothes?" asked Lanman, looking suspiciously at the leathery-faced detective.

"Later, we may need to get some of your hair," said Miller.

"Is this normal procedure, to take hair and clothing?"

"In a case this serious, we need it."

"I don't quite understand why, but if it helps catch the person that killed my family, I'll do whatever it takes," said Lanman, shrugging his shoulders.

Miller spoke with an emergency room nurse and got a hospital gown for Lanman to wear. After undressing, Lanman handed his clothing to the detective, who placed them in a bag. Taking the man's clothes didn't sit well with Miller, but he would follow the orders given him. Even worse, he needed a hair standard from Lanman. Plucked hair.

Lanman sat on the bed clad in only a hospital gown. Medical personnel plucked head hair from five separate areas of his head. Over one hundred hairs had to be collected for the standard, he was told. Sitting quietly through the ordeal, he tried to sort out his thoughts. In almost a dreamlike stupor, he tried to function. He answered the detective's questions. Some of the questions made no sense to him. He had nothing to hide. For a brief moment after finding the bodies, he worried about becoming a suspect, but the loss of his family pushed that thought out of his mind until now.

After the detective left, Lanman was surprised to see his pastor, Hal Santos, standing outside the cubicle in the treatment room. Santos had received a call from Lanman's neighbor and was told about the murders. The six-foot-four man left his Wednesday bible class at the Full Gospel Tabernacle Church in Fairview Heights and drove to St. Elizabeth Hospital to comfort the husband of the slain family. Jolaine had been stronger than John in her religious beliefs, but John was glad to see Pastor Santos. Lanman spoke to the large man as he entered the treatment room.

"I'm glad I hugged her before I left," he blurted out, beginning to cry.

He rambled on for a short time while the dark-haired pastor listened with a heavy heart. His fourteen years in the ministry taught him to let the bereaved vent their grief. Lanman was trying to deal with his. After receiving medication, he fell asleep in the hospital bed. His nightmare had stopped.

While Lanman slept, investigators were being called to assist in the investigation. St. Clair County Sheriff Mearl Justus made the decision to activate the Major Case Squad to investigate the Lanman murders. Detectives from other police agencies in the Metro-East area would combine their expertise to form the elite Major Case Squad (MCS). Detective Sergeant Steve Nonn of the Madison County Sheriff's Department was selected as commander of the squad. The command post for the unit was located on the second floor at the St. Clair County Sheriff's Department. Detectives that had been selected to work the case arrived at the command post.

As the Major Case Squad assembled, Captain Lay remained outside the Lanman residence. He assigned road deputies at the crime scene to start a neighborhood canvass. Busch completed the overall photographs inside the house. He walked back into the master bedroom where the bodies of the woman and child lay lifeless on the light blue carpet.

He remembered the first double homicide he worked where a mother and her five-year-old son were butchered inside their home. Ten years had passed but that scene was still with him: The kitchen floor covered with large pools of clotting blood . . . the woman spread-eagle on the floor, hacked with a large butcher knife. Fragmented teeth were strewed about from a stab wound to her mouth. Her finger had been severed. Busch remembered the smell. The pungent smell of blood. He had found the boy's body in the bedroom, on top of the bed. Along with the numerous stab wounds, the child's stomach had been cut open. A small Ronald McDonald doll lay blood-spattered beside the small victim. Busch could not help but feel sickened by the brutality of the murders. His own child had been about the same age as that slain boy. He had learned to channel his outrage for the loss of life into a driving force to develop evidence that would catch the person guilty of such heinous crimes.

Busch stood at the corner of the master bedroom and looked at the positions of Jolaine's and Kenneth's bodies. For the next hour, he studied their positions and the blood spatters to interpret what the killer had done to the victims. This would help him become familiar with the type of individual he was up against.

Many murder investigations go unsolved because investigators are in a hurry to remove the victim's body from the scene. Busch felt he owed it to the victims to do everything possible to gather evidence that would lead to the person responsible for this savage act. He was not worried about the newspaper reporters and TV crews that waited anxiously outside.

He was joined at the crime scene by St. Clair County Coroner Rick Stone. Stone had been a homicide detective with the City of East St. Louis, Illinois, for fifteen years before he became coroner. He, too, had seen his share of senseless deaths.

"Man, that's a damn shame, someone doing that to the young boy," said Stone in disgust.

"But you can bet that whatever the reason was, it wasn't justified," said Busch.

"Why the boy, too?"

"Hell, Rick, I don't know what we have here yet. You've worked enough of these type cases to know that it is going to be a long time before we get to the bottom of this."

"I know, it just makes me mad to see these types of killings."

"I need to take pictures from floor level on the other side of the bed yet. The pattern of blood on the woman's clothing suggests that she wasn't standing when she was killed. From the blood spatters on the headboard, I think she was lying on the bed."

Busch lay on the floor on the east side of the bed. He set the flashlight on the floor above him to provide light in the darkened area beneath the mattress. Peering through the camera lens, he focused on the woman's body. He photographed the position and the bloodstains on her clothing. Looking across underneath the bed, he could see that there were no blood smears on the bottom of the mattress or on the carpet next to her. She had not crawled under the bed. She had been placed there.

The inspector reached up and rolled the flashlight higher above him to move the light beam toward Jolaine's head. He paused. On the carpet above her lay an orange notebook. Returning to the other side, the two men worked to remove her body from under the bed. Busch stopped abruptly. There was a handwritten note on top of the notebook. He photographed the note in its original position before retrieving it. Busch and Stone read the note, shocked by its contents. It read:

"A woman and 2 men hit me they called each other croupa, Bob Dlarry and Vael. They bragged about killing ardrey cardenas. There IL LPN CRX15 and KDH 221."

"How in the hell can these people be connected to the Cardenas case?" said Stone.

"Let's keep a low profile on this note. If the news media gets wind of it involving the Cardenas case, this investigation will turn into a nightmare. I want to find the one who killed these people." Audrey Cardenas, a twenty-three year old journalism intern at the *Belleville News-Democrat,* was found brutally murdered on June 29, 1988.

About the same time as the note was discovered inside the house, a second startling discovery was made by St. Clair County Deputy Kelly Oliver. A neighbor of the Lanmans, Vicki Sartory, had completed her workday at 2:00 P.M. and was heading home. She normally would arrive home before her daughters got out of school, but the early dismissal program at school had altered the schedule. Vicki's ten-year-old daughter, Brooke, and her younger sister would arrive home twenty minutes before their mother.

With concern for her children, the working mother hurried home. Turning the corner, she noticed an unfamiliar car parked across the street from her house by the open field. She had an uneasy feeling about the safety of her daughters. Parking her car in the garage, she hurried into the family room and called out for them. No response. She quickly climbed the staircase and with relief found the two children playing in their rooms.

Now that her mother was home, Brooke wanted to ride her bike. The pretty fifth grader rode down her driveway and out into the street. She stopped at the rear of the car parked near the field and looked at the license plate. She studied the numbers and then rode away. A short time later she returned home and put her bike back in the garage.

Around 4:45 P.M., Vicki, seated on the couch in her living room, heard the sound of a car door shut and a car engine start up. As it pulled away, sunlight reflecting off the vehicle and shining through Vicki's bay window caused light images to dance across the living room walls.

Deputy Oliver jotted down the information while the woman talked about the strange car in the neighborhood.

"What kind of car was it?" he wanted to know.

"It was light blue, a metallic blue."

"Did you get a license plate number?"

"No, I didn't," said Vicki, in an apologetic tone.

During the interview, Brooke stood beside her mother. She heard the officer ask about the blue car. Taught by her parents to be well-mannered, she waited until her mother had finished speaking.

"I know the number, I put it into my long-range memory," said Brooke, who then recited it to the officer.

Deputy Oliver was excited. He wrote down the license plate number. It was said to be an Illinois plate. He had found two witnesses that could put the blue car within a hundred yards of the crime scene for over an hour. The license plate number given by the young girl was relayed to Captain Lay, who still remained outside the Lanmans' residence.

Inside the Lanman house, Inspector Busch began his detailed examination of the first of the two bedrooms where the murders took place. He knelt beside Jolaine's body to study the injuries. The smell of blood was heavy as he examined her neck. The bloodstains on the front of her sweatshirt across her breast indicated that she had also been stabbed in the chest. The bloodstains did not trail downward. This suggested that she had been in the prone position when they were inflicted.

A man's white shirt was wrapped around her neck. A black handled pair of scissors was embedded up to the handle in the front of her neck. Looking down into her blood smeared face, Busch wondered why this woman and her young son were chosen as victims.

Busch unzipped the plastic body bag and placed it on the floor beside Jolaine's body.

Let's secure her body in this bag. I'll seal it and sign the tag. I don't want anyone opening the bag at the morgue. I want to check the body for hair and fiber transfers later," said Busch.

"However you want to work it is fine with me," said Stone, assisting in placing the body in the white body bag.

"I'll need at least a few hours here to get an idea what all this bastard did while he was here. Hold the bodies until I get finished with the crime scene. I'll call Dee Heil and let him know that I want to check the bodies with our laser."

"Let me know when you're ready to have the bodies transported, and I'll get the ambulance back here and have a deputy coroner accompany them to the funeral home," said Stone.

The body of Kenneth Lanman was placed in a body bag and moved near the kitchen door near his mother's body to await the ambulance's arrival. Busch walked outside to speak with Captain Lay about the note found under the bed. Lay was transmitting a license plate number on his portable radio as Busch waited to talk to him.

33

The fresh air outside was a pleasant break from the death scene.

Lay completed the radio message and motioned for Busch to accompany him to the side of the driveway so they could talk without the news media overhearing.

"We got a lead that a car was spotted over there by that empty lot," said Lay, as he pointed the antenna of the portable radio in that direction.

"Did you get a plate?" asked Busch.

"Yeah."

"Who did it come back to?"

"I just ran it as you walked up," said Lay.

"Found a note under the bed that talks about three people involved in the Cardenas murder, giving partial names and license plate numbers," said Busch, as Lay's portable chattered with the information on the license plate check.

"Dale Anderson," repeated Busch, after hearing the radio traffic on the license plate check. "Isn't he the one that kept popping up in the Cardenas case?"

"Yeah, I'm surprised you remembered his name," teased Lay.

Lay and Busch had worked together as undercover agents back in the 1970s. Busch had a good memory for details but was usually not good at remembering names.

"Hey, fuck you," said Busch, grinning about his inability to retain names. "What's Anderson's connection with these people?"

"None, that I know of. He worked as a jailer

34

for us for about a year. He's a strange fucker. We're sending cars over to his house now," said Lay.

"Let me know what's going on over there. I'm going to be tied up here for a couple more hours. If Anderson is arrested let me know right away," said Busch, as he walked back into the house.


In the master bedroom several men's shirts were sitting on the bed. Busch noted that the shirts were clean, probably put there by Jolaine after she had washed them. On top of the bed, toward the headboard, two peach-colored pillows and a heart-shaped toss pillow lay in a heaped pile. Their position appeared out of place. He noticed that there were tiny specks of blood on them but not on the bed around the edge. Busch lifted up the first one and then the toss pillow. He could see a heavy saturation of blood under the remaining one, but there was something under it.

Lifting the pillow, he could now see what it was.

"You rotten bastard," whispered Busch under his breath while he stared at the object. A small blue and white stuffed Teddy Bear had been placed facedown in the pool of blood on top of the bed. Busch felt the rage building inside him. The killer had a sick sense of humor. Had he placed the stuffed bear in the pool of blood to taunt the investigators, or was there some kind of message in the fact that three pillows were used to cover the bear? Three people had been named in the note.

Jolaine's purse was on the bed. Her keys and wallet were in the purse. Robbery did not appear to be the motive in the slayings. Busch read the note from under the bed again.


Several things about the note bothered him. The "IL LPN" meant Illinois License Plate Number which sounded more like the writings of someone connected to law enforcement than a housewife. The second puzzling question was how could the woman write the note while the named intruders were there. *She certainly didn't do it after being stabbed,* reasoned Busch while he sorted out things in his mind. The third issue was the license plate numbers. She would have to have seen both cars or would have to have known the people and been familiar with their license plate numbers.

Busch didn't know the people named in the note but felt the note was the key to finding the killer. Had the note been prewritten and placed at the scene? It suggested that three people were responsible for the murder of Audrey Cardenas, but someone had already been charged with her murder: the drifter, Rodney Woidtke. Busch reflected back on the bits and pieces of what he knew about the Cardenas case. A case that never sat well with him. A case with too many unanswered questions.

The note from the Lanman Case had dredged

up unanswered questions about Rodney's guilt or innocence. It also pointed a finger at three people for Audrey's death and the Lanmans'. Busch placed the note in an evidence bag. He entered Kenneth's bedroom. Again he battled with his emotions. Being a professional he couldn't afford the luxury of emotions. Personal feelings cloud the mind and dull the investigative senses.

On top of the dresser sat Kenneth's shoes. Busch fought back tears as he examined them. He didn't know the boy but just the thought of someone killing a child upset him. Pushing his personal feelings out of his mind, he got back on track. The bed in the boy's room was made, but there was a slight wrinkling on the surface. Since Kenneth was found wearing socks and his shoes were atop the dresser, he may have been asleep on top of the covers when he was attacked by the killer. The blood on the brown carpet was in two small patches. The distance between the patches was consistent with the theory that he was beaten in the back of the head while he was facedown on the floor and rolled over one time to expose the neck. There was no other blood on the carpet. The killer probably wrapped a shirt around the child's neck to take him to the master bedroom, where he put him under the foot of the bed.

Busch leaned over and examined the tiny specks of blood on the headboard. The pointed tails of the blood droplets indicated a directional path from which they came. The woman may have been slain first. She was killed on top of the bed where the blood pooled. Her body was placed underneath by the killer. The skirt of the bed was lifted up by the killer as her body was pushed under. A bloody cloth impression was left on the bed skirting. Probably cloth gloves.

Residents of the Villa Madero Subdivision gathered near the Lanmans' home on Chula Vista. TV camera crews had set up shop on the green lawns around the Lanmans' house. Chula Vista became congested with people and vehicles. Reporters and news broadcasters were busy interviewing neighbors to get their reaction to the brutal murders.

The sun had dipped behind the roofs on the west side of the subdivision, dropping the temperature by several degrees. The ambulance pulled in front of the house so that the bodies could be taken away. Stone supervised the removal of the victims from the crime scene. Cameramen and photographers scrambled to get coverage of the stretchers bearing the body bags being loaded into the ambulance.

Busch watched the ambulance pull away. He waited. As always, once the bodies were gone, the crowd and news media rapidly disappeared. The news media would head for the sheriff's department where the command post of the Major Case Squad was forming.

# Four

At 7:00 P.M. the twelve investigators that comprised the Major Case Squad assembled and were immediately briefed on what little information was known on the case. This was Steve Nonn's first time to fill the slot as commander. He would be lead investigator in the double murder. A prestigious position. The responsibilities that accompany the title of "Commander" change from case to case. Nonn would soon learn how demanding that title would be.

As commander, Nonn was faced with several logistical problems at the start. Half of the MCS members were seasoned investigators. The other half were inexperienced in homicide investigations. Nonn tried to organize the two-man units with one experienced detective and one less-experienced detective.

Another problem was that several of the MCS members were from the Madison County area and were unfamiliar with the St. Clair County area and its local police officers. Nonn had paired up the teams when possible with a man from each county. To his surprise, the unit began working with top efficiency due to the dedicated effort of each man on the team.

Nonn was unaware that soon he would be called upon to make decisions in matters of life and death. His abilities as commander would be tested. He was confident. He had sixteen years of police experience behind him and a team of hard-working detectives.

Commander Nonn was apprised of the status at the Anderson home. St. Clair County deputies had already arrived and set up a stakeout on the house. There was one car, a yellow Oldsmobile, parked in the driveway. The one-story, brick ranch was located on a corner lot in a quiet sub-division in Belleville, six miles west of the Lanman house. Officers reported all the windows were covered with sections of cardboard.

Nonn ordered the surveillance to continue while more information was gathered. Squad members were assigned to check into the background of the Lanmans. Other investigators arrived in the Villa Madero Subdivision and initiated a thorough neighborhood canvass. A two-man team was sent to assist in the surveillance of Anderson's house.

Nonn wanted to have a working knowledge of the death scene. He drove out to the Lanman house. There, he met with Busch and learned about the note under the Lanmans' bed. He, too, was baffled by it.

Nonn was one of the officers who composed the seventeen members of the MCS that worked the Cardenas case. He and fourteen other field officers totalled 940 man-hours during the five-day investigation in 1988. Driving back to the command post, Nonn remembered that Sunday afternoon call and being assigned to the Cardenas case. The call came from Commander Vic Logan, who was handling the Cardenas investigation.

On Sunday morning, June 26, 1988, a decomposed body in the creek bed on the grounds of Belleville East High School was discovered by a school custodian at 11:00 A.M. By 1:00 P.M. the area around the creek bed had been secured with yellow plastic tape bearing three inch letters, "Police Line Do Not Cross." Around 4:00 P.M., while Inspector Dee Heil and other officers were at the scene with the body, an unidentified white male walked into the open field, one-hundred yards west of the creek bed.

The man was arrested for obstructing a peace officer as a result of crossing a marked police line. The transient was identified as Rodney Woidtke. Woidtke had an earlier history of mental problems and had received treatment. The twenty-seven year old was found to have writings among his belongings that told of sexual problems and the need to be with a woman. It appeared that he had a deep fear of being labeled a homosexual.

Woidtke was interviewed during the evening of June 26, 1988. During that interview, he denied any involvement in the homicide but later told the interviewer that he had attempted to sexually assault the victim and had been scratched on his arms by the struggling girl. He told of striking her in the back of the head, causing her to fall to the ground. He then carried her to the wooded area where he left her while she was still breathing.

On June 27, 1988, the dental charts of Audrey Cardenas were compared to the dental remains of the unidentified body. Dr. James McGivney, DMD, positively identified the body found the previous day as being that of Audrey Cardenas. That same day, Woidtke was reinterviewed and gave a similar story as his first statement. He requested that any future interview with him be conducted by a woman.

On June 28, 1988, Woidtke was interviewed by a female officer, his story still vague and rambling. In all three interviews, Woidtke had given different descriptions of the clothing worn by the victim. His statements had numerous inconsistencies about how the victim was clothed, manner of death, and exact location of the body.

An autopsy conducted on June 26 failed to determine the cause of death. The advanced state of decomposition hindered the pathological examination. The body was larva-infested which made the internal examination difficult. There was no indication of trauma. Xrays revealed there were no skull fractures. There was tissue damage to the area of the neck below the chin. Animals and insects had attacked the neck leaving an injury site the size of a baseball.

On July 1, 1988, at 1:00 P.M., Nonn and the other sixteen members of the MCS were informed that the unit was deactivated. The Cardenas Case was turned over to the Belleville Police Department with Woidtke as the prime suspect. He was charged with the murder. During the following year, several court hearings occurred on the issue of Woidtke's sanity. On July 8, 1989, the transient from Bakersfield, California, went on trial for murder. He waived his right to a jury trial and chose a bench trial. St. Clair County Associate Judge Richard Aguirre presided. After three hours of deliberation, Aguirre found the defendant guilty. He set Woidtke's sentencing date for September 28, 1989.

Nonn returned to the command post and was set upon by news reporters inquiring about the Lanman murders. He briefly explained to them that the investigation into the double murder had just begun and there would be a news release at a later time. He didn't want to be burdened with the news media now, he had an investigation to run. He hoped to assign an officer to make news releases to control the information flow to the press. As it turned out, the sheriff wanted Nonn to handle the press releases. This complicated things. He was swamped with phone calls at the command post by reporters.

Nonn removed his glasses and set them on the conference table. He rubbed the bridge of his nose. He waited for the update from the crime scene technician at the Lanman house and the surveillance team at Anderson's house.

At 1:00 A.M. on Thursday morning, Busch closed and locked the door at the Lanman house. He had spent seven hours processing the scene where the two had died. His findings were noted and photographed, and he requested the scene be secured for twenty-four hours until he released it. A sheriff's deputy was stationed outside.

Busch had radioed Dee Heil to meet him at the Sheriff's Department, where he was headed to do a briefing with the Major Case Squad. Walking up the stairs to the second-floor command post, he began to feel tired. He had been up for twenty-five hours and would probably be working another seven or eight before he would be able to rest. Over the last thirteen years, he had become accustomed to pushing his endurance on long cases.

Squad members listened as the crime scene was described to them. Their faces were solemn. Inspector Dee Heil met with Busch at the briefing. After the briefing the two men talked in the parking lot of the Sheriff's Department.

"What do you think about the note?" inquired Heil.

"I'm not sure what's going on yet. You worked Cardenas, and both of us know there are a lot of unanswered questions on that case," said Busch.

"What's the connection with Anderson and these victims?"

"I have no idea, so far there is no connection. Remember we talked about Anderson at the end of the Cardenas investigation. Wasn't he arrested for impersonating a police officer? Told someone he was investigating the Cardenas murder?"

"Yeah, he worked for Public Aid and was having problems with Belleville PD."

"Well, let's go laser the bodies. You want to stop at that drive-through hamburger place near the funeral home? I haven't eaten since lunch yesterday, and the way it's going it may be a long time before I get a chance to eat again."

"Sounds good to me. I'll meet you at the funeral home," said Heil.

They sat in their squad cars on the parking lot of the funeral home and ate the greasy breakfast of hamburgers and fries. Heil unloaded the large metal case which housed the portable laser unit. Both men carried their equipment into the prep-room of the funeral home. It was dark and quiet. The funeral director turned on the lights. Busch unzipped the white body bag which contained Jolaine's body, photographed and charted her wounds. The bright lights above the morgue table gave a stark and cold illumination to the evil work of the killer. Unwrapping the white shirt from around her neck, he noted that the scissors had forced a section of the shirt down into the wound in the neck. This meant the victim had been stabbed several times in the throat. The shirt was placed around her neck and she was stabbed again. When the blood soaked shirt was removed, a necklace of stab wounds was visible. The pregnant victim had been stabbed through her sweater, four times in the heart. Wearing surgical gloves, Busch separated the bloody strands of matted hair on the woman's head. The back of her head revealed large wounds from a blunt object.

Heil set up the portable laser on a chair next to the morgue table. He handed Busch the safety goggles with the orange lenses, which he put on. They would protect his eyes if the laser light were reflected off something shiny. After securing a pair of goggles for himself, Heil flipped the switch to turn the laser on. A brilliant, blue-green light traveled down the fiber-optic quartz cable. Busch turned off the overhead lights to allow the laser operator to focus the four-inch sphere of light on the body.

Looking through the goggles, which filter out the blue-green light leaving only the yellowish visible laser light, the forensic examiners now covered the surface of the victim's body four inches at a time. Hairs, fibers, body fluids, and other substances take on a fluorescence when exposed to the Argon-Ion laser light. They found no latent fingerprints.

Busch unzipped the body bag that contained the boy's body. Heil shook his head as he viewed the small boy on the morgue table. Kenneth's body was lasered. No latent fingerprints. Busch logged the clothing as he examined and packaged the tiny garments.

"It takes a no-good bastard to do that to a child," said Heil.

Busch had taken on a cold, professional attitude toward the body lying on the table.

"Look at the stab wounds in his neck and in his chest. The person that inflicted these wounds has no conscience. He'll be a son of a bitch to interview. It took time to do all this. He wanted to enrage us. Hell, besides the blunt trauma to the head, there are bruises on his back," said Busch.

After working five hours over the morgue tables, Busch completed his work as far as he could prior to the autopsies. Returning to the crime laboratory, he unloaded the evidence collected in the investigation. Daybreak found him en route to the command post for an update on the case. The autopsy was scheduled for 8:30 A.M. which would allow for time to complete the briefing.

Driving down the highway, Busch went over the case in his mind. Why were these particular people killed? Was there a connection between the Cardenas case and this family? If so, the connection wasn't on the surface. On the other hand, if there was no connection between the two cases, that meant that the victims were selected at random, which made the killings even more vicious.

Somewhere in all of this there was a common denominator, but what was it? Busch wanted to learn as much as possible about Dale Anderson.

Although Busch had not worked the investigation into Cardenas's death, he knew that most of the investigators who worked the case had written Anderson off as a kook.

At the command post, Commander Nonn sat behind the long conference table piled high with incoming reports from the men out in the field. He looked up from the report he was reading, and said to Busch, who was seated, "Have you finished with the bodies?"

"No, they're going to be posting them around 8:30 A.M. We used the laser on the bodies but didn't get shit, replied Busch as he placed his square-toed boots up on the conference table and leaned back in the chair.

"What kind of injuries were on the bodies?" Nonn wanted to know.

"Well, the woman was stabbed with the scissors and beaten with a blunt object. The boy was also stabbed with scissors, beat in the head with something blunt, and I think he was stomped on by the killer."

"The squad should all be in here by eight. Do you want to give them an update on the bodies or wait until the autopsies are completed?"

"Let's wait until we get done with the posts," said Busch as he rubbed his eyes. "What's the scam on Anderson? Are they still sitting on his house?"

"Yeah, there hasn't been any movement there. He won't answer the door or phone. We've got guys working on getting information on him," said Nonn.

"That was my next question," said Busch. "What is the connection with him and Cardenas? Didn't you work on that case?"

"Belleville took that over after the MCS five-day rule expired. I know that Anderson got arrested by Belleville in June of 1988 on a weapons charge," said Nonn. "I think he called Cardenas's father in Texas, either during the investigation or shortly after it."

"That note under the bed at Lanmans' is fucked up. Did you check out the plates it mentions?" asked Busch.

"The plates come back to two workers at the Public Aid Office in Belleville. They are two of the three people named in the note: Charlotte Kroupa, Maurice Vale, and Robert DeLaria," said Nonn.

"They're the ones named in the note," said Busch.

"I guess so. The names in the note were three of Anderson's bosses before he got fired," said the commander.

Busch left the command post to attend the autopsies. Nonn answered the ringing phone. Officers assigned to do a background check on Anderson reported that Anderson had covered the windows with cardboard in July of 1988, shortly after he was arrested by the Belleville Police for flourishing a revolver while *Belleville News-Democrat* reporter Carolyn Tuft was interviewing him.

A neighbor of Anderson reported that Anderson had driven his blue Oldsmobile into the garage around 5:00 P.M. Wednesday and had not ventured out of the house since then. A stakeout team had been camped outside of his house since 6:30 P.M. on Wednesday and observed Anderson's wife and son arrive home and go inside. Through information gathered from Anderson's neighbors, investigators believed the suspect was inside with his wife and two children.

Nonn listened as the officer continued with the information. Dale Anderson had been unemployed since August of 1988. He was terminated from his job at the Public Aid Office. His wife, Linda, worked at a child day-care center in town. She had last worked on Wednesday, and had not gone in on Thursday morning. Her place of employment had not heard from her, and she was not scheduled to be off. Her yellow 1976 Oldsmobile sat parked in her driveway outside the garage.

The two Anderson children had been at school on Wednesday, but had not returned to school on Thursday morning. After hearing the update, Nonn hung the phone up and leaned back in the chair. *There could be a couple of reasons why the family remained inside the house,* thought Nonn. *The wife and children may be held there by the husband.* Reluctantly, Nonn envisioned the other reason, they could all be dead. He would have to play the waiting game. It was too early in the investigation to take action. To enter Anderson's house forcibly without a search warrant would be asking for trouble in the double murder investigation. Nonn wanted a search warrant. He decided to send additional manpower to canvass the Lanman neighborhood. Detective Marion Hubbard wanted to help. He drew the autopsy assignment.


Busch returned to the funeral home where the autopsies of the Lanmans were scheduled. Detective Hubbard arrived and greeted him. He viewed the bodies of the victims. Raj Nanduri, the pathologist, donned her apron and surgical gloves. She had performed several hundred autopsies over the years, many of which Busch had observed.

Nanduri was a native of India and a skilled pathologist. Busch liked working with her on cases because he could see that she was relentless in her quest for pathological evidence. She left no stone unturned. Working with Busch over the years, she had learned to ask the street-slang speaking investigator what he meant by some phrases that he used. These inquiries would usually get her a grin and an explanation from the inspector.

During the autopsy of the pregnant woman, the pathologist reflected the sex and approximate age of the fetus. Busch noted the information as he observed the autopsy standing beside the brown-eyed doctor. He felt angered about the fact that the person responsible for the death of the unborn child would never be charged with its murder. Experienced with the judicial system, Busch knew that the State would have a difficult time proving that the killer was aware that the woman was pregnant when she was slain. After

51

four hours spent with the autopsies, Busch headed for the 1:00 P.M. briefing at the command post.

The phone at the command post rang repeatedly. Information poured in from the field. Thursday afternoon was a hectic time for Detective John Betten of the Fairview Heights Police Department, who had been assigned as Field Report Officer for the MCS. He had the tedious and all-important job of sorting information from the field into investigative leads that would be selected for further follow-up. Betten kept Commander Nonn apprised of all developments in the investigation.

Detectives David Hoffmann and Joe Michaelis, MCS members, had located two witnesses, besides the young girl, that had seen the blue car in the area of the crime scene on the day of the murders. This information would be critical for the basis of a search warrant that would be drafted later. St. Clair County Assistant State's Attorney Dennis Hatch was drawn into the case by his inquisitive nature. The Wednesday evening news broadcast about the murders on TV would be the means by which the prosecutor would become involved in the most complex murder case of his career.

Dennis Hatch had turned thirty-six, just two weeks before the Lanmans were killed. He had spent the last seven years working as an assistant state's attorney in St. Clair County, a county that handles sixteen thousand felony cases a year with just eight full time prosecutors.

Wednesday evening, Hatch had left the county court building and walked across the street to the 101 Club, a local bar that many of the courthouse employees frequented.

Sipping on a draft beer, Hatch's attention was caught by the news commentator talking about a double murder in Belleville. The bartender turned up the volume on the overhead TV set, but information was sketchy. Hatch finished his beer and left to head home. Walking two blocks to his car, he decided that he would stop by the Sheriff's Department; it was only eight blocks away.

Hatch was given a brief synopsis of the case by Steve Nonn. He was amazed. He had heard of Anderson before, regarding the weapon charge. *The note was interesting,* thought Hatch. The Cardenas case was prosecuted by Scott Mansfield, the chief Assistant State's Attorney of St. Clair County. He would talk with Mansfield and John Baricevic, the State's Attorney, Thursday morning. He cautioned Nonn not to enter Anderson's house without a search warrant.

# Five

On Thursday morning, John Lanman opened his
eyes only to find the white ceiling of the hospital
room sectioned off with a sliding curtain track
above him. He realized that it wasn't a bad dream.
*They were gone.* He felt empty and alone.

Later that morning, he learned from the nursing
staff that the doctor had approved his discharge
from the hospital. A set of clothes from his neighbor, Mark Nixon, lay on the chair beside the bed.
Still drowsy from the sedative, he dressed himself
and sat on the edge of the bed. He waited for his
neighbor, Vic Sartory, to give him a ride back to the
empty house.

The Sartorys had been friends and neighbors
since the Lanmans had come to the neighborhood.
Vic backed his car out of his driveway and headed
toward the hospital to pick up John Lanman. What
should he say? How do you talk to someone whose
family was just murdered? Vic placed the morning
issue of the newspaper behind the front seat of the

car. If John asked for the paper, he would give it to him. *Better to receive the news from a friend,* thought Vic, *than to get it from a stranger.*

Vic walked down the corridor to John's hospital room. John was talking with Pastor Santos when he entered the room. Vic looked at John and forced a smile. John looked terrible. His eyes were sunken and had dark rings around them. He moved slowly and seemed unsure what was going on. He didn't talk much. After checking out of the hospital, they walked to Vic's car before John began to speak.

"What's going on, Vic?"

"We don't have very much information yet," said Vic.

Vic thought it would be easier if he showed him the newspaper than trying to explain. He reached behind the driver's seat and picked up the *Belleville News-Democrat,* handing it to him. The headlines read: TWO FOUND SLAIN IN HOME. The article came with a large photograph of John Lanman leaning against a squad car outside the house.

"Oh God, I can't believe this is happening," said John.

"We just don't know much of what's going on. Brooke got a license plate number on a car parked across the street. The police are checking on it," said Vic.

"Way to go, Brooke," said John. "Good going, Brooke," he repeated.

Vic felt proud of his daughter, but he had other emotions, too. Fear, anger. . . . If that was the car involved in the murders, his entire family could be in danger. He was outraged at the person who was so brazen as to come to this quiet neighborhood to kill a woman and child. *In broad daylight.*

John read the newspaper article slowly. He wanted answers. His eyes caught the line: POLICE WOULD NOT SAY WHETHER LANMAN WAS A SUSPECT. His anger grew. He tossed the newspaper on the floor of the car. Vic pulled the car into his driveway, looking at John. He could tell John was angry.

"I'm going to stand out here all day and answer questions. It looks like a circus out here with all the cars. I want to find out what's going on," said Lanman.

Vic didn't say anything as John and he walked over to the Nixon's house. Pastor Santos was standing on the front lawn talking with the Nixons and John's brother, who had just arrived in town. The news media stirred when they saw Lanman. Cameramen lugged the heavy cameras as they walked toward him.

"What do you want to do about these news people?" asked Vic.

"Let's get this over with. Let's talk to them. Vic, I want you to help me if you can. I have no idea what's going on. I don't have any information. Just get the bastard so he doesn't do this again," said Lanman.

Before Vic could speak, the reporters and cameramen converged on them. John spoke briefly but was unable to give them any new information. Then the personal questions started. John turned away.

\* \* \*

Later that afternoon, John asked the officer stationed outside his house if he could get some of his clothes. The officer relayed the request to Inspector Busch inside the crime scene. Busch motioned for Lanman to enter the garage. He stopped the large man who accompanied Lanman.

"Who are you?" said Busch.

"I'm Hal Santos."

"He's the pastor at my church," said Lanman.

Santos looked at the investigator. His face looked mean. His eyes were piercing. It wasn't anything that the investigator said, but the pastor sensed that Busch was very confident in his work.

"I'll have to accompany you as you get your things from the house," said Busch.

"I just want to get some clothes to wear," said Lanman.

"While you're here, could I get some information from you? I need to know what items should and shouldn't be here," said Busch.

"If I can help, I will. Whatever it takes," said Lanman.

"I found a white plastic timer on top of the bed in the master bedroom. Does that belong there?"

"Yeah. We used that when Kenneth would do something wrong. We would set it for five or ten minutes, during that time Kenneth would have to stay in his room. But he was such a good kid, he usually carried it around as a toy to play with," said Lanman, his voice choked with emotion.

*Damn,* thought Busch, *that question reopened emotional wounds for this grieving father.* Now he had to ask about the scissors in his wife's neck.

Then describe them. *Always so many questions*. He hated these types of cases.

"Was there a pair of metal scissors with black handles here in the house?"

"I think so. There were two pairs. One had green handles and the other had black," said Lanman.

Busch had found the green ones among the assortment of pens and pencils in a glass on the nightstand in the bedroom. These were too lightweight to make a suitable weapon for the person that carried out the murders. He had brought whatever he beat the victims with and taken it with him when he left. He brought the rope that was around the woman's neck. The large bow tied in the rope at the back of the woman's neck had been done for a purpose.

# Six

By Thursday afternoon the news media had gotten wind of the surveillance of Anderson's house. During shift change for the stakeout team, neighbors ventured out into the road to inquire about the presence of the police in the quiet neighborhood. Lawmen refused to say why they were there, except to caution homeowners to stay away from the Anderson property.

By early evening the intersection at the front of Anderson's home was lined with spectators and news reporters. Nonn sent additional officers to insure that nobody crossed the perimeter that now skirted the suspect's property. The phone lines at the command post were swamped with calls from reporters.

Commander Nonn met with St.Clair County Sheriff Mearl Justus and Belleville Police Chief Robert Hurst. The case had now taken on a multiple jurisdictional aspect. Anderson's house was in the city limits of Belleville. Nonn requested the meeting with the two police administrators to discuss the situation. By 6:00 P.M. on Thursday, twenty-four hours had passed since the stakeout on the home had begun. Nonn was concerned with the well-being of Anderson's wife and children.

In the strategy meeting with Justus and Hurst, Nonn discussed the possibility of a hostage situation developing when Anderson was confronted at his house. He reflected the feelings of the MCS members and himself that a course of action on the house should be executed as soon as possible.

Cautioned by the State's Attorney's office to obtain a search warrant before going inside, Nonn assigned MCS members to work on getting a search warrant for Anderson's house. Detective Sergeant David Nester of the St. Clair County Sheriff's Department would soon become a key investigator in the case.

Detective Nester had been with the Sheriff's Department for twelve years. Nester, a well educated man with a bachelor's degree in political science, and working on a graduate degree in the administration of justice, had stopped his educational pursuit just short of his master's degree to join the Sheriff's Department in 1977.

On September 27, 1989, Nester had worked the morning shift from 7:00 A.M. to 3:00 P.M. Returning home by 3:30 P.M., he spent the afternoon and evening with his family. At 10:00 P.M., Nester watched the local news report and learned of the double murder in the Villa Madero Subdivision. Shortly after the report about the Lanman Case, Nester got a call from Captain Lay. Lay was looking for officers to relieve road deputies who were assigned to the surveillance of Anderson's house.

Nester volunteered to relieve one of the men. Dressing in his uniform, he told his wife, who was pregnant with twins, that he would be working a stakeout and would see her the following day. His eight-year-old son and four-year-old daughter had already gone to bed.

After working an eight-hour surveillance, Nester was assigned to assist the MCS in applying for a search warrant. He arrived at the State's Attorney's office at 10:00 A.M. and waited in the reception area to talk with the prosecutor who would be handling the case.

Dennis Hatch arrived at work early. He was excited about the Lanman case, and entered Baricevic's office with the suggestion of assigning a prosecutor to the Lanman investigation. Ten minutes later, he walked out into the reception area, looking for Nester. Hatch had been assigned to the case.

Nester covered the facts of the case with Hatch. Hatch absorbed the information as he tapped a pencil on the desk top. He thought about the note. The handwriting would be what would link Anderson to the murders. He wanted Anderson's handwriting standard. The car description and license number had focused the investigation on Anderson, but the handwriting would be the deciding factor. He would not issue an arrest warrant for Anderson on the license number alone. The investigators had to secure handwriting samples. Hatch agreed to draft a search warrant for Anderson's handwriting standard and samples of his writing. The process would take several hours.

Nester relayed the prosecutor's discussion to Commander Nonn. This was the green light the investigators were waiting for. Everyone was concerned about the woman and two children inside, where no movement had been seen since Wednesday evening. Chief Hurst agreed to handle the assault with members of the Belleville Police Tactical Team.

At 8:00 P.M. on Thursday, Commander Nonn held a briefing at the command post with MCS members. He informed the officers that an 8:30 P.M. meeting was scheduled with Belleville's Tactical Unit. The men seated around the conference table cheered. They felt the sooner Anderson was confronted, the better chance his family had to survive. Many officers had expressed the concern that Anderson may have already killed his family.

Busch, seated beside Nonn at the end of the conference table, watched the face of the commander as he answered the 8:20 P.M. phone call. After a brief conversation on the phone, the weary man hung up the receiver.

"The tactical unit called it off for tonight. They want to hit the house around six in the morning," Nonn said with an irritated tone.

"Why are they waiting until morning?" demanded Busch.

"It's not my call, Busch, Hurst is handling the tactical unit. Everyone is to be here at 5:00 A.M.," said the commander.

The men walked out of the command post tired and frustrated by the latest development. Some had been without sleep for fifty-two hours. Busch arrived home at 9:00 P.M. on Thursday; he showered and quickly fell asleep after speaking briefly with his wife. Normally he would set his mind to wake at a given time and would usually wake up within ten minutes of that time. But with the events planned for 5:00 A.M., he set the alarm clock.

The buzzing sound in the distance of his consciousness became louder as Busch fought to wake up. Opening his eyes and staring at the red numbers that showed 4:30 A.M. on the clock face, Busch headed for the shower. He dressed as he usually did every workday in slacks, shirt, and tie. Walking to his squad car, he put on his black gunbelt which held a 9-mm automatic pistol, gold Inspector badge, handcuffs, and extra ammo clip. He headed for the command post that was four miles away.

West Main Street in Belleville was dark, and the early morning commuters were slowly beginning to appear on the roadway as Busch made his way through town. As he pulled into the parking lot at the Sheriff's Department, he waved at the county unit pulling away. Other vehicles and personnel were arriving at the command post. The briefing room had been moved to another part of the building to accommodate the large number of people now involved in the case.

Members of the Belleville Tactical Unit along with Chief Hurst filed into the room. MCS personnel and other officers now assigned to the operation took seats awaiting the briefing. Sheriff Justus and Chief Hurst stood at the front, waiting for everyone to arrive. Commander Nonn was locked in traffic at a train crossing by a long, slow moving freight train north of the city.

Sheriff Justus began. It was quiet as the large man spoke to the multiforce unit that had assembled. Justus, in a sober tone, unveiled the plan of action that Nonn, Hurst, and himself had devised. For precautionary measures, several officers were selected to handle the crowd of spectators that were accumulating at the intersection outside Anderson's house. News media personnel and their equipment were also camped there. The line of spectators around the suspect's house would have to be moved back even farther before the tactical unit deployed their men.

Chief Hurst covered the briefing of his tactical unit. Their mission would be in two phases. Phase One would be to enter the Anderson house to ensure the well-being of residents and secure the house. Phase Two would be to diffuse any type of hostage situation that might develop. Members of the tactical unit were aware that Dale Anderson was known to have a large number of guns from prior contacts with him.

The final part of the overall plan was to execute

the search warrant for the handwriting samples. Once the house was secured, Detective Nester and Inspector Busch were to execute the search warrant. All members of the investigation were cautioned that at the present time, legal advisers felt there was not enough evidence to warrant an arrest.

The tactical unit made preparation for the assault. Each man checked his headset unit to ensure that they would have total communication capability with each member of the team. Lives may depend on it. They donned their body armor and then their weapons. Again the plan of action was covered in every detail. The parking lot of a bowling alley eight blocks away was selected as a final meeting place before the assault. The convoy of police vehicles left the Sheriff's Office en route to the parking lot at the bowling alley.

The early morning sun had just begun to rise as the police units neared the subdivision. The convoy pulled into the parking lot where they were met by Commander Nonn. He ordered the first units that were assigned crowd control to depart on their assignments. Nonn waited for a radio response from the first unit.

Nester, seated in his car in the parking lot, was busy preparing the handwriting standard kit for the interview with Anderson. He was excited about being selected to interview the prime suspect in the case.

Busch, now seated in his squad car, was directed by Nonn to pull in behind the SWAT van when the convoy started toward the house. Waiting for the order to move, Busch wondered what made Anderson tick. He knew that in a short time he would be face-to-face with the suspect. Busch had spoken with hundreds of killers during his career and had learned that most, even though they were cold-blooded killers, would usually respond well with people interviewing them if they were treated with a certain amount of respect. To catch a killer one must know what he is about, how he thinks, and why he did what he did. Given the chance, most will talk; they want to tell their version.

Time passed slowly for Busch as he waited for the signal to move. He thought about his trip in 1980 to Quantico, Virginia, where he met John Douglas of the Behavioral Science Unit at the FBI training center. The unsolved 1978 homicide case, where a young woman was found sexually assaulted and murdered in her home in Illinois, had taken Busch and three other investigators to Quantico to meet with the legendary Douglas for his assistance in the case.

The Behavioral Science Unit was in its infancy stage at that time, but Douglas had already made a name for himself in the field of criminal profiling. He sat down with the Illinois investigators and studied their case. Busch had explained the crime scene to Douglas and displayed photos. During the investigation from 1978 to 1980, evidence of a bite mark developed by image enhancement of a morgue photograph of the victim's neck gave investigators a new lead. They considered the exhumation of the victim's body to examine the bite mark.

Douglas had listened to the information while he viewed the crime scene and morgue photographs. After the hour-long meeting, he told the Illinois lawmen that he agreed with them that the crime scene had been altered by the killer to throw them off. He advised them to publicize the exhumation of the girl's body and said that the killer would contact them. Douglas predicted that the person responsible for the woman's death would want to become a part of the investigation. Douglas had gone as far as to predict what type of vehicle—and even what color the vehicle would be—that the killer would now be driving.

Returning to Illinois, the investigators had publicized the exhumation and did receive the call from the suspect as predicted by Douglas. The alibi given by the suspect in 1978 had a large time gap in it. He couldn't account for his time during the murder. A court order for dental impressions of the suspect's teeth was granted. He was taken to a dentist for casts of his teeth. A forensic odontologist compared the cast taken to the bite mark on the girl's neck. They matched. The suspect was arrested and convicted of the murder. Douglas was also correct on the color and make of vehicle driven by the man convicted of the murder.

The exposure to the effectiveness of knowing

human behavior as shown by Douglas inspired Busch. He understood the importance of communication between suspect and investigator. Profiling usually came about through research of crime statistics and interviews with perpetrators to learn their behavioral characteristics. To be a good hunter you must know the habits of the creature you pursue.

# Seven

Nonn was advised by radio that the area was secured. The tactical unit vehicles moved swiftly toward Anderson's house. Busch pulled in behind the tactical van with Nester following him. The tactical team deployed themselves around the house as Busch pulled his squad to the curb across the street from Anderson's driveway. Standing behind his squad, he watched the faces of the crowd as the SWAT team took position. A member of the SWAT team asked that Busch block Anderson's driveway with his car. Busch pulled the squad car into the driveway, parking near the door of the garage. Then leaving the squad, he walked to the east side of the house.

One more attempt was made to contact the people inside. TV cameramen, with cameras perched on their shoulders, watched through their lenses as St. Clair County Deputy Ralph Owens walked across the lawn toward the front door. Deputy Owens attended the same church as Anderson and had talked with him in the past. He knocked on the front door announcing that there was a search warrant to be served. The sound of Owen's voice carried across the now quiet street. Spectators waited quietly for a response.

Five minutes passed before Owens walked away. SWAT team members converged. While two rifle-men covered the back, two tactical officers carried a large metal battering ram up to the back door. Two other officers positioned themselves beside the rear door. Only two hits were required from the battering ram before the rear door broke open with a thud.

The crowd at the front waited anxiously. One young spectator ventured out into the street.

"I wanna see what's going on," the youngster mumbled to the officer.

"Son, if the shooting starts, bullets don't have eyes. They can't tell if you're a good guy or not," said the veteran officer as he escorted him back behind the police line.

The two armed lawmen entered the kitchen through the broken door. The interior was dark from the cardboard covering the windows. They waited a moment while their eyes adjusted to the dim light. While they crouched near the broken kitchen door, they listened for any sound of move-ment in the house. *Nothing.* It was quiet and dark. They spoke through the headset and advised other tactical members of their position. To the left of the kitchen door, an entranceway led to the living room. The dining room opened into the kitchen and living room. From the dining room, the hallway to the bedroom started.

After securing the kitchen, living room, and dining room, the officers approached the west end of the house. A long hallway ran west of the kitchen. The door to the room on the left of the hallway was open. In the dim light of the bedroom, the officer could make out what appeared to be a human form on the bed. The officer moved closer. He could now see the body of a young boy lying on the bed. He listened for the sound of breathing, but there was none. He whispered into the headset that he had located the boy, but he was not breathing. The expressions on the faces of the other team members outside, who were wearing headsets, reflected the bad news.

"What's going on?" said Busch to the team member standing beside him.

"They've located Anderson's son in his bedroom, and he's not breathing. They're going to check the girl's bedroom next."

"Fuck, I was hoping it hadn't come to that," said Busch.

"Wait, they're still in the boy's room," the tactical man said as his headset crackled again. A smile crossed his face. "They're bringing the two children out. They're okay!"

Commander Nonn and additional officers responded to the rear door of the house. Karen and Paul, wearing only sleeping apparel, were escorted through the mid-forty-degree morning air to warm cars parked down the street.

Paul Anderson told investigators that his father had said that the police wanted to kill him. That was why he held his breath when the officer entered his bedroom. Paul's sister, Karen, was upset and shaken by the ordeal. She was worried about her mother. Both children were taken to the command post to be interviewed.

Standing against the wall in the hallway, outside the master bedroom, the team leader slowly reached for the doorknob on the bedroom door. With a gentle turning action, he checked to see if it was locked. There was no give. He signaled to the other officers in the hallway that the door was locked.

He listened outside for several minutes, heard movement inside the bedroom, and alerted the other officers. Fearing for the safety of Linda Anderson, the bedroom would not be forcibly entered. When the sounds inside the bedroom stopped, the team leader identified himself and requested Anderson to open the door.

In a calm voice, Anderson replied, "What do you want?"

He was informed by the officer that the Sheriff's Department had a search warrant for his handwriting standard and sample writings from the house. After hearing about the search warrant, Anderson still refused to open the door. Concern for Linda Anderson's safety was still the focal point of the tactical unit. They had not heard her talk during the exchange.

"Let us speak with your wife," demanded the officer.

"She doesn't want to talk to you," Anderson said.

"We just want to make sure she's okay. Why don't you let her come out of the room?"

"She's fine. She doesn't want to come out," came the reply through the bedroom door.

Anderson told the tactical officers that he didn't trust them. After twenty minutes of talking, the officer heard the sounds of a woman coughing. They then knew that she was still alive. During negotiations between Anderson and the tactical officers, Anderson asked to speak with Deputy Owens, who agreed to speak to Anderson through the bedroom door.

"Dale, I have a search warrant for your handwriting. You can read it if you like. Will you come out and talk with me?"

"I want to read the warrant. Slip it under the door."

"Okay, I'll slip it under the door," said Owens.

The search warrant slid under the bedroom door.

# Eight

Linda watched her husband in silence as he picked up the typed paper and began reading. She was confused about what was happening. Standing beside Dale Anderson, she read down the paper until her eyes caught the word "MURDER." She stepped back from her husband of eighteen years, not out of fear but out of disbelief. A murder investigation was focused on him. He had told her a different reason why the police were outside.

Her heart pounded as she read the search warrant. *There must be some mistake. Why did the police think Dale had something to do with a murder?* The events of the last two days raced through her mind as she searched for answers.

Wednesday morning, September 27, she had awakened around 5:30 A.M. Dale was in bed beside her, still asleep. She showered and dressed in preparation for work at the day-care center in town. She prepared breakfast for Paul, Karen, and herself. After breakfast, she would drop Paul off at school on her way to work. Karen's school was five blocks from the house, so she would walk to school.

Dale had told Linda, several months after he was arrested in July of 1988 for the weapons charge involving the newspaper reporter, that he had been placed on home assignment by the Public Aid Office. He explained to her that the home assignment meant that he worked out of his house and would not have to go into the office. She didn't question the arrangement since she knew that during his previous working day he would visit Public Aid recipients at their home. Months later, she learned that Dale had lost his job at the Public Aid Office. He blamed what happened on his former supervisors. He expressed his dislike for them and talked about the civil service hearing on his termination. He had filed for the state civil service hearing after he was terminated, and the case was scheduled later in the year. Now unemployed, Dale was usually asleep when she left for work, as he was this Wednesday morning. Closing the front door of the house, Linda left for work.

At 6:30 P.M., Wednesday, she pulled her yellow Oldsmobile into the driveway and parked. Followed by Paul, she went into the house where she found Dale listening to his portable scanner through a headset, as he watched TV. Karen was in her room. Linda began cooking dinner. By 7:30 P.M., the family sat around the dining room table. Linda and the children talked, while Dale listened to the police scanner through head-phones.

Later that evening, Linda noticed that a police car was still parked near the intersection at the front of the house. She had seen the squad car there when she pulled into the driveway earlier but didn't think anything about it. Now she mentioned it to her husband.

"I know they're out there. I may be in trouble with my probation officer for not letting him come inside. I'm still on probation for that gun thing. I'm not going to allow him to come into my house."

"Will you get in trouble if you don't let him in?"

"I may have violated my probation. They probably want to arrest me. I don't think you and the kids should leave. The cops will harass you if you go outside. I think you should stay home from work tomorrow and the kids should stay home from school."

Linda didn't like the idea of missing work, but Dale's voice was firm. Dale had never been physically mean to her. They had always discussed family matters although Linda was the one that handled the day-to-day activities of the children. She was the dominant parent with the children. Dale managed the finances.

At 10:00 P.M., Linda went to the bedroom, where she watched the news on TV. It was

76

through the evening newscast that she became aware of the double murder in the Villa Madero Subdivision. During the broadcast, it was reported that a man had been seen in the general vicinity in which the woman and her son were slain. Shocked by the story of the murders in her hometown, she hurried down the hall to talk to Dale, who was watching the report in the living room.

"Dale, I just heard on the news that there was a murder in Belleville."

Dale had little or no comment. He was listening to the police scanner again with the earphone plugged into the scanner. After her comment about the murders, she paused and began to think. There were several police cars around their house. She didn't want to believe that her husband could be involved in a double murder, but now she began to wonder if he may have been mistaken for someone else.

"Is there any way you could have been in the neighborhood where those people were killed? Maybe someone mistook you for somebody else."

"Oh, no. I don't even know where that is. I don't even know where Villa Madero is."

She couldn't tell if he was telling the truth. His calmness made her feel confident that he had nothing to do with the killings, but in the back of her mind there was the little question that he may have been in the area and someone thought it was Dale who killed the family.

He had been a good husband. Linda remembered back to when they first met in college. She was eighteen and a freshman at Illinois State University. Dale was also a freshman. They dated all through college and went to the graduation ceremony together. After college they both became student teachers for a while. Dale taught at the high school in La Salle. Linda taught in a grade school in Peru. They returned to Belleville in March of 1973, and were married in August of that year.


By eleven o'clock on Wednesday evening, Linda and her family were asleep while patrol units outside kept a watchful eye on the house. Thursday morning was uneventful. Dale read books, watched TV, and listened to the police scanner. Their children played in their rooms and watched TV. Linda did laundry and cooked meals. Early in the evening, Dale walked over to the cardboard covered window and peered out. He smiled as he viewed the large number of officers and spectators in the street.

"Look at all the cops. They're afraid of me. It's going to take a lot of cops to take me."

"Dale, what's going on? Tell me what this is about."

"Must be because of my probation violation."

He would not say much to her other than he had made a violation in his probation status by not allowing the probation officer into his home. When she quizzed him about the matter further, he wouldn't answer. He seemed hungry with power as more people gathered outside. She decided not to rock the boat with too many questions. He kept boasting about how many cops it would take to arrest him. She felt uneasy and uncertain about what he might do.

Thursday night, they were asleep by 11:30 P.M. Friday morning, Linda awoke to the sound of breaking glass and splintering wood. She sat up in bed and looked around. Dale, also awakened by the noise, calmly told her to get dressed. He seemed unconcerned about the safety of his children, as he locked his bedroom door. Now dressed, he sat on the edge of the bed, listening and waiting, like a skilled chess player, awaiting the next move by the police.

# Nine

Busch stepped through the shattered door into the kitchen. He paused. The darkness surprised him. While he waited for his eyes to adjust, someone bumped into him. It was Nester. He, too, had come from outside into Anderson's kitchen and did not see Busch.

"I've been in underground caves that weren't this dark," said Busch.

"Man, how can they live like this?" Nester said in a low tone.

Busch peered down the dim hallway. He could see the two SWAT officers standing outside the bedroom door. Deputy Owens spoke to Anderson through the door. He assured Anderson that no harm would come to him if he came out of the bedroom. Busch listened for a response. From behind the door came a nasal-toned voice.

"Am I under arrest?"

"No, they have a court order for your handwriting standard. If you don't comply with the order then the judge may issue an arrest order," said Deputy Owens.

Minutes passed. Nester and Busch stood beside the dining room table while they watched and waited. The bedroom door opened slowly. Linda Anderson emerged from the room with her husband behind her. Anderson held his wife by her arms, shielding himself.

Anderson was searched for weapons. He had none on him. Anderson shuffled slowly down the hallway toward the living room. He stood behind the table and watched as the tactical officers left the house. Busch waited for Anderson's reaction. Anderson huddled beside his wife at the dining room table while he spoke with Deputy Owens.

Nester and Busch were responsible for the next phase of the investigation. They were joined by Inspector Heil in the dining room. Nester identified himself to Anderson, even though he felt Anderson knew him from working at the Sheriff's Department. He then introduced Busch and Heil. Anderson commented that he had seen Heil before but not Busch.

Busch came face-to-face with Anderson for the first time. When he stuck out his hand, the gesture surprised Anderson, who hesitated momentarily, then extended a pale hand. After Anderson had met the three investigators, Nester asked him if he would go to the Sheriff's Department to be interviewed and complete the handwriting standard.

"If I'm not under arrest, I don't want to leave the house," said Anderson.

"I need to interview you," said Nester.

"Why can't you do that here? I don't want to leave the house."

Nester was perplexed with the situation. He knew if he pushed the issue about Anderson leaving the house it could jeopardize the investigation. As long as Anderson did not violate the court order and complied with giving the handwriting standard, there was nothing the detective could do. Nester pushed on with the interview.

"It would be better if we went to the county to do this. I need to talk to you, and one of the other detectives can talk with your wife," said Nester.

"No, I don't want to leave. You can talk to me here," said Anderson.

Linda Anderson volunteered to be interviewed at the Sheriff's Department. She asked about her children and was told that they had been taken to the command post. She seemed concerned about them but still asked her husband if she should leave. His mood had changed. He sensed that the investigators were not going to arrest him and now appeared cocky. He dwelled on the issue of not leaving his house, and showed no interest in the status of his children.

Busch watched Anderson as he talked with Nester, noticing that Anderson appreciated the attention the investigators were giving him. Anderson liked being in control. He was accustomed to having things his way. The dark setting of the house had been noted by Busch. How would Anderson react if that was altered somewhat? He had kept the house dark for over a year. Busch strolled over to the glass patio doors, behind the dining table, that were covered with large sheets of cardboard. Anderson stopped talking and watched him.

"Let's get a little light in here. I can hardly see," said Busch as he removed the cardboard at the patio doors.

The bright morning sunlight exploded into the dining room and sent beams of light into the kitchen and living room. Anderson blinked as the room brightened but made no comment about the new arrangement. Busch walked back to the dining table and sat down. He smiled at Anderson, who now seemed at ease with the investigators.

Nester, seated across the table, asked Anderson if he remembered him from the Sheriff's Department. Anderson, who had worked as a jailer in 1980, began to talk about fellow jailers that he had worked with. Nester had picked a topic that opened the lines of communication between the two. They talked for thirty minutes about members of the Sheriff's Department, past and present. Deputy Owens excused himself from the round table discussion and left the house. Nester, Heil, and Busch stayed.

Busch picked up on the fact that Anderson liked anything that had to do with police work. Anderson was smart. He knew that he had control of the situation. He was well versed in law and knew that he could end the interview at any time. The only two things he had to comply with were giving his handwriting standard and allowing handwriting samples to be collected. *Like a card game in Vegas,* thought Busch. Anderson was the dealer and played by his rules. The investigators would have to play the hand dealt them. The stakes were high. Two had already died.

Busch chose his words carefully as he requested Anderson's compliance with the search warrant for samples of handwriting on documents inside the house.

"Dale, I need to take photos of any items I collect."

"Take as many photographs of the house as you need. I have nothing to hide. I'll help you search the house after I complete the handwriting standard. Go ahead, search. I have nothing to hide," said Anderson with a smirk on his face.

Busch began taking pictures. He started with the living room, noticing that there were several videotapes on top of the TV with writing on the covers. *All cop shows. Anderson has a fetish for police work,* mused the veteran investigator, whose police career had come about by chance.

Busch entered the bedroom on the left side of the hallway. It was Paul's room. Nothing unusual. He checked the second bedroom on the left, Karen's room. It was clean and well kept. Busch removed the cardboard from the bedroom windows after he photographed each room.

Opening the door to the master bedroom, he saw a queen-size bed, two dressers, and a TV. A small bathroom was located off the northeast corner of the bedroom. Walking into the bedroom, Busch noticed wooden clubs and metal baseball bats in the corner. Soap. Small used bars of soap, all the same size but of different brands, were piled high in bags on the dresser along with stacks of business cards from lawyers. Four identical-looking, brown, combination-lock briefcases sat on the floor. They looked out of place with the rest of the room. The combination locks on all four briefcases were set on the same numbers.

Nester, seated to Anderson's left at the dining room table, continued the interview. He had also picked up on Anderson's cop fetish. Anderson had a preoccupation with anything involving police work. Nester stayed with the subject of Anderson's time as a jailer as long as possible. Now he had to change the topic of conversation. In a tactful move, he asked Anderson where he went after he left the Sheriff's Department.

The interview moved smoothly with Anderson talking about leaving his jailer position and going to work at the Public Aid Office. Nester felt uneasy about the calmness of the man. Even though Anderson made no threatening gestures toward him, Nester had the sense of being in the presence of something evil.

Anderson explained to Nester that he was currently on a leave of absence from his job at the

Public Aid Office. Nester confronted him about having been terminated by his employer. Anderson, pushing back his glasses on the bridge of his nose, admitted that he lost his job but was quick to reply that he expected to be reinstated soon. Anderson was now on a first name basis with the three investigators. He asked questions when Busch and Heil walked past the table.

"I'll help you search if you want me to," said Anderson, as Heil and Busch entered the dining room.

"Dale, I think Nester would like you to work with him," said Busch.

"What about my cats? Belleville broke down my door and the cats are gone," said Anderson.

"We can check outside and see if they're there," said Busch, motioning for Heil to join in the search.


Anderson was an interviewer's nightmare. He would change the subject or complain about something every time Nester began to focus on key issues of the investigation.

"Can't we get that guy to move? I don't think that's right. I don't want him there," said Anderson, pointing to the cameraman in a neighbor's yard behind Anderson's house.

"Do you want to go to the county where we won't be interrupted?" asked Nester.

"We're better off here," said Anderson.

Nester decided to back off the issue of Anderson leaving the house. He slid the writing forms across the table toward him, explaining how the handwriting forms were to be filled out. Anderson listened with interest as Nester went through each form. Reaching for the two writing pens clipped to the pocket of his blue shirt, Anderson smiled. The smile gave Nester a cold chill down his spine. Anderson seemed amused about something, but the investigator didn't know what it was. With each passing moment, it became more evident that he was dealing with a very clever and dangerous man.

Heil and Busch walked around the house looking for Anderson's cats. Photographers scurried to take pictures of the two men. A member of the MCS approached Busch and Heil as they rambled around in the yard.

"What are you looking for?" asked the detective.

"We're looking for some pussy," said Busch, then grinning at the expression on the detective's face.

Heil chuckled at Busch's statement to the detective. As the detective walked along with them, Heil explained that Anderson was playing mind games with them.

No cats. Heil and Busch rejoined Nester and Anderson at the dining room table. Anderson sat at the table writing on the forms. He stopped writing to inquire if he were filling out the forms properly, like a grade school student seeking approval from an idolized teacher. To stroke his ego,

Nester complimented Anderson on his penmanship during the left-handed phase of the handwriting assignment.

After writing for a few minutes, Anderson stopped and began to complain about the Belleville Police Department. He glared at the broken kitchen door. Tightening his facial muscles, he asked, with a sarcastic tone, "Who's going to fix my door?" Nester avoided the question and tried to get Anderson back on track with filling out the handwriting forms. Anderson verbally blasted the Belleville Police Department again. Nester sat quietly for a moment, then asked Anderson if he wanted to take a break. Getting up from the table, Anderson walked toward the master bedroom. Busch followed behind him. Stopping at the bathroom door of the bedroom, Anderson turned and looked at Busch.

"I need to use the bathroom," said Anderson.

"Okay, I'll have to search it, before you use it," said Busch.

Anderson stood by the bathroom door as Busch checked the shower stall, toilet, and sink in the bathroom for any weapons. He stepped out; Anderson stepped in and closed the door behind him. Busch waited. The bathroom door opened and Anderson finished wiping off his eyeglasses with a bath towel. *He cleaned his glasses twice before when Nester escorted him to the bathroom off the dining room,* Busch remembered. *Perhaps he was making sure all the tiny blood spatters from the victims were cleaned away.*

* * *

Anderson returned to the dining table, again staring at the broken kitchen door and door frame. His round chin went white and exposed a cluster of ugly dimples as he began to speak.

"Who's going to fix my kitchen door? Belleville liked doing that," said Anderson.

"Dale, if the police broke your door then they'll fix it," said Busch in a calm voice.

"I think whoever broke it should fix it," said Anderson.

"I agree, I'm going outside to radio Mearl Justus and see if we can get that door fixed," said Busch.

Anderson felt that he was in control again. He had the police working for him. He went back to filling out the handwriting forms. Nester put his hand over his mouth to hide his smile. He knew that Busch had used the door issue to get Anderson back to writing, but now Busch would have to confront the sheriff about having Anderson's door fixed.

Busch walked outside to his squad car and radioed for Sheriff Justus to meet with him. Ten minutes later Justus arrived at the crowded intersection and parked on the side of the road. The large man met Busch on the front lawn. Busch had worked with Mearl before and counted on his cooperation. He also knew that the request could elicit a scolding, depending on the sheriff's mood at the time.

Mearl listened as Busch explained that fixing Anderson's door could help build a bridge of confidence between the investigators and the suspect. Mearl agreed to send two men out to repair the door. He asked how it was going inside.

"Anderson's jacking us around. He knows why we're here. He likes to play games. I'm glad Nester is interviewing Anderson. He has the patience to deal with him," said Busch.

"Have you found anything yet?" asked Mearl.

"We've been taking it slow with Anderson. He stalls a lot. We don't want to piss him off so it's going to take time," said Busch.

"I'll send someone over to fix that door," said Mearl, as he turned toward the crowd waiting at the intersection.

TV cameramen and reporters cornered the sheriff as he walked back to his car. They shouted questions: Why were the police in the Anderson house so long? Is Anderson the prime suspect in the Lanman murders?

Mearl straightened his blue blazer as the cameraman focused on him for a live interview. He was a good public speaker and had been in police work for twenty-six years. He would give the news media a brief explanation without giving any details.

"We came here this morning to execute a search warrant at Anderson's residence. We had some concerns about his safety and that of his family. Obviously everyone is okay," remarked the sheriff before departing.

Busch returned to the dining room. He was glad to see that Anderson was still writing on the forms. Busch told Anderson that Mearl had agreed to repair the kitchen door. That appeared to satisfy him. Busch entered the master bedroom and collected a steno notebook with writing from the dresser. He logged the item of evidence on the evidence receipt. Anderson walked into the bedroom en route to the restroom. He stopped. Busch had picked up one of Anderson's briefcases. Seated on the edge of the bed, Busch placed the briefcase on his lap. He noticed that Anderson was watching him.

"What's in the briefcases, Dale?" asked Busch.

"Just papers," said Anderson, with a nervous twitch.

"Feels awful heavy for just papers."

"Just papers, that's all," said Anderson.

"I noticed that the combination locks on the four briefcases were set on the same number."

"I don't remember the combinations."

Busch turned the dials of the combination locks on the briefcase. Anderson watched intensely. He repeated that he had forgotten the number to open the case. Busch watched Anderson's eyes. The pudgy-faced man just stood there as Busch turned the dials again. The latches on the case sprang open. Anderson's eyes widened but Busch held the top of the briefcase closed. He relocked it and placed it on the floor. Anderson sighed with relief. Busch decided that to open the lid at that time could jeopardize the investigation. He would wait until he had a legal right to view its contents.

When Anderson returned to the dining room, he was relaxed. It was 11:00 A.M., three hours had elapsed since Nester began the interview. With the bathroom trips and distractions created by Anderson, very little progress had been made on the lengthy handwriting forms. Nester was fearful of pushing the time factor. He needed the handwriting forms completed. He would stay with his first approach. Slow and easy.

"Dale, you want to take a break for a while?" asked Nester.

"We could," said Anderson.

"Let's take a lunch break. What kind of food do you like, Dale?" said Busch.

"I like McDonald's," said Anderson.

"McDonald's alright with you guys?" said Busch.

Nester and Heil agreed on Anderson's choice. Allowing Anderson to select the type of food he wanted boosted his ego. He was the important one in this investigation. He liked the attention. Anderson placed his order.

The food order was given to a road deputy stationed outside. Busch was surprised at the size of the crowd around Anderson's house. People now sat in rows on neighboring lawns. Pizzas were being delivered to hungry spectators. The circus atmosphere stopped there. Inside the house, the three investigators joked and laughed with Anderson, but they had not lost sight of their objective.

Busch had seen what was done to the Lanmans.

He knew that he had to mask his real feelings. To deprive Anderson of his newfound esteem could be dangerous at this point. Anderson was far from ignorant. He would be able to spot an ill attempt at friendship.

The food order arrived. The four men ate at the dining room table. Anderson turned on the TV on the kitchen counter to watch the news.

"Dale, can you turn off the TV while we eat?" inquired Busch, fearful of derogatory news commentary on Anderson.

"I want to watch the news," said Anderson in a stern tone.

Nester and Busch exchanged glances. Nester raised his shoulders to indicate to Busch that there wasn't much either could do. Nester watched through the open living room door as a news crew prepared to film live from the edge of Anderson's front lawn.

# Ten

The crowd of spectators outside Anderson's house grew restless as the news crews began their live Friday afternoon coverage. Nester bit into his McDonald's hamburger, and Anderson started on one of the chicken sandwiches. Busch reached into the large McDonald's bag and took out a salad, fries, and Anderson's second chicken sandwich. He slid the food across the table to Anderson. Heil and Busch took their lunch from the bag, but Busch deliberately left Anderson's apple pie inside to see if he would notice. He did.

"Is there an apple pie in there? I ordered an apple pie," said Anderson.

"One apple pie coming up," said Busch, grinning. "If you eat like this every day, you'll be bigger then Heil."

"Fuck you, Busch," said Heil in response to Busch's comment.

"Shame on you, Twiggy, for talking like that," said Busch.

Anderson peered down the dining room table at the 275-pound Dee Heil. He laughed at the expression on Heil's face after being called Twiggy. Anderson enjoyed the police humor, but turned his attention to the news broadcast which began with coverage of the Lanmans' house. It was quiet in the room while the four men watched the TV on the kitchen counter.

A portrait of the Lanman family was shown, followed by a live interview with John Lanman.

"How frustrating is it for you personally that an arrest hasn't been made?" said the reporter.

"Well, from the people I talked to from the Major Case Squad, they all have been very nice and very kind. I'm sure they have their job to do, and they are doing it the best they can. My only hope is that they catch whoever did this, and that the evidence is conclusive. So we can put an end to this once and for all," said Lanman.

The news continued with live coverage in front of Anderson's house.

"State's Attorney John Baricevic told us that he does not expect an arrest anytime soon," said the reporter. "Apparently authorities are looking for the evidence that would make that arrest possible."

A photograph of Dale Anderson appeared on the TV. Busch watched Anderson for any type of reaction. Anderson listened and watched with a smile on his face.

"Meanwhile Dale Anderson is well-known to local lawmen. His neighbors describe him as weird and strange. He's been known to tell people that

95

he is a police officer. Police sources say he carried fake badges and often told people he was an undercover police informant. Neighbors say he once claimed to work for the CIA," said the reporter.

Busch looked at Nester and rolled his eyes to emphasize how bizarre the situation had become. Never had Busch been involved in an interview where a suspect in a double murder watches TV, and the news media is chastising the suspect.

The news coverage talked about the 1988 Cardenas case and labeled Anderson as a suspect. Carolyn Tuft was interviewed on TV. She talked about the incident on June 7, 1988, where she went to Anderson's home to interview him about having his bosses arrested. He flourished a holstered revolver, telling her not to misquote him or she would be sorry. The news broadcast ended with how potentially violent Dale Anderson was.

"I guess they're disappointed that we didn't shoot it out," said Anderson, looking at Busch.

"I'm not concerned with what the news media wants, but I am concerned with the death of the woman and the three-year-old boy," Busch told him.

Anderson denied ever seeing the Lanmans until their photos appeared in the news. The negative coverage about Anderson didn't faze him. He ate both sandwiches and the rest of the food he had ordered. After lunch, the four men talked about police work which Anderson thrived on. Nester thought the time was right to press on with the investigation and get the handwriting standard completed. As Nester located the final pages of the form for Anderson to finish, Busch spoke with Anderson.

"Dale, we need to search your blue Oldsmobile."

"You have a search warrant. Go ahead and search it."

"The search warrant doesn't cover your vehicle. Before I can search it, you'll have to sign a consent-to-search form, you know all about this search warrant stuff, don't you, Dale?"

Anderson smiled and signed the form for his car to be searched. He accompanied Busch out to the garage where the car was located and then returned to the dining room to complete the handwriting forms. Busch went to the master bedroom to collect samples.

Busch stopped working when he heard Anderson's voice get louder. He listened for a moment. From the dining room came Anderson's voice again. Busch went to see what was going on, and was surprised to find Mike Boyne sitting at the table with Anderson. Busch motioned for Nester to follow him to the living room.

"What the fuck is going on?" said Busch.

"Anderson wanted to talk with Boyne, now they're talking about when Anderson got arrested in 1988," Nester told him.

"It doesn't look like it's going too well. Anderson is getting pissed," said Busch.

"He was almost finished with the handwriting forms," said Nester.

"Hey, I don't give a fuck about 1988, just tell Boyne to back off Anderson for now."

Nester interrupted the conversation between Anderson and Boyne. He told Anderson that he could talk with Boyne later, but the forms needed to be completed. Boyne assured Anderson that he would come back later and they would talk.

Busch had worked with Boyne in an undercover unit back in the 1970s. Both had entrusted their safety many times to each other during covert operations. Although Boyne was smaller than most people would envision an officer to be, his courage put him heads above the rest. He was well versed in police work, having worked for the East St. Louis Police Department before joining the Belleville Police Department. During Boyne's police career, he had been involved in shoot-outs and ordeals where he risked his own life to protect others. Busch liked and respected him.

Busch noticed that Anderson became irritated quickly with any exposure to the Belleville Police Department. That was in direct contrast to the interest Anderson had shown in police work. He otherwise remained cool and calm.

Fearing that Anderson's antagonistic attitude toward the Belleville Police Department might jeopardize the Lanman case, Busch approached him about a consent-to-search agreement for a complete search of the house for any items of evidence. At 2:50 P.M. Anderson signed the agreement, and again a smirk crossed his face as he said, "Go ahead and search. Take anything you want. I don't have anything to hide."

Returning to the master bedroom, Busch opened the drawers of the dresser. He found sections of nylon rope among items of clothing, several wooden paddles, and other sexual devices. *Someone was into masochism.* Searching the third drawer, Busch found six pairs of white cloth gloves and several sets of latex gloves. He examined the cloth gloves closely. They had two separate weave patterns to them. Busch had seen that pattern before, in blood on the bed skirting of Lanman's bed.

Placing the gloves into an evidence bag, Busch felt that the gloves would be important but would not be enough to base a case on. He showed the items to Anderson as he logged them on the evidence sheet. Busch described each item. When he came to the paddles, Anderson corrected the investigator on what the items were.

"Those are just pieces of wood," said Anderson.

"They look like paddles to me," said Busch. "Each one has a handle and some are taped around the edge. What do you use these for, Dale?"

"They're just pieces of wood," said Anderson, who became flush.

Busch listed them as pieces of wood with tape and red stain visible. Judging from the look on Anderson's face, Busch guessed that they were used either by Anderson or on Anderson during marital games. Since a red stain was visible on them, they were collected to determine if there was blood present.

Anderson had finished the handwriting forms. They were packaged by Nester and sent with a member of the MCS to St.Louis, Missouri, where document examiner William H. Storer awaited the arrival of Anderson's writing standards to compare to the note found at the Lanman house.

# Eleven

The other members of the Major Case Squad were busy while the search of Anderson's house was going on. Detectives Rick McCain and Mick Dooley revisited Villa Madero, knocking on doors and interviewing homeowners.

Commander Nonn, working on a hunch that the "For Sale" signs may have attracted the killer, assigned Detectives Joe Michaelis and David Hoffmann to canvass the subdivision east of Villa Madero. Michaelis and Hoffmann located Jill Hindrichs, who also had her home for sale and had received a visit from a stranger the day of the Lanman murders.

Jill Hindrichs said she had walked toward the front door when the bell rang. Glancing at her watch, she saw that it was almost two in the afternoon. *Who would be here at this time of day?* She answered the door and spoke to the chunky-faced man standing on the porch.

"Hi, can I help you?"

"I'm here to see the house," said the stranger.

"Pardon?" said Hindrichs, as she watched the man in the blue baseball cap.

"Can I go through your house and see it?"

"No," she said. "I can't let you see the house unless a real estate agent is with you."

The stranger assured her that his wife had called the real estate agent. Standing near the door, he clung to the large bulky leather bag that hung to his right side. He carried it like a newspaperboy, the strap of the bag around his left shoulder. His insistence to enter frightened her. She cautiously slid the chain lock into place on the front door while she talked to the man with the overbite.

Jill told him to wait outside while she got her real estate agent's business card. Opening the chained door slightly, she handed the card to the middle-aged man. He stared at her for a brief moment while he ran his hand along the bulging side of the bag at his waist. His hand moved toward the opening in the bag, but stopped as he looked down the street. Then he thanked her and walked away. She watched him walk down the street until she lost sight of him. *Strange,* she thought as she closed the door. *He didn't even have a car parked nearby.*

Jill Hindrichs was able to give a good description of the suspicious man. Hoffmann and Michaelis learned that the stranger was around five feet eleven inches tall with a short haircut and wore eyeglasses. They called the information into the command post. They were given another lead to follow up on. It was a woman named Cheryl

Scott who lived in the subdivision three-quarters of a mile northeast of Villa Madero.

The detective parked in front of Cheryl Scott's home. A large "house for sale by owner" sign was posted in her front yard. Hoffmann and Michaelis were allowed in after they identified themselves as members of the Major Case Squad. The interview with the thirty-nine-year-old homemaker began.

On September 20, 1989, Cheryl Scott and her six-year-old son were at home. Around 4:00 P.M. there was a knock on the front door.

"Hi, I'm Dave Johnson and I'm here to see about the house," said the man, who acted as if he had made an appointment. Cheryl let him in the front door. He walked around inside as she pointed out different aspects of the home. He viewed the outside of the house briefly. Turning to her, the chunky man in the tight clothes asked to see the inside again. Walking back inside, the stranger stopped and looked around the room.

"This is exactly what we're looking for," he said, pushing his glasses on the bridge of his nose.

"I have a handout with the statistics of the house, if you want one," said Cheryl.

"You have a basement?"

"No, there's a crawl space that you can get to in the walk-in closet."

He seemed interested to see the crawl space, but began to ask peculiar questions as they stood in the bedroom. His mannerism alarmed her. She went back into the living room. Again he wanted her to come into the master bedroom and show him the closet.

"I'm just trying to get an idea of space," said the man, clutching the bulky satchel tightly under his right armpit.

Cheryl felt that she had made a mistake by allowing this total stranger into her home. The man kept within arm's reach of her everytime she moved. She looked around to see where her son was. He was playing Nintendo in his room. What should she do? She was leery of going back into the master bedroom with the pudgy man, who wanted to see the crawl space again.

They stood in silence in the laundry room. He stared down at her. His blue-gray eyes were cold and uncaring. He had a smirk on his pale face. To break the silence, she asked him what kind of work he did for a living. In a nasal-toned voice, he answered with caution. Noncommittal about a company's name, he claimed that he maintained and repaired hospital equipment in the area. He hinted that he was from Springfield, Illinois.

The loud knock on the front door startled them both. A woman walked into the house, calling out to Cheryl.

"I'm getting a beer," she said as she sat down at the kitchen table.

With a sigh of relief and a nervous tone in her voice, Cheryl yelled out to her neighbor.

"Go ahead. You know where it is."

The man showed concern that someone had entered the house. He no longer wanted to ask "prospective home buyer" questions. He appeared frustrated by the arrival of the neighbor. He headed for the front door and tried to avoid the kitchen area where the woman sat drinking a beer.

"Do you want to go out through the kitchen door?" said Cheryl, hoping her neighbor would turn around to see him.

"No," he said in a calm voice.

Cheryl now felt safe since her friend arrived. As she walked to the front door, she noticed that he had no car parked outside. He picked up on the fact that she was looking for his car and mentioned to her that he had parked down the street earlier to look at another home that was for sale.

The detectives were not surprised when Cheryl described the stranger as around six feet tall, early forties, short hair, and with an overbite. They returned to the command post and filed their reports of the interviews with Jill Hindrichs and Cheryl Scott. Detective John Betten, Field Report Officer, flagged the reports and alerted Commander Nonn about them.

Nonn felt that statements from Hindrichs and Scott could be used to obtain an arrest warrant for Anderson. It would take time to accomplish. Nonn would have to be cautious about the arrest issue. A legal mistake at this time would be fatal to the Lanman case, and Nonn was concerned about Anderson leaving the house before an arrest warrant was issued. If that happened there was nothing he could do.

Assistant State's Attorney Dennis Hatch received the information about the interviews with Hindrichs and Scott. He weighed the importance of the statements in his mind. The statements by themselves were not enough to arrest Anderson.

Since investigators had found a note, the handwriting on the note could possibly link Anderson to the murder scene. Hatch felt that the MCS was on target with their investigation, but they needed more to connect Anderson to the case.

Commander Nonn and Hatch kept in close contact on every development in the case. Nonn desperately wanted something ironclad to link Anderson to the Lanman case. He wondered if evidence would surface during the Lanman investigation that might tie Anderson to the Cardenas murder.

Nonn assigned detectives Phil Delaney, Roger Cook, and Dave Jacobs to check the vacant fields near the murder scene for any items of evidence. Nonn provided additional manpower for a search of trash Dumpsters on several routes that Anderson may have taken from the murder scene to his house. MCS members checked local storage companies to see if Anderson had rented any storage units in town. Court records were checked for any rental property in Anderson's name. All met with negative results.

Nonn ordered the unit to concentrate on witnesses. The commander wanted to lock Anderson in on time and place. Nonn wanted enough information about Anderson to check any alibi given by Anderson. These puzzle pieces about Anderson, gathered by Nonn, would later be arranged by skilled Hatch to form a portrait of a very evil man. But for now, Nonn would have to wait for Anderson to give a statement to Nester. Time was passing, and Anderson was still at home.

# Twelve

Nester returned to the dining room table. Anderson waited patiently while the investigator opened his notebook to begin the interview. Nester asked Anderson about his activities on the morning of September 27, 1989. Anderson talked about how typical Wednesday was. His wife had left for work, and the kids were in school. Since he was unemployed he had no plans for the day. He worked around the house but did not go anywhere.

Expecting the condensed version of Wednesday, Nester moved the time frame of the question to Thursday the twenty-eighth, with intentions of returning to more detailed questions later. Anderson ignored Nester's question about Thursday and commented on the evening of the twenty-seventh.

"I knew the police were out there."

"Why didn't you go out there or answer the door?" said Nester.

"Because I've had a bad experience with the Belleville Police," said Anderson.

"Why didn't Linda go to work and the kids go to school on Thursday?"

"The family had colds," said Anderson in quick response to the question.

Nester moved to the issue about the two cars in the garage. Anderson verified that Linda drove the yellow Oldsmobile and he drove the blue Oldsmobile. Nester wanted to pin him down on the locations of the vehicles on Wednesday, the day of the murders.

"Did you leave the house on Wednesday, the twenty-seventh?"

*"No."*

"Did you let anyone use your car?"

"No, it was in the garage."

"So you never left the house on Wednesday?"

Anderson thought for a moment as he looked at Nester. He appeared to be weighing the question to guess which response to give. With his hands clasped together as though in prayer, he answered.

"I might have gone to the store."

"Were you home when your kids came home from school?"

"Yes, I was home around 3:00 P.M. to 3:30 P.M. that afternoon."

Anderson frequently stopped the interview to make phone calls just to test the detective's tolerance. Nester used Anderson's own ego against him. When Anderson walked away from the table during the interview, Nester would wait until he returned to continue.

"Dale, if you don't want to talk to me you don't have to," said Nester.

"I'll talk to you. I want to help in the case," said Anderson.

"You can cease any conversation, and I'll leave at your command," said the detective, testing the eagerness of Anderson to stay in the center of attention.

Nester pulled out a Miranda form and read it to Anderson again and handed the form to him. Anderson read down the list of his rights per the Miranda Decision. Looking back at the detective, he slid the form back to him.

"I know all about that, and I'm not interested in exercising my rights. I've got nothing to hide," said Anderson with a confident tone.

The two men talked about the Villa Madero Subdivision. Anderson denied ever being in that area. He admitted that he was familiar with the area near there and had played miniature golf down the highway from the subdivision. Nester offered Anderson a chance to form an alibi for being seen in the subdivision.

"Could you have driven through Villa Madero when you played miniature golf?" said Nester.

"I would not have gone through that subdivision," said Anderson emphatically. "Not Villa Madero or any other subdivision in that area for over six months."

Sliding the front page of the *Belleville News-Democrat* that was sitting on the dining room table toward Anderson, Nester asked him if he

110

knew the people on the front page. Anderson looked down at the Friday edition of the newspaper which he had read earlier that morning. In bold letters across the top of the paper: HUSBAND TELLS OF TRAGIC DISCOVERY. Below the headlines was a family picture of the Lanmans.

"I don't know them. I never saw them before," said Anderson, his facial expression never changed.

Nester went over the interview with Anderson again to lock him in on a statement covering four points:

(1) He had been home alone Wednesday, 09/27/89, and had no appointments or commitments.

(2) He was in sole possession of the blue Oldsmobile and had not allowed anyone to have the car that day.

(3) He was familiar with the Villa Madero area, but to the best of his recollection, had never been in the subdivision for any reason and knows no one in that area.

(4) He did not know the victims or the family and had never been to the house.

Anderson read the four points Nester outlined. He agreed that all four were accurate. Nester asked if Anderson was planning to move from the house he currently lived in. Anderson had been very calculating during the entire interview, to the point of being almost robotic in his actions. He measured his words and thoughts before speaking. If Nester asked a question he didn't like, he would stare at the detective as if to intimidate him, his blue-gray eyes fixed on the interviewer.

Detective Mike Boyne walked past the front door of Anderson's house, which brought Anderson out of his seat in the middle of the interview. He wanted to talk to the Belleville officer. Nester tried to continue the interview but Anderson demanded to talk with Boyne. Boyne came into the house and sat down at the table at Anderson's request. Nester walked into the living room where Busch was examining files and papers that sat in boxes on the living room floor.

"Look at some of this shit," said Busch. "Dale's got all kinds of documents concerning Cardenas. He's got eleven copies of a Sunday paper dated 9-24-89, that's three days before the Lanmans were murdered. Guess whose face is on the front page? Woidtke." Busch handed Nester a copy.

"Why so many copies?" mumbled Nester as he read. "It is about Rodney Woidtke being sentenced for Cardenas's murder."

"Yeah, there's a connection here with the Lanman murders, but I'm not sure what it is yet. I'm going to read some of this stuff. Nobody has eleven copies of a newspaper unless the article is very important to them."

"This case gets stranger as we go along," said Nester.

"Dale's a clever son of a bitch. It's all a fucking game for him," said Busch. "Not your run-of-the-mill St. Clair County jailer, I hope."

Nester laughed and took the ribbing from Busch. It was a strange feeling investigating someone on a double murder that once worked at the same place he did. He had only seen Anderson at the jail, he really didn't know the man.

"Dale seemed too willing to give that handwriting standard and let us search the house, what do you think?" said Nester.

"He's definitely good for the Lanman murders. I'm afraid he knows something about the note we don't know. He's too damn confident on the handwriting."

Anderson and Boyne were in a loud discussion in the dining room again. Busch and Nester came back in. Anderson seemed irritated with Boyne, arguing that the Belleville Police Department had no right to confiscate his guns when he was arrested in 1988 for the weapons charge filed by Carolyn Tuft. Busch stood near the kitchen counter while he watched Anderson. This was the first time Anderson had shown any anger. As he talked about the Belleville officers, he slammed his clenched fist on top of the table.

Boyne defended the actions taken by his fellow officers back in 1988, when Anderson's guns were seized. That infuriated Anderson. His voice became higher-pitched as he told Boyne that he

113

wasn't treated with respect from the Belleville officers when he was arrested. Boyne listened as Anderson expounded on how he was wronged. Anderson wanted Boyne to have his guns returned to him. Boyne told him that he did not have the authority to release the weapons. Anderson's temper began to emerge.

The tension worsened. Busch intervened. If the discussion was allowed to continue Anderson might make demands that the guns be returned, and that would only cloud the issue. Busch asked to talk with Boyne. Nester returned to the table and renewed the interview with Anderson.

Boyne and Busch walked to the garage. After discussing Anderson and his weird outlook on things, they agreed not to let past history confuse the primary interview.

Boyne returned to the dining room and spoke to Anderson briefly, then left so Nester could finish the interview. Nester asked if Anderson had any plans of moving from his present home. The question took Anderson by surprise. He told the detective that he liked the house and hadn't considered moving. Nester asked if he had looked at any houses for sale during the last year.

"No, I haven't been looking, and I like my house. I'm getting hungry. Can we get something brought in?" said Anderson.

Nester placed orders for the four men. The MCS usually ate their meals at Bonanza during an investigation. Anderson knew this. He wanted a steak and all the trimmings. His knowledge about the MCS began to emerge. It would be months later before Busch would discover how attuned the suspect was to the MCS.

When the food was delivered, they ate in the dining room. Busch turned the conversation to movies. He talked about the movie *Raiders of the Lost Ark*. Soon, Anderson was talking about movies. He liked the movie *Cool Hand Luke,* where Paul Newman played a prisoner in a Southern prison. For the next hour, they ate and talked. The setting could have been anywhere, a fraternity house, boot camp, just four guys thrown together.

After supper, Anderson watched TV from the couch in the living room, while he manicured his nails with a long metal fingernail file. Busch sat in the chair in the living room, scanning through boxes of files on the floor. Nester, still seated at the dining room table, reviewed his notes to finish the interview with Anderson. Heil joined Busch in the living room to search for evidence. Standing near the bookshelves, Heil noticed that the recessed area of the living room wall looked suspicious. With his finger, he applied pressure to the wooden panel that covered the 2 X 2 foot section, and the panel popped off exposing a wall safe.

"Did you know about this?" asked Heil, pointing the safe out to Busch.

"No. By God, Heil, you surprised me with that. Say, Dale, did you see what Heil found?"

"That's just a wall safe. There's nothing in it. Just old insurance papers," said Anderson with a look of surprise.

"Let's look inside and see," said Busch.

"I don't remember the combination. There's nothing in it but papers, just insurance papers."

"You're not getting selective-amnesia, are you, Dale?" said Busch.

"No, I can't remember the number right now. Maybe it will come to me later. It's been years since I've opened that."

Anderson walked into the dining room and sat at the table. Nester looked up from his notes.

"Dale, can you explain how your car and a man fitting your description were seen in the Villa Madero Subdivision near Chula Vista Street around the time of the killings?"

"Either they're mistaken or they're lying about seeing me there," said Anderson, the dimples forming in his chin.

"Were you at the Lanman house?" said Nester. "Did you kill the Lanmans?"

"No. I could not do such a thing."

"Can you prove that you weren't in Villa Madero?"

"No."

"I think you killed the Lanmans. Your facts don't match the information."

Nester waited for a denial to come from Anderson. It never came. His demeanor stayed the same. He excused himself from the table and walked to the bathroom. After brushing his teeth, shaving, and changing his shirt, he returned with Nester to the dining room.

Busch had placed the boxes of files from the living room and the briefcases from the bedroom against the wall of the dining room. He told Anderson that these items would be collected as evidence. Anderson showed no outward sign of concern.

At 8:50 P.M., there was a knock at the front door of Anderson's house. Deputy Willie Smith of the St. Clair County Sheriff's Department came in. He told Anderson that Assistant State's Attorney Dennis Hatch had issued a warrant for his fingerprints.

Anderson walked to the kitchen and called the St. Clair County Sheriff's Department, where his wife was. He asked to speak with her. His voice was calm.

"It's not going too good. I probably won't see you tonight," he said into the receiver.

Holding the phone in silence for a moment, he motioned for Nester to join him in the kitchen.

"Am I under arrest?" said Anderson, with the mouthpiece of the receiver resting on his chin.

"No, Dale, you aren't under arrest. You can go and come as you please," said Nester.

"I don't want to talk to you any more tonight. Maybe I'll talk with you tomorrow. I want you to leave. I think it's best if you leave."

Anderson continued the phone conversation. He asked to speak with his children. He told them not to say anything. After a pause, he told them not to make any additional statements.

117

Nester honored Anderson's request that he leave. He gathered up his notes and papers from the table and walked out the door at 9:00 P.M. Busch, who was standing in the dining room, waited for Anderson to finish his conversation.

"What about Heil and me? Do we have to leave too? I still need your help in collecting this stuff," said Busch, hoping to maintain that investigative link between himself and Anderson.

"You guys can stay. But I think I might leave later. I can leave any time, can't I? Nester said I could."

"Dale, as far as I know there's no log-chain on your ass. I guess you can leave whenever you want," said Busch. "There is a lot of evidence here that we need to go over, like the combinations to the briefcases."

"I don't remember the numbers. There's just old papers in them. I guess they want me to go to the county to be fingerprinted," said Anderson. "I may just leave. They have already talked to my wife and kids."

"That's your business. My job is to collect evidence in this murder case," said Busch, walking back to the dresser in the bedroom with Anderson.

Anderson opened the top dresser drawer. He removed his wallet. He turned to Busch, who was standing beside him.

"I'm not coming back, am I?" said Anderson. "They'll probably arrest me soon."

"Probably so," said Busch. "Like you told your

118

wife on the phone, it don't look good for you."

At 9:30 P.M., there was a second knock at Anderson's door. Detective John Betten came in. He read the arrest warrant to Dale and then handed the warrant to him. Dale looked at the warrant. In bold print under the offense column read: "FIRST-DEGREE MURDER, [2 COUNTS] NO BOND."

Anderson turned to Busch and instructed him that nobody could use the bathroom and everyone except him and Heil should leave his house. Anderson was taken from the house in handcuffs by Detective Betten. Busch walked outside behind Anderson and Betten. The crowd in front of the house hadn't dwindled. Some spectators had been there since Wednesday night. The front of the house was aglow with lights from the TV cameramen's floodlights. Flashes from camera strobes silhouetted the trees in the yard against the black sky.

Busch stopped at the end of the sidewalk, surprised by a loud round of applause and cheers of approval from the crowd as Anderson was placed in the squad car. As the crowd disbanded, Busch loaded the packaged evidence into his car. It would be hours before he had everything secured for the evening. Tomorrow he would spend the day going over Anderson's house again to insure he hadn't missed anything, and if need be he would get a court order to forcibly enter the wall safe.

Deputies were stationed outside until he returned.

The car pulled away from the side of the road. Glaring lights of the news media illuminated the interior. Anderson sat between Detectives Roger Cook and John Betten in the back. The trip to the county jail was quiet.

Anderson was taken to the interview room in the jail, where Nester spoke with him. He appeared eager to talk. Before the interview started, Mearl Justus walked into the room, and Anderson greeted him with a complaint.

"Sheriff, I've got something to say to you. Some of the jail officers aren't acting in a professional manner."

"What do you mean?" said Justus.

"They've been saying things to me. They shouldn't do that; I used to be a corrections officer," said Anderson.

"Are you fucking crazy," bellowed Justus. "You just killed a lady and a three-year-old baby. I don't think that. . . ." Justus stopped in the middle of his sentence and stormed out of the room.

"He didn't take that very well, did he?" Anderson said to Nester, seated across the table from him.

"Dale, he just said what everybody else is thinking."

"I'll talk with you tomorrow," said Anderson.

# Thirteen

Friday had proven to be another emotionally draining day for John Lanman. Faced with making funeral arrangements for his wife and son, he walked into the funeral home accompanied by Pastor Santos. They waited for the funeral director in the lounge area. Lanman nervously jingled coins in his hand before he placed them in the soda machine and pushed the selection button. A can of diet soda clanged to a halt at the opening of the machine.

The funeral director stepped into the room and apologized for the delay. He took them to the viewing room where caskets were displayed. Walking among the silk-lined containers, Lanman's eyes watered as he approached the area where the small caskets were stored.

"Why did he have to kill them?" Lanman whispered, "Why Kenneth?"

Santos had no answer for the question. Lanman

put his hand on the one Kenneth would be buried in and pointed to the casket for his wife. After the selections were completed, the funeral director excused himself momentarily to answer a ringing phone. In the lounge, Lanman sat at the table briefly and then paced the floor. Pastor Santos waited for him to sit down again. After lighting a cigarette, Lanman returned to the table.

"We need to pray that they catch whoever did this, so it doesn't happen again," said Lanman.

"We can pray that the officers have guidance," said the pastor. "I'm sure that they'll find the one responsible."

Lanman crushed out the half-burnt cigarette in the ashtray on the table. With a shaking hand he lifted the soda can to his lips and drank the remaining contents. He stared at the door that led back to the display room.

"Don't ever leave home without kissing your wife and child goodbye," sobbed Lanman.

Santos handed him a Kleenex from the box on the table. He wiped his eyes with the tissue. The emotion in his statement caught Santos off guard, and his eyes teared as he thought about what Lanman had said.

After completion of the funeral arrangements, Santos drove him back to the Nixons' house which had become the meeting place for Lanman's relatives. Out-of-town family members stayed at local hotels, since the Lanman house was still secured by the police.

The news media was camped outside Lanman's

house. Friday was busy for them, working double coverage interviewing neighbors of Lanman and Anderson. After the arrest of Anderson, they flocked to Villa Madero.

The fear that gripped the neighborhood lessened as news of the arrest spread. People caught up in the murder investigation were not as reassured. All of the witnesses would have to deal with their fears on an individual basis. Most were women and children. They would soon learn that justice doesn't come easily. There is always a price associated with it, not in money but in courage.

Linda Anderson proved to be a woman of great courage and strength. Friday morning, she walked out of her house and got into her father's car. He was shocked by what had happened but was still supportive of his daughter, which Linda was thankful for. She thought about what Commander Nonn had said to her as she was leaving the house: "Linda, you need to do the right thing. You need to think of the kids and yourself." His words ran through her mind as they neared the Sheriff's Department where Karen and Paul had been taken.

In the detective section, Linda and her father found Paul and Karen, clad only in their nightclothes, seated in chairs near one of the detective's desk. Linda was glad to see them. She hugged them and told them that everything would be okay. Karen seemed upset about being dressed in nightclothes; she was at that age where appearance meant everything. Paul, on the other hand, was busy eating a glazed donut from the box of assorted donuts on the detective's desk.

Linda was offered coffee and a donut by a detective. She took the coffee. It tasted good and helped perk her up. Paul and Karen left the Sheriff's Department with their grandfather.

Linda Anderson sat across from Detective Paul Bargiel in the interview room. While she waited to be interviewed, she thought about her childhood days in Belleville. When she was very young, her mother told her that the police were there to help. That had always stuck with her. She had been raised to respect the police and, as a mother, she passed that on to her children.

The detective's voice was calm as he asked the first question of the interview. Linda answered without hesitation. She knew that the truth was the best answer to any question, and she was being truthful with him.

She didn't have any reason to fear the police and knew nothing about the Lanman murders. She did know now that Dale had lied to her about the probation issue, and had used the family as a shield for himself. She had made up her mind; she wouldn't lie for Dale. Whatever trouble he had gotten himself into he would have to face the consequences.

She answered the general background questions

124

about herself. When asked if she was aware of any plans to sell the house they currently lived in or purchase another house, Linda looked at the interviewer strangely. *What was he talking about,* she pondered. The expression on her face caused Bargiel to smile, which he did several times as the two continued the question and answer session.

When asked about the windows being covered, she told the detective that Dale put the cardboard up on all the windows after the problems in the office in 1988. She was allowed to take the cardboard down during the day. Dale used the excuse that he could sleep better in total darkness. Thursday was different; he wouldn't let her take it down and she wasn't to answer the door or phone.

She described her husband as a man that usually kept his temper in check, but could get angry and be violent toward others but never toward his own family. She'd seldom seen him emotional.

Linda had become numb to her husband's quirks: His obsession with the news reporter's death and his personal investigation into it, the hatred for his ex-bosses, and the search for evidence against them.

She talked about her job as director of a children's day-care center, where she made good money. They were still able to make ends meet even after Dale lost his $25,000 a year job. Dale began receiving Social Security benefits after his termination. He told her the money was for job-related stress brought on by his ex-bosses.

* * *

Many of the questions made no sense to her: the one about the large bag with the shoulder strap that Dale owned. She admitted that her husband owned a bag like that, but she didn't know where it was now. She was comfortable with Bargiel. He dressed sharply and sounded intelligent. She felt he was a person that was trustworthy. When asked to take a polygraph, Linda looked at the blond-haired detective.

"Sure, I'll take one if you think it will help."

"They'll go over the questions with you before you take it," said Bargiel.

"Will there be any good times in my life again?" said Linda, feeling the need to rebuild her life.

"Yes, there will be," said Bargiel with a smile, "You'll get through this."

Linda appreciated the vote of confidence from the investigator. She was determined to get her life back on track. She would take it one day at a time. Today she would take a polygraph. Walking down the hall with Bargiel, she entered the small room and was greeted by Detective Robert Baldwin. He would administer the polygraph. Baldwin explained the testing procedure to her and discussed the questions to be asked.

Linda was seated in the examining chair, which had extended armrests. A standard blood-pressure cuff was placed on her upper right arm. Two rubber corrugated tubes were placed around her, one across her upper chest, one across her abdominal region. Silver concave-shaped electrodes were placed on the first and third finger of her left hand. Finally, she was ready to begin the test.

It felt strange having these things attached to her. She sat quietly and listened to the questions. The examiner's voice was low and came from the side, as she faced straight ahead staring at a blank wall. Baldwin allowed time between the questions to mark his observations on the chart as the inked needles moved across the narrow paper strip. Linda showed no physical or emotional changes on the chart during the test. She was being truthful. She passed the polygraph test.


After completing the test, she went to her parents' house, where she spent the evening with her children. Later, Friday night, she received a phone call. Dale's voice sounded tense. He told her that he was going to leave the house shortly, before they could arrest him. Linda was still not convinced that her husband could be capable of such a terrible crime. A small flicker of hope for Dale remained with her but grew weaker with each passing hour. After hanging up the phone, she sat back in the chair and closed her eyes.

At 10:00 P.M., Linda received a second call at her parents' house. This time it was Detective Bargiel. He asked if she could come to the Sheriff's Department. It sounded urgent. Ten minutes later, she met with Bargiel in an interview room on the second floor.

"We need to interview you again. There has

been some new development in the case," said the detective.

"I'll help with whatever I can," said Linda.

"Our evidence man has found some paddles in Dale's dresser. There may be specks of blood on them. Do you know about the paddles?"

"Those are Dale's," said Linda.

"Why does he have them?"

She paused for a moment before answering, her eyes focused on the floor. "Dale likes to be spanked with them."

"He has you spank him?"

"Not all the time, but from time to time he has me spank him."

"Does he use them on others?"

"Not that I know of. He wanted to use them on me, but I'm not into that."

"Why would there be blood on one of them?"

"I don't know about that," said Linda, turning toward the door as the sound of footsteps echoed in the hallway.

The door to the interview room opened and Sheriff Justus entered the room. He pulled a chair up near Linda and sat down. He told her that Dale had been arrested and was in the booking room downstairs. She asked if he was arrested for the murders of the woman and boy. Justus nodded and asked if she would be alright.

She wanted to know why they thought Dale had committed the murders. Sheriff Justus told her about the witnesses seeing Dale's car near the crime scene, the house-buyer ruse, and the note naming Dale's ex-bosses. Her heart sank when she heard about the note. Now she was convinced in her own mind that she was married to a murderer.

# Fourteen

Busch locked his weapon into the metal wall unit at the county jail. He motioned to the guard behind the glass- and steel-enclosed control console that he was ready to enter the jail. The electronic locking system clicked, then with a loud thud the large metal barred door slid open. Busch stepped inside. Again the sound occurred and the door slammed shut behind him. He walked to the metal door that led to the booking area. The guard pushed buttons inside the console and the door sprang open.

Busch looked at his watch. It was 8:30 A.M. He wondered if Anderson would be as friendly this Saturday morning, since his arrest last night. Busch walked to the hold-over cell and peered inside. There sat Anderson on the metal bunk in the orange jumpsuit that county prisoners wear.

"Dale, my man. What's going on with you? I need to fingerprint you this morning."

"They haven't treated me with respect since I've been here," said Anderson, with a tone of irritation.

"Dale, this isn't the fucking Hilton. You used to work here. You know what the rules are," said Busch. Anderson seemed to like the fact that Busch acknowledged he once worked there. He smiled and stood up. Busch asked the jailer to open Anderson's cell.

"I would like to talk to you about the case. You've treated me like a man. Everyone else is mad at me," said Anderson.

"Dale, I do this shit day in and day out. I treat people the same way they act," said Busch, inking Anderson's fingers.

"Are you going back to my house?"

"Yeah, I have a lot of other areas in the house to search, and we have to open the wall safe."

"I might give you the combination to the safe later."

"Dale, it doesn't matter to me. If I have to, I'll get a court order and open it. I don't have time to talk to you now, I need to complete the search of your house. I'll talk to you when I get time."

"My wife needs to get clothes for herself and the kids. Can she get that while you're there?"

"Sure, tell her I'll be there in about fifteen minutes and she can get whatever items she needs."

"I'll give you the safe combination," said Anderson.

"What about the combinations for the briefcases?"

"Maybe later," said Anderson with a smile, as he made a collect call from the pay phone in the booking area.

Twenty minutes later, Busch spoke with the deputy

131

stationed outside Anderson's house and walked in. As Busch walked into the living room, the house still had a dark and ominous feeling about it. He had radioed for Nester to meet him at the house. Busch sat on the couch and waited.

Ten minutes passed before Nester arrived. The look on his face told Busch something was wrong.

"Give me the bad news first," joked Busch.

"The handwriting expert says the note at Lanman's house wasn't written by Anderson," said Nester.

"Son of a bitch, that's why he was so confident. He must have made her write the note," said Busch.

"Nonn wants me to get some of Jolaine's writing to compare to the note. It's Saturday and John Lanman is attending the funeral service today," said Nester.

"That poor woman. She must've known that she was going to be killed when she was writing the note," said Busch, pausing as a visual picture formed in his mind. "That bastard, that's why he had the rope around her neck. He could control her while she was writing."

"What did Dale have to say when you fingerprinted him today?"

"He gave me the combination to the safe," said Busch.

"He did? What about the briefcases?" said Nester.

"I guess he thought I wasn't ready for that yet. He told me that would come later."

Busch read the numbers from his notepad as he turned the dial on the wall safe. Three turns to the left, two turns to the right and back again left, stopping on the last number. He twisted the handle downward and the door opened. Busch shone the flashlight into the safe.

"Whoa, looks like Dale forgot to tell us about the other things in the safe," said Busch, attaching the strobe to his camera to photograph the contents.

"Dale must have known we would look in the safe," said Nester.

"He didn't think we would find it. If it wasn't for Heil finding the safe, this stuff wouldn't have been discovered," said Busch, while slipping on rubber gloves to remove the things from the safe.

"A .357 magnum revolver?" said Nester. "That could be considered a form of insurance policy, I guess."

"Here's another revolver, a .22-cal. and a black-jack, a green towel with a speck of blood. . . . Holy shit," said Busch, "look at this."

"What is it?"

"It's some kind of ID card of a Cardenas Compos Jorge. It's in Spanish. By the photograph on the card, it looks like a young boy. Who in the fuck is Jorge Cardenas, and why does Anderson have his ID card locked in his safe?"

"I don't know. We better let Nonn know about this."

"Give him a call and I'll collect the other papers in the safe," said Busch.

There was a knock at the kitchen door. Busch looked out and saw Linda Anderson standing on the patio. He opened the door for her to enter. She handed him a small piece of paper.

"What's this?" said Busch.

133

"Dale told me to give that to you," said Linda.

Busch unfolded the paper. Written on it was the combination to the safe and three digits under that.

"Dale called and gave me the numbers. He told me you wanted them," said Linda.

"He already gave me the combination to the safe. Is the three digit number for one of the briefcases?"

"I don't know, he said you would know."

Linda gathered clothing for her children and herself. Nester and Busch helped her. She was surprised that they took the time to do that. Walking through the house, she tried to think of all the things her children would need until they could return to the house. Busch cautioned her; it might be several days and she should take extra clothing. She liked him. He seemed genuinely concerned about her and the children. He took the time to find Paul's soccer uniform. Now Paul could play with his team today. She hoped others would realize she had nothing to do with the murders.

"You and the kids may have some rough days ahead, but time will pass and things will work out," said Busch.

"I hope so. They're good kids and we didn't have anything to do with this," Linda said in a soft voice.

"Kids at school can be brutal at times. Make sure you prepare your kids for that. You'll get through this."

Linda was surprised at how understanding the bearded investigator was. He listened to her problems and offered suggestions. None of the officers she had talked with showed any resentment toward her. She walked with them as they carried the clothing to her father's car. She had to hurry to make Paul's soccer game.

Busch placed the four briefcases on the table. Nester stood nearby. Sliding the briefcase directly in front of him on the table, he turned the cylinders of the combination lock to the numbers Anderson had given him. With his thumbs he pushed the release buttons on the briefcase. The lid of the case sprang open. Busch shook his head and grinned.

"Dale's been a naughty boy. Look at this. Here we have several pairs of surgical gloves, sections of cord, an eighteen-inch metal bar, a brown baseball cap, and assorted papers," said Busch.

"I wonder what Dale's excuse for those are?" Nester remarked.

"I'm sure he'll have a good excuse. Let's see if the same numbers open the other briefcases."

Busch tried the second briefcase. It opened. Inside were surgical gloves, sections of cord, a hunting knife, a push-button knife, and a note from Anderson's probation officer dated 9-18-89. Busch smiled when he saw the date on the note. It meant that Anderson had opened the briefcase as early as nine days before the Lanman murders. Anderson had told Busch that the briefcases had not been opened in months.

Placing the third briefcase in front of him, Busch opened it with the same combination. Inside lay a ten-channel programmable scanner, the portable model that snaps onto one's belt. The earphone was still attached. In addition to the scanner, the briefcase contained surgical gloves, newspaper clippings on Audrey Cardenas, assorted papers, two large pocketknives, and a pair of black handled scissors.

The fourth briefcase contained an FBI crest pin, knives, surgical gloves, a ten-inch blackjack, three revolver holsters, and assorted papers.

"I can't wait to read through all this stuff," said Busch, closing the fourth briefcase.

"What do you make of all that?" said Nester. "The gloves, cords, and knives make it look like these are assassin's kits."

"With Dale, I wouldn't rule anything out. He had syringes, needles, and a scalpel in the brown suitcase in the bedroom. Unless he's a doctor, I would call those items suspicious, especially the brass knuckles," said Busch.


It was nine o'clock that evening before Busch returned to the jail. The ID card of Jorge Cardenas still bothered Busch. *What did it mean?* Nonn had contacted Audrey's parents, and they didn't know who Jorge Cardenas was. Busch planned to speak with Anderson shortly. He would tell him what items were seized from his house.

Busch left the briefing at the MCS on the second floor and entered the jail. Anderson grabbed the bars of his cell and placed his face against them when Busch entered the hold-over section of the jail.

"Were you able to get into the safe?" Anderson asked.

"Dale, if you want to talk to me, I got to tell you that you can have an attorney present. I'm here to let you know what items I collected from your house to-day," said Busch.

"I want to talk to you."

"I'll have to advise you of your rights, Miranda Decision."

"I know my rights. I'll talk to you."

Busch asked the jailer to open Anderson's cell. Anderson stepped out of the cell and walked with Busch down the hallway between cell blocks. The guard in the control room opened the door of the interview room by remote control. Anderson and Busch went inside, the door clanged shut behind them. They sat opposite each other at the corner of the interview table. Busch placed the legal pad on the table. Dale watched in silence.

"Dale, we opened your safe and briefcases. I'm going to hold on to the items that were in them."

"Will I get them back?"

"I listed everything on evidence receipts. It'll be up to a judge or a state's attorney to decide that," said Busch.

"Belleville took all my guns and didn't give them back."

"Dale, if you want to talk about what's going on now we can, otherwise I've got shit to do."

"I can tell you the whole story," said Anderson.

"Can I tape this?"

"No."

"It sounds like it may be a long story. I don't know if I can write as fast as you talk," said Busch.

"I don't want you to tape me."

"Okay, Dale, go for it, but take it slow."

* * *

Anderson started with his background when he began his job as a jailer in 1978. He moved quickly to his assignment to the Public Aid Office in East St. Louis in 1980, where he met Maurice Vale.

"Vale is the key person in this," said Anderson. "He was my supervisor in East St. Louis until he transferred to the Belleville office."

Anderson reflected that he and Vale were friends at first, and it was Vale that helped him transfer to the Belleville office. Their friendship gradually began to deteriorate. It was Anderson's opinion that Vale was a person so tight with money, that he began to bilk money from Public Aid clients. According to Anderson, when the clients reported this to him, he talked to Vale, but he said that Vale wanted Anderson to cover up the complaints. Anderson said that he began collecting reports to expose the corruption which he said was going on. He also stated that he discovered his other two supervisors, Robert DeLaria and Charlotte Kroupa, were also involved in the supposed scheme.

Busch took notes as Anderson made these allegations. He stopped him to ask the spelling on the supervisors' names, hoping to get the similar incorrect spelling that was in the note, but Anderson wasn't taking the bait. He looked at Busch suspiciously and then spelled the names.

"What happened after you learned that your three supervisors were involved?" said Busch, playing into Anderson's story.

"I told all three of them that I was going to report them and send the reports to Springfield," said Anderson. "That's when they grabbed me, hit me, and took my briefcase away on 5-23-88 around 10:30 A.M."

Busch was surprised that Anderson had the date and time memorized. He would soon learn that Anderson would give several days and dates as the interview continued.

"So, what did you do?"

"I called the Belleville Police Department. This is how this whole fucking nightmare began," said Anderson. "I signed complaints on the supervisors for aggravated battery, but in the first week of June of 1988, the charges were reduced to disorderly conduct.*

Busch had not heard Anderson cuss before, it seemed out of character. He wanted to keep the interview flowing so when it slowed he would prompt a reply with a question to show Anderson he was interested.

"Why was that?" said Busch.

"Because they bought the cops off. Carolyn Tuft of the *News-Democrat* wrote a story about me having my bosses arrested and that starts all this shit off."

"What do you mean . . . that starts all this shit off?" said Busch, realizing that Anderson had already had the conflict with his bosses before Cardenas came to town.

---

*In fact, the supervisors were charged with disorderly conduct when they were issued a citation at the police department. The charges were proved to be groundless, however, and were eventually dropped. — Author

"I got put on leave from work. I'm at home when a *News-Democrat* reporter named Audrey Cardenas comes out to my house and wants to do a follow-up story on me having my bosses arrested."

"Audrey Cardenas came to your house?"

"Yeah, she came over and said, 'What's going on down at Public Aid?' "

"When was that?" said Busch, surprised at Anderson's statement.

"It was Saturday, 6-18-88, but she had been there a few days before. She wanted to write about the Public Aid story. She told me that the three supervisors had threatened her with bodily harm or death."

"The three supervisors: Vale, DeLaria, and Kroupa?" said Busch.

"Yes, those three," said Anderson. "I told Audrey that they were just upset, they wouldn't really harm her. Then on Sunday, 6-19-88, Audrey was kidnapped and murdered. My wife and I got upset when we heard about the murder."

"You should've told the police about this," said Busch.

"Carolyn Tuft wanted to talk to me but I wouldn't talk with her. She had me arrested on 6-7-88 on a gun charge. Anthony Smith [another reporter at the *News-Democrat*] had me arrested for impersonating a police officer on 6-13-88. After I was released on 7-15-88, I filed a lawsuit against the Belleville Police Department. They arrested me again on 7-21-88 for impersonating a police officer because I had a conversation with Joe Cardenas, Audrey Cardenas's father."

"You talked with Cardenas's father?"

140

"I told him that I believed that Vale, DeLaria, and Kroupa killed Audrey or paid someone to kill her."

"Dale, we found an ID card of Jorge Cardenas in your safe. Why do you have that in your safe?" said Busch.

"It shouldn't have been in the safe," said Anderson's ending his sentence with a glaring look at Busch.

"Where should it have been? Is he related to Audrey?"

"I don't know why that would be in my safe," said Anderson.

"Why do you have surgical gloves, cords, and knives in the briefcases?"

"I just store things in them."

"Let's take a break, Dale. I'm getting writing cramps from all of this. I got to meet with MCS upstairs. I'll get back with you later," said Busch.

Commander Nonn listened to the information that Busch had collected during the interview. However, because the information received seemed to add unnecessary confusion to an already complex investigation, the decision was made to discontinue any further interviews with Anderson.


The note from the Lanman murder sparked interest into the unanswered questions that still smoldered in the Cardenas case. *Belleville News-Democrat* publisher, Gary Berkley, pushed for the Cardenas case to be reopened after receiving a letter written by a teenage friend of Karen Anderson.

On October 1, 1989, Berkley published the letter

in the Sunday addition of the paper.

"In June 1988, I was at the home of Karen Anderson when *News-Democrat* reporter Audrey Cardenas arrived to interview Dale Anderson. Karen Anderson, Linda Anderson, and I talked to Audrey Cardenas during the interview. Audrey Cardenas said she had interviewed Maurice Vale, Robert DeLaria, and Charlotte Kroupa. She said these three threatened to murder her if the *News-Democrat* newspaper printed any more articles about them. Audrey Cardenas said these three people really frightened her."

Nonn tossed the Sunday paper onto the conference table at the command post. His tolerance with the news media was wearing thin. From the start of the Lanman case, some witnesses were interviewed by news reporters before investigators could talk with them.

Although the teenager's letter from 1988 was news for the newspaper publisher, it was old news for the Belleville Police Department. The police had received the letter after they'd arrested Woidtke for the Cardenas murder and they considered it a hoax. It was believed that Cardenas had never met Anderson.

Nonn, after reading the paper, sent Detective Mike Boyne to the home of the young girl that Sunday afternoon. Boyne learned that there had been two letters written on July 29, 1988, by the teenager at the request of Dale Anderson. He had given her copies of the letters he wanted her to write but said they would have to be in her own words.

"On 6-7-88 at 7:30 P.M., I was at the home of Karen Anderson when *News-Democrat* reporter Carolyn Tuft arrived to interview Dale Anderson. Karen

142

and I were in her house and talked to Carolyn Tuft during the interview. Linda Anderson was also at the house during the interview. Dale Anderson did not have a gun in his hand at any time while Carolyn Tuft was at his home. Dale Anderson did not place a gun on a table at any time while Carolyn Tuft was at his house."

Her second letter was about Audrey Cardenas interviewing Anderson at his home, which had been published fourteen months after she had written it. She admitted she had never met Audrey and was writing the letters because Karen's father had asked her to. She didn't understand the importance of the letters or what she was involved in. She, too, had become another pawn in the game.


Nonn had been schooled by Captain Robert Hertz of the Madison County Sheriff Department. Hertz's policy on news releases was simple but enforced. Only a typed copy of the information prepared by the commander would be given out to the news media. Nonn was in a county that he was unfamiliar with and relied on others to assist him on news releases—that was his first mistake. There was another problem. Information was being leaked to the press.

The quest for news was getting worse as time passed. Nonn knew that he had made his second mistake by not asking for a sealed affidavit when he applied for a search warrant for Anderson's house. In the affidavit sent to the court, the names of the three supervisors in the note were listed. It was now public knowledge who they were.

Nonn slammed the phone down after talking with

a reporter that called in about Anderson's ex-supervisors.

"Christ!" said Nonn. "Those people carry this too far. They're wanting to name the supervisors, and they're totally innocent of any wrongdoing, but their names will be linked to the murders."

"The news media accuracy is always something you can count on," laughed Busch as he walked toward the door to leave but stopped. "They usually get enough information to mess up your case but not enough to be accurate."

"I should have had that affidavit on the search warrant sealed," said Nonn.

"Man, there's so many leaks in this boat, it wouldn't float. I see this all the time. After a while the press will have all the details of the crime on the front page. The bad guy couldn't tell you something that wasn't printed in the paper if he wanted to."

"I can see telling the press that a person died a violent death and just leave it at that. What good does it do to have each and every detail printed?" Nonn said in a disgusted tone.

"Steve, let's keep this between you, Nester, and myself," said Busch, stepping back into the room. "I usually keep a fact or two about the crime scene secret during briefings because of problems with leaks. The rope around Jolaine's neck had a large bow tied at the base of her neck. There was a space between her neck and the rope. I'm sure now it was used to control her while she was writing the note," said Busch. "Also there was a bloody cloth impression on the bed cover at Lanman's house, two separate weave patterns. I collected cloth gloves at Anderson's house that look very similar."

Nonn felt a little better. At least there was something they could hang their hat on later, if Anderson decided to confess.

The issue about the possible link between Cardenas and Anderson raged on. St. Clair County State's Attorney John Baricevic promised to be open-minded about any new evidence, but felt reopening the Cardenas investigation at the present time would be premature until the Lanman case was adjudicated.

Brian Trentman, the attorney for Rodney Woidtke, had a different point of view. The note at the Lanman crime scene and the arrest of Anderson was considered by Trentman as grounds for a new trial for his client. A new trial could mean freedom for the California drifter. Trentman would not be the only one who would dig back into the past for answers.

# Fifteen

John Lanman arrived at the funeral home Sunday afternoon. He felt the crisp wind against his face as he walked up the front steps to go inside. It seemed cold to him for being only the first day of October. The warmth of the world he once knew had vanished.

John noticed the scent of fresh flowers in the hallway. The fragrance intensified as he entered the viewing room where his wife and son were. Shaking his head from side to side as if to say no he wouldn't accept the fact of their deaths, John moved closer to the caskets. Small pink and red roses blanketed the satin linings of the coffins. Flowers from friends, neighbors, and relatives lined the floor of the viewing room. The back of the chapel was filled with the overflow of flower arrangements.

By early evening, the capacity of the funeral home was exceeded by the six hundred mourners that filled the pews and stood along the walls to pay their respect. Pastor Santos accompanied

John in greeting the long line of people that filed past. Santos had canceled his Sunday service at his church to conduct the memorial service for the Lanmans.

After the service, John returned to his next-door neighbors' home where his relatives joined him. His house was still sealed and secured by the police. Later that evening after all the people had left, John walked to the back of his property. He stood there leaning on the fence and looking at Kenneth's toys. The song from the memorial service, "Amazing Grace," still echoed in his mind. Strangely, he felt as though a weight had been removed from his body.

Somehow, John realized he'd accepted their deaths. His wife and son would be buried on Monday in Decatur, Illinois, at the wishes of Jolaine's parents.

Returning to the neighbors' house, John received a request from Inspector Busch to meet him at the Sheriff's Department. John met with him on the second floor in the detective section.

"John, I know this is bad timing. I need to get a set of your fingerprints for elimination reasons," said Busch.

"What ever you need. I'm here," said Lanman. "Do you have a lot on this guy?"

"John, I can't discuss the details and status of the case with you. There're a lot of cops still working. The MCS is tying up loose ends in the investigation, and we're getting the forensic evidence together. That's why I needed your fingerprints. Just covering the bases so nothing goes astray."

Busch didn't want to try to explain to John the lengthy process of the evidence submission and all the preparation which lay ahead. Busch wasn't sure himself what some of the outcome and findings would be on the forensic evidence. He was curious about Anderson's files and what was in some of Anderson's writings that he had only glimpsed at when he seized them. He felt that the answers to many questions lay among the boxes of papers stacked high in the evidence vault in his office. With the constant barrage of additional murder cases coming in, it would be some time before the documents could be studied by him, but he was determined to make time to go through each page.

Busch was surprised by the office visit from Dennis Hatch in the week that followed Anderson's arrest. Hatch met with Busch at the Metro-East Forensic Science Laboratory.

"What kind of evidence do we have in this Anderson Case?" Hatch asked, with a raised eyebrow to taunt the investigator.

"Do you want the short version, or do you have something important to do?" countered the inspector in response to the prosecutor's question.

"You mean you don't have all this submitted yet," said Hatch.

"It will be months before we even get to the bottom of it all. I have already submitted the physical evidence and subdivided most of the exhibits. But there are several thousand documents that I seized that have to be read and catalogued," said Bush.

Hatch looked at the boxes of documents stacked high against the wall. He surveyed them from different angles as if sizing up a tree to notch for cutting. He was all business now as he turned to speak with Busch.

"I don't know how we can list all of the documents and know which documents are important in this case."

"Anderson has journals and notes in that paperwork that may explain why the Lanmans were killed," said Busch. "There's something going on with Anderson during the Cardenas case, but I'm not sure what it was. I know some people in our Intelligence Section that could help us. We could put this on a computer and do cross matching through dates, names, and time," said Busch.

"That sounds good. Keep me informed on the physical evidence. Oh, by the way, Dave Nester from the county and Phil Delaney from my office will be working with me," said Hatch.


On the drive back to his office, Hatch's mind became preoccupied with trial strategies and the many legal hurdles that lay ahead of him in this case. His thoughts turned back to the earlier years of his life and the struggle to become an attorney.

Although Hatch came from a large family of attorneys, he had not always wanted to be a lawyer. His college years were spent at Notre Dame in South Bend, Indiana, where he met Monica Fortune, a liberal arts student from New York who he would later marry.

He spent several years as a grade school teacher, and enjoyed teaching and coaching. But the teacher's salary barely paid the bills and after his son was born, he decided to make another career move. He enrolled in law school and worked odd jobs to make additional money for his family. Monica helped by working as a waitress part-time to supplement his income. During his third year in law school, he interned at the St. Clair County State's Attorney's Office during the summer of 1984. That is when he realized that he wanted to be a prosecutor.

Graduating from law school in 1985, he was hired as an Assistant State's Attorney and assigned to the Child Protection Unit at the St. Clair County State's Attorney's Office. His sights were set on the Felony Section, and within a year he was reassigned to felony cases.

Hatch parked the car at the curb outside the courthouse and climbed the two flights of steps before entering the elevator. He had a suspicion that the Anderson case would be one of the most challenging trials in his career.

# Sixteen

Busch sat at the long examination table in the evidence packaging room at the Metro-East Laboratory. He opened the first package of documents seized from one of Anderson's briefcases. A blue plastic checkbook cover lay on top of the pile of papers. Busch opened the checkbook cover and found a newspaper clipping of an article on the Kristina Povolish murder case.

Busch raised an eyebrow at finding the article. Kristina Povolish was a nineteen-year-old woman from Belleville, whose nude body was found in a ditch south of Belleville on July 28, 1987. She had been strangled and her clothing scattered along the side of the country road. She had been last seen walking late at night in downtown Belleville. The case remained unsolved.

Two other pieces of paper were with the article: Maurice Vale's business card from the Public Aid Office and a newspaper clipping with a photograph of Audrey Cardenas. Busch was surprised at finding the three items tucked away together in the checkbook cover.

The next item discovered in the briefcase brought a grin to the face of the investigator. It was a letter. His eyes scanned the single page that lay before him. At the top of the letter was the seal of the State of Illinois with the Department of Law Enforcement letterhead. The Department of Law Enforcement was defunct, Busch knew this for a fact, he had worked for them. That was the title for the State Police's Investigative Section when Busch was hired by the State. The title was changed in 1987 to the Illinois State Police. Busch read the typed letter:

## DEPARTMENT OF
## LAW ENFORCEMENT
### Audrey Cardenas Homicide Case

On 6/20/88, Audrey Cardenas was reported as a missing person. On 6/26/88, the body of Cardenas was discovered at Belleville East High School. On 6/19/88, Cardenas was last seen alive by Belleville Police Officer John Klee at the Belleville Deutschfest at Hough Park. Klee was observed to be intoxicated and harassing Cardenas. He has refused to take a polygraph exam. John Klee is a murder suspect.

Cardenas, age 24, was an intern at the *News-Democrat*. She was from College Station, Texas and moved to Belleville in 6/88. The week of 6/13/88, Cardenas interviewed several employees for the Il Dept of Public Aid, 218 W. Main, Belleville, Il. She interviewed Maurice Vale, Robert DeLaria, Charlotte Kroupa, Mary Reibling, and Dale Anderson. Anderson has been employed with the State of Il since 1980. Prior to that time he was a Deputy Sheriff with the St. Clair County Sheriff's Dept. Cardenas was doing a follow up interview to the 6/4/88 article by Carolyn Tuft concerning the arrest of Vale, DeLaria, Kroupa. Investigation has determined these three people gave a bribe to the Belleville Police Dept to have their charges reduced from Battery and Theft to Disorderly Conduct. Then they gave a bribe to the City Prosecutor Patrick Flynn to prevent their cases from going to trial.

Anderson provided information and evidence to Cardenas concerning his four co-workers committing crimes including public aid fraud and forgery. These four people threatened to murder Cardenas if the Newspaper printed any more articles about them. Cardenas uncovered additional evidence that these four people were involved in a criminal conspiracy with John Baricevic, Francis Touchette, Jerry Costello, John Klee, and Harry Seper and some County Judges. There are witnesses and evidence to charge Vale, DeLaria, and Kroupa with the murder of Cardenas.

In 7/88, Anderson was charged with

some Misdemeanor offenses. Investigation has determined the charges against Anderson are unfounded. He agreed to take a polygraph exam. The people that made a complaint against Anderson refused to take a polygraph. In 8/88, Investigation has determined Vale, DeLaria, and Kroupa coerced and bribed some public aid clients to make a false complaint against Anderson.

On 8/16/88, Rodney Woidtke was charged with the murder of Cardenas. However, there is no witness or evidence to charge Woidtke with murder.

Busch leaned back in the chair after reading Anderson's letter, taking a moment to digest the information. It was clear that Anderson had no limits on conspiracy theories. Although Anderson's fantasies entangled everyone, he still focused the murder on the same three people. In the letter Anderson seemed to profess Woidtke's innocence. Had the drifter walked into the middle of a well laid plan of murder by Anderson to frame his bosses, or was Anderson taking advantage of a sexual murder by Woidtke to frame the trio? Busch continued reading through the volumes of paper when he came to a file folder marked: "7-29-87 Kristina Provolish Murdered."

Inside the folder were newspaper articles on the Provolish murder and one article from Chicago (AP) with the headline: "Investigation reveals possible link to policeman in killings."

On a separate sheet of paper in the folder, Anderson had written down the names of the murdered woman's parents and their address. The next folder was marked: "9-6-86 Unidentified woman murdered body in Summerfield."

Inside the folder were newspaper clippings on the investigation. Busch had worked that murder, and the case was unsolved. The woman died of strangulation and had been sexually assaulted with a knife.

If Anderson was keeping files on cases as they occurred, this suggested that he had an interest in murder cases of young women as early as 1986, or he was researching old, unsolved murder cases. Again it only led to more questions. Was Anderson looking for an unsolved murder to blame his bosses with? Did the cop fetish in Anderson push him to make files on the local cases? Or was there still another reason? The Cardenas murder seemed to be perfect timing for Anderson if it was Woidtke that killed her.

The next group of papers inside the briefcase had another surprise for Busch. A list of eleven mailing addresses written in the usual Anderson's handwriting style which Busch had become accustomed to seeing. At first, the addresses didn't seem to have any importance until Busch read the next page which was a letter.

155

To: I D P A
From: Charlotte P. Kroupa 218 W Main
Belleville, Il 62220
A report needs to be made concerning
Maurice Vale and Robert Delaria.[sic]
I was a witness when they murdered the re-
porter Audrey Cardenas in 6/88.
They are guilty of attempted murder, bat-
tery and theft of $800.00 against an office
caseworker in 6/88.
I have evidence to prove it.
They have been bragging about it.
They have threatened to murder me.

Busch cursed after reading the letter. He knew
what the letter was designed for—the murder of
Charlotte Kroupa. Anderson had written out the
two letters for his daughter's friend to copy in
July. Now, the Kroupa letter dated December 11,
1988.

Busch theorized that Anderson had planned to
make Kroupa copy the letter in her own handwriting and then he would kill her. After her
death, copies of her letter would be sent to the
addresses listed which comprised three newspapers, the FBI, Illinois State Police, State Civil
Service Commission (which was to rule on the
discharge of Anderson at the IDPA), AFSCME
(Anderson's union), and Joe Cardenas.

In Anderson's mind this would show everyone
that Vale and DeLaria had murdered Cardenas

156

and they had to kill Kroupa because she was going to expose them. Anderson wanted to discredit his bosses at any cost. Lives of women and children meant nothing to him. He wanted to become the super investigator he had always dreamed about being. Busch would soon discover that Anderson had also assumed the personality of David Hendricks, the clever investigator inside him that worked as a special investigator for the State of Illinois. Hendricks would surface several times in Anderson's diary.

Busch was confident his theory about the Kroupa letter was correct. He also felt that Anderson had taken a prewritten note with him when he entered the Lanman house and made Jolaine copy it before killing her. Busch doubted if Anderson would chance leaving the details of the note to memory. One thing for sure, Anderson made a mistake with his letters and note. He had become repetitious and used similar phrases. In the note found at the Lanman house: "They bragged about killing." The Kroupa letter had: "They have been bragging about it." *Small little details like these would help build a case against this ruthless bastard that took the lives of a pregnant woman and a small child,* thought Busch.

There were other similarities visible to the investigator in the letters written by Anderson's daughter's friend, the Lanman note, and the Kroupa letter. In all the documents the theme was identical. Anderson's bosses were responsible for the death of Audrey Cardenas.

The secretary's voice over the office intercom broke Busch's concentration when she called his name. A crime scene call had come in, and Busch was the duty man for the week. He placed the papers back into the evidence vault and left the office. The remaining secrets among Anderson's writings would sit quietly on the shelf in the dark confines of the vault until the investigator returned.

# Seventeen

Linda Anderson sat at the kitchen table and tried to reassure herself that things would be alright. She was left to care for Paul and Karen, while her husband sat in jail, charged with murdering a pregnant woman and small child. The initial shock of Dale's arrest had passed, and now she had to decide what was best for her children and herself. Dale had brought the situation on himself, and she would not let her children be drawn into it. Although she wasn't normally strong-willed, she had decided she must tell the children the truth. She would not sugarcoat it, lie for their father, or make excuses for what had happened.

A friend of Linda's once told her that with her personality she could find some good in everyone, probably even the devil. Linda no longer believed that old saying. There were no redeeming qualities left in Dale. She knew that he would try to use her and the kids to his advantage. She would fight to save Paul, Karen, and herself from Dale's grasp, a grip that was still felt even though he was behind bars.

During the week that followed Dale's arrest, Linda was told by her employer that her services were no longer needed at the day-care center. She had been a faithful employee for many years, but the publicity surrounding her husband had caused concern. Parents did not want to leave their children with a woman whose husband was accused of brutally murdering a small child. As in any small town, Linda was looked upon by a few as having something to do with the murders. She faced the undeserved stigma and held her head up high. Having done nothing wrong, she would not be intimidated by whispers behind her back whenever she went out. She cherished the support from neighbors and friends.

After receiving her severance pay and joining the ranks of the unemployed, she set out to reconstruct her life. First, she had to deal with Dale. She had made up her mind to divorce him. He was not the man she once knew. She would try to erase from her mind all the years she had spent with him. She busied herself with filling out job applications and searching for work while Paul and Karen were in school. Her savings were dwindling, but she was certain that she would find suitable employment soon.

She hired an attorney and started divorce proceedings, only to find herself caught up in another web of legal entanglement spun by her spouse. He had plans for his wife. She, too, had become a pawn to be played at a later time.


The temperature in October of 1989 was the only thing cooling off in the metro-east area. The *News-Democrat* was hot on the issue about the Lanman murders being linked to the Cardenas case. In the October 3 article, the *News-Democrat* printed the similarities as pointed out by Woidtke's public defender, Brian Trentman:

*(1) The manner of death.* "The (Lanman) murders apparently were committed through the use of a sharp instrument, possibly a scissors, which was left in the throat of one of the victims." Trentman said he speculated that Cardenas's throat was cut, although a cause of death could not be determined because her body had decomposed.

*(2) The Cardenas and Lanman murders occurred in the Belleville area.* "There aren't that many murders in Belleville," Trentman said.

*(3) The physical resemblance between Cardenas and Jolaine Lanman.* Both were petite with dark-colored hair.

*(4) Anderson allegedly posed as a law enforcement officer investigating the Cardenas murder.*

161

*(5) Trentman also said the timing of the Lanman killings—a day before Woidtke's scheduled sentencing—raised his suspicions.* "Either he (Anderson) did kill Audrey Cardenas and didn't get the attention for it, or he didn't do it but for some reason wants the attention out of it," Trentman said.

The stories in the *News-Democrat* that followed the October 3 article helped generate a review of the Cardenas case. State's Attorney John Baricevic appointed his former chief prosecuting attorney, John English, to review the two cases. Baricevic outlined for the news media the reasons he felt convinced that Woidtke had killed Cardenas:

*(1) Dr. Daniel Cuneo, a clinical psychologist, testified Woidtke was capable of homicidal tendencies.*

*(2) Woidtke could not have known that Cardenas had a set of keys clenched in her fist and a barrette in her hair if he had just stumbled upon the body. In his confessions to killing Cardenas, Woidtke told investigators of the keys, barrette, and pipe, which was found under Cardenas's body.*

*(3) A woman jogger in O'Fallon reported that Woidtke had stalked her and she had called the police. Another O'Fallon woman said he had followed her and "stole a kiss."*

*(4) When State Police Agent Debra Morgan interviewed Woidtke, Woidtke made bizarre sexual innuendoes. Evidence indicated Cardenas had been sexually assaulted.*

*(5) Woidtke's past included that he had attacked his mother and had psychological problems in college.*

*(6) Baricevic stated that the Woidtke murder trial was incorrectly reported. He said a footprint near Cardenas's body in the dry creek bed was size eight-and-a-half to nine, not size twelve, as reported by the* Belleville News-Democrat. *Woidtke wears size eight; Anderson wears from size seven to eight-and-a-half.*

Days after the State's Attorney's Office comments appeared on the pages of the *News-Democrat*, Anderson made his first appearance in court on the issue of retaining a public defender. Dressed in an orange jumpsuit issued to prisoners at the county jail, Anderson stood beside his newly appointed lawyer, St. Clair County Public Defender Clyde Kuehn.

Kuehn informed the judge that if a link between the Cardenas case and the Lanman case developed, he would have to withdraw as Anderson's attorney to avoid conflict of interests in the Public Defender's Office.

Prosecutor Dennis Hatch's first encounter with Anderson came at the indigency hearing. During

Hatch's inquiry into Anderson's assets, Anderson refused to answer the questions.

"Do you understand that you can be held in contempt?" asked the presiding judge.

"I haven't had any sleep since Friday," said Anderson, turning to Kuehn for support.

Hatch pointed out that Anderson had resources to obtain money for a private attorney, reflecting on Anderson's two bank accounts, a home, and two cars.

"There is no indication before the court that he cannot afford an attorney. We ask the court to have the public defender withdrawn from this case," said Hatch.

"Any money that might be available in the bank accounts, she's going to deny me access to," said Anderson, referring to his wife.

"We don't know from the documents presented whether there is access to these funds. I think it would be imprudent at this time to reconsider. I would support the court's continued investigation into his indigency. For the short term the court should keep the public defender in this thing," said Kuehn.

Anderson won the ruling and was allowed to retain a public defender at the taxpayers' expense. He managed to convince the judge that it would be almost impossible for him to convert his assets into cash. Anderson claimed that his wife controlled the money and that he had no say in the matter.

* * *

Two days after the ruling to provide Anderson with a public defender, Anderson was back in court. His attorney, Clyde Kuehn, had filed a motion to withdraw as defense counsel for him. Anderson knew about Kuehn's reputation as a highly qualified attorney, well skilled in defense tactics. Anderson fought to block Kuehn's withdrawal, citing to the court that he had not been given time to review the withdrawal motion.

"I would object to this motion," said Anderson, as Kuehn outlined to the court his reason for the motion.

"I wish to disagree with what Mr. Kuehn said. I feel it could possibly be permanently harmful to my case if this motion was granted," said Anderson.

The judge ruled in favor of Kuehn, but gave Anderson three weeks to hire private counsel or return to court on another indigence hearing.

In the divorce proceeding, Dale had refused to sign the papers to grant Linda the divorce, because he needed money for private counsel. Since the divorce was not final, the property in joint ownership would then be a source of payment for his attorney. Dale used his knowledge of the legal system to his advantage. In compliance with a court order, Linda had to pay Dale's attorney, Gary Bement, fifteen thousand dollars to defend him. Linda was astounded. It seemed unfair that he should be able to use the money for a defense attorney even though she received full ownership of the house and cars under the proposed divorce settlement. Unemployed and caring for two children, the fifteen thousand dollars would pay a lot of bills.

She realized the wheels of justice turn slowly, but they seemed to grind to a halt in her divorce. Linda's attorney suggested that she wait until after Dale's trial to finalize the divorce to ensure no legal snag in the husband-wife confidence issue.

Imprisonment hadn't stopped Dale's scheming mind. From inside the jail, he placed calls to newspaper offices and promised a newsworthy story. Reporters responded to the invitation. Through the thick glass of the interview room at the jail, he toyed with the reporters. His motive: generate publicity to force the court to grant him a change of venue in his upcoming trial.

Anderson spoke to the reporters in a calm voice while he claimed to be a devoted family man, an innocent man, who was caught up in a nightmare of the justice system run amuck. Touching on the shame and humiliation his family had to endure over his wrongful arrest, he quickly said that he would be victorious and be able to rejoin his wife and children.

His voice became stern when he talked about

the evidence in the upcoming trial. He assured reporters that the State would find no blood on any of his clothing and suggested that would be the State's downfall. Turning to the reporters, Anderson made a request. "Do me a favor, use a picture of me in a suit and tie. It makes for a negative impression if you see someone in a jumpsuit. It doesn't present me in a favorable light."

Anderson liked to challenge the system. On January 25, 1990, he walked with an air of confidence into the courtroom the first day of the motion to suppress hearings. Tucked under his arm was a bulging expandable file folder that drafted the paperwork contained in his attorney's briefcase. He sat at the defense table clad in a white shirt, unbuttoned at the collar, and slacks that looked too small for him. He busied himself with arranging papers on the table in preparation for the proceedings.

Gary Bement had filed two motions for his client. The first motion was to suppress all oral statements made by Anderson, and the evidence collected at Anderson's house, contending it was illegally received. The second motion was to change the place for trial because of intense media coverage.

Before Bement could finish addressing the court, Anderson became impatient with him and wanted to cover other issues.

"Did you want to go ahead, Mr. Bement?" asked Judge Jerry Flynn.

"We will go ahead, Judge. Sometimes we have a little difficulty communicating exactly what he wants to do and that's the reason for the delay," said Bement.

Anderson was called to take the witness stand. Walking slowly up to the court clerk to be sworn in, Anderson turned momentarily to glance at the prosecutor. Dennis Hatch watched his face as he took the oath before being seated. Anderson appeared excited about testifying.

Hatch had come out second best in his first court encounter with Anderson on the indigency hearing. This suppression hearing on the evidence was of paramount importance. To lose the evidence seized at the house would be devastating to the prosecution.

"Were you in your house when the police came into your house?" Bement asked of the witness.

"On September 29 of '89, it was approximately 5:00 or 6:00 A.M. My wife and I and the children were asleep in our home when a large number of armed police officers broke in our home with battering rams and pointed guns at us and threatened our lives. We thought we were all going to be murdered in our beds," said Anderson.

Bement let Anderson talk about the SWAT team entering the house and the Nester and Busch interview of his client. He wanted to focus on the search.

168

"How long were they in your house before you understood the reasoning why they were at your house?" said Bement.

"I am not sure how long that was. I didn't have a clock. The police turned off the electricity to our home before they broke into it with the battering ram."

"At any time during the fifteen hours that you and the police officers were at your home, did you tell them that you didn't want to give them any information and that you wanted an attorney to be present?"

"Yes. In fact, when Deputy Sheriff Ralph Owens first broke in the house with the SWAT team, I told them we would like to have one or more FBI agents present because my rights were being violated, and I also requested an attorney be present during questioning and they refused to do that."

"Specifically what was the response after you asked Sergeant Owens to have an attorney?"

"He told me that I could not have an attorney present during questioning. Like I say, the men took turns questioning me. They kept stepping on my feet. Punching me to get me to answer questions. This is not right the way they did that," said Anderson.

Hatch raised his eyebrow at Anderson's statement. Anderson was alleging police brutality, and went on to name Nester, Busch, and Heil as the officers who beat him. Hatch jotted notes as he listened to the testimony.

Anderson continued with his story about the beating he received at the hands of the officers. He maintained that he never signed anything, was never given a copy of the search warrant for handwriting samples or handwriting standards.

When Bement finished his examination, Hatch leaned forward in his chair as if to study his notes before beginning his cross-examination. He remembered every word Anderson said, but wanted time for the witness to become uneasy with no immediate dialogue.

Hatch started the questions in an easy tone, covering the SWAT team's entrance into the house. Anderson responded by telling of the twenty officers pointing guns at him and his wife. Hatch moved swiftly into the issue of Anderson wearing his eyeglasses that morning.

"Now, these policemen come into your house. Did you recognize any of them?" said Hatch.

"Not immediately because I wear glasses and I didn't have my glasses on when I was asleep. I can't see very well," said Anderson.

"Did you put your glasses on?"

"At some point I did put them on."

"Well, you have no idea how long it took you to put your glasses on?"

"You have to remember the police occupied my house for approximately fifteen hours."

# Have you seen this woman?

## Audrey Cardenas

Audrey Cardenas, 24, new to the area, has been missing since Sunday, June 19, 1988. She has dark hair, is approximately 5-feet, 2-inches tall and weighs about 100 pounds. Anyone who may have seen her Sunday, possibly jogging, or since, or who has any information on her whereabouts is asked to call the following:

**Belleville Police** or **Belleville News-Democrat**

**234-1212** **234-8420**

The poster circulated by the Belleville Police before the body of Audrey Cardenas was found.

Rodney Woidtke, the man convicted of the Cardenas murder.

Jolaine Lanman.

Kenneth Lanman.

The Lanman home.

Kenneth's cloth teddy bear left in a pool of his mother's blood on her bed.

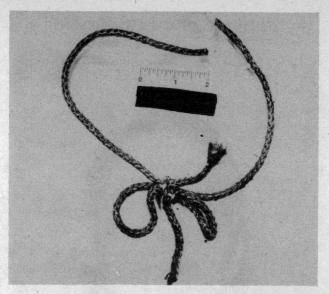

The rope removed from the neck of Jolaine Lanman's body.

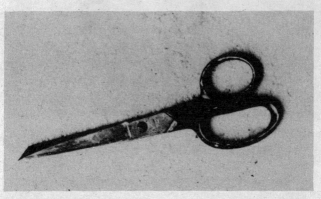

The household scissors used to stab Jolaine and Kenneth to death.

# THE FACES OF DALE ANDERSON

As photographed by police.

In happier times.

Age six.                    Age nine.

In high school.             In college.

Anderson's home.

Police gained access to Anderson's home through his kitchen.

The collection of paddles, sex toys and pornography found in Anderson's home.

ESCUELA SECUNDARIA FEDERAL

E. S. 314-13
S. PCO. DEL ORO. CHIH.

La presente acredita a

CARDENAS CAMPOS ....

como alumn  regular de esta Escuela, del

3ER. Grado. "C"

S. Fco. del Oro, Chih.  Dic. ......... de 1971

Presidente ...... de Alumnos          El Director de la Escuela

Eduardo .......... López          Profr. José ... José Delgado

ID card found in Anderson's wall safe.

Inspector Alva Busch.

St. Clair County Sheriff's deputy Detective David Nester.

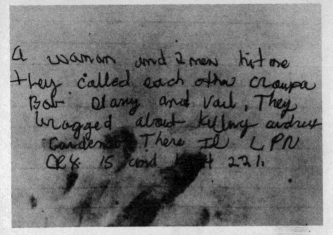

The blood-stained note (*left*) found near Jolaine Lanman's body.

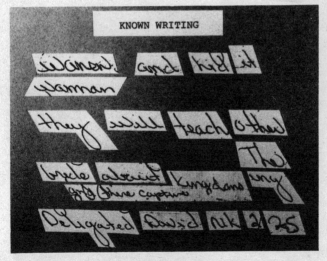

KNOWN WRITING

Samples of Jolaine's handwriting used to compare against the note found at the crime scene.

Brooke Sartory, the Lanman's young neighbor who was instrumental in helping investigators find Anderson.

Prosecutor Dennis Hatch.

"We are all aware of that. My question is—"

"You are not letting me answer, Mr. Hatch."

"Go right ahead, Mr. Anderson."

"After a day of trauma like that, I was in such shock, I don't have a lot of recall of small details like you are asking."

"So, the police could have advised you of your Miranda rights then?"

"No. They clearly did not advise me."

"So you remember that. You are absolutely sure of that with all the shock and trauma, you know that for sure."

"Yes, I know that for sure."

"But you can't remember whether or not you put your glasses on?"

Hatch moved from one point to another to test Anderson's reaction. Anderson wanted to explain his viewpoint on each issue, but Hatch kept moving with questions. He didn't want to deal with Anderson now; that would come later in the trial. Hatch would have to win the motion to suppress or there would be no trial. His plan of attack was to break Anderson's credibility through cross-examination, and to use the officers' testimonies to rebut Anderson's story.

During the cross-examination, Hatch dealt with the allegations of the beating. Anderson told the court that due to injuries sustained from the investigators, he was kept in the jail infirmary for two to three weeks after his arrest. Hatch wasn't worried about the brutality charges, there were booking photographs and medical personnel at the jail to impeach Anderson's testimony. Hatch touched on that slightly before moving on to the meat of the suppress hearing.

"Could you take a look at those, please? Can you tell us what those are?" Hatch said, handing Anderson two documents.

"They are 'consent to search' forms for a car and a house," said Anderson, glaring at the prosecutor.

"Okay. And is that your signature at the bottom of both of those?"

"I'm not sure. I don't recall signing either one of these forms, although the police did have me sign my name dozens of times on papers for handwriting tests while they were at my house. But I don't recall signing either one of these forms."

"You are familiar with your signature, aren't you?"

"Yes, I am."

"Is that your signature?"

"I can't be sure. It doesn't look like the way I normally sign my name."

After completing cross-examination, Hatch put on State witnesses to rebut Anderson's testimony. Anderson's statement about being placed in the jail infirmary due to a beating from police had opened the door for the prosecutor. Hatch used the nurse at the jail to document the extent of

Anderson's injuries the evening he was arrested.

Anderson had a small abrasion on the second finger of his left hand near the knuckle. The nurse put on a Band-Aid at his request. Her report reflected that Anderson's heart and lungs sounds were checked showing no signs of abnormality. No bruises were observed on his chest, back, or arms. Anderson was later placed in the infirmary at the request of the court psychologist.

Judge Jerry Flynn ruled on the two motions filed by Anderson. He denied the defense motion to suppress Anderson's oral statements and ruled that the evidence seized at the defendant's house could be used by the prosecutor. Hatch had won a crucial round on the evidence. Judge Flynn delayed his ruling on the change of venue for two weeks. Hatch knew he still had an uphill battle and that there would be other pitfalls along the way.

The trial date had been set by Judge Flynn for the nineteenth of February.

On the eighth of February, Hatch entered the courtroom for the ruling on change of venue. He was surprised to see Anderson seated in a wheelchair.

Hatch noticed that Anderson seemed upset with his attorney. Bement and Anderson appeared to be having words at the defense table.

Only after the hearing began did Hatch understand what the problem was. Anderson had written a three-page letter to the court with complaints about Bement in hopes of using the court to order Bement to obtain police and lab reports. In the letter, Anderson cited his attorney with: "Gary Bement has harassed my wife for money and caused severe damage to my marriage and family . . . seldom meets with me to discuss my case and prepare my defense . . . refused to take my phone calls . . ."

Anderson demanded that the court order the following documents to be granted to him: results of a polygraph test conducted on his wife, Linda; all police reports and polygraph test results on the Cardenas case; copies of all notes written by Jolaine Lanman and a handwriting report; Department of Public Aid files on Anderson; documents regarding Jolaine Lanman's twenty-five thousand dollar life insurance policy; determination of ownership of Jolaine Lanman's scissors; a list of Anderson's clients at the Department of Public Aid; lab test results on blood found on John Lanman's clothes.


Hatch immediately picked up on where Anderson was going with the letter to the court. Hatch began to appreciate the cleverness of Anderson's letter, which had two main purposes.

First, Anderson wanted to have several options

for his defense. His wife's polygraph results could be used to his advantage during the trial. Jolaine's life insurance policy, ownership of the scissors, and lab test for blood on John Lanman's clothing suggested that Anderson would try to blame the husband for the murders.

The second part of the letter to the court was an attempt to allege incompetency by counsel in hopes that if he was found guilty at the conclusion of the trial, he would have grounds to appeal. Hatch smiled at Anderson's cleverness and waited to see what his next move would be. Looking across the room he watched as Anderson barked orders at Bement.

Bement asked to address the court on the matter of his client's letter. "I am not going to go on what I think are wild-goose chases. I consider myself an experienced attorney. Some of those records have nothing to do with the case I've been hired to defend," said Bement. "I can only assume . . . he no longer wishes me to represent him. I feel Mr. Anderson should have the opportunity to have an attorney he is happy with."

Judge Flynn leaned forward on the bench and looked directly at Anderson. After a brief moment, he spoke in an authoritative tone when he addressed the suspect.

"I have not noticed anything in the court proceedings that Mr. Bement has failed in any way on your behalf. Nothing is keeping you from ditching him and getting another attorney. I would strongly urge you to sit down with Mr. Bement and work out any differences," said Flynn, denying Bement's motion to withdraw from the case.

Hatch waited for Anderson's reaction. Anderson had pushed too hard this time to get what he wanted and had backed himself into a corner. Hatch was not surprised when he heard the nasal-toned voice say, "I think Mr. Bement and I can work out any differences."

The next allegation the court heard about was the bad treatment Anderson alleged occurred at the county jail. He claimed to have fallen and could not walk, causing the need for the wheelchair. Hatch quickly dispensed with Anderson's wheelchair ploy by testimony from the jail superintendent, who informed the court that Anderson requested the use of the wheelchair after claiming to be dizzy.


Judge Flynn heard arguments from both Bement and Hatch, but granted Anderson a change of venue due to publicity, even though the accused had generated additional news coverage through interviews from jail. The location of the trial was changed to Randolph County, just south of St. Clair County.

The courthouse in the riverfront town of Chester, Illinois was selected. The move would pose a logistical problem for the prosecutor. He needed more time to prepare for trial. The summoning of the prospective jurors in Randolph County would take time, but there was still much work to be done on court preparation. Witness scheduling was a major concern. One of the main witnesses in the case, Al Busch, was out of the country on a scuba-diving adventure in Central America. Seventy other witnesses had to be located and scheduled for trial.

Judge Flynn set the trial date for March 26, 1990. Summons were sent to people in Randolph County notifying them they had been selected for jury duty.

# Eighteen

The murder rate in the metro-east area continued to rise as the new year started off. Busch's case load increased along with it.

The Lanman case had consumed most of Busch's spare time since September. He worked on the Anderson files every weekend, reading through boxes of papers, then making copies for Glenna Mell and Lex Bitner, analysts in the Criminal Intelligence Section of the Illinois State Police assigned to work with Busch. He met with the analysts and gave them copies of the documents. Mell and Bitner read the material and then began systematically cataloging thousands of pages to feed into the computer.

Early one Saturday morning, Busch arrived at his office to delve into Anderson's writings. The weekend was a good time to read through the material; there would be no distractions from ringing phones or normal workday interruptions. Opening the files, he soon entered the evil, calculating mind of Dale Anderson.

Among the writings were files with dated pages. Each file contained personal information on a given person, their family, and conversations Anderson had with them. Anderson kept the files current. The dates started in July of 1988, when he was actively seeking legal counsel after the incident with Carolyn Tuft, and ran through September of 1989. His diary started in June of 1988.

Busch could see that Anderson's quest was to use the legal system to rise above the situation he was in. His strange activities at work appeared to have started months before Cardenas was murdered. Busch was unable to get the total picture of what was going on in 1988. He needed more data on the Cardenas investigation. Names were turning up in Anderson's writing that Busch didn't know. He remedied that by obtaining a complete case file on the Cardenas investigation which, when coupled with Anderson's diary, proved to be of considerable value in putting the pieces of the puzzle together.

Teresa Anglin, Linda Cox, and Dave Hendricks were names that appeared in the diary. Busch soon realized that Linda Cox was a co-worker at the Public Aid Office, which in and of itself was of little interest until Busch found a receipt from a local florist in Anderson's briefcase. Silk flowers had been sent to Linda Cox at the Public Aid Office on June 29, 1988. The name on the receipt was "Dave Hendricks."

179

The card attached to the receipt said: "Linda, Hope this brightens your day. I would like to see you. Love D.H."

Busch paused after reading the card. The only Dave Hendricks he could think of was the one in northern Illinois, who was charged with the murders of a wife and two children with an axe.

The next slip of paper from the briefcase was a hotel room receipt from the Ramada Inn, only five miles from Anderson's home. The room was rented by "Dave Hendricks" on June 26, 1988, and listed a Chicago address. Busch flipped through the stack of papers of Anderson's makeshift diary until he located the section dated around that time frame.

"Sat 6-25-88 3 P.M. I saw Linda Cox at swimming pool. She was with a friend. Tammy — — — — — —, Granite City."

Anderson wrote down all of Linda's personal history and her family members' names, the type of car she drove, and her license plate number.

"Sun 6-26-88 9:15 am I called Linda about lunch today in FVHS (Fairview Heights) at Olive Garden Rest at 1:30 pm with a friend Dave Hendricks, IL State Police officer, Springfield around 12:20 pm."

Anderson notes that Linda's air conditioner is broken and she can't make lunch. He writes about her relatives staying with her this week.

"Mon 6-26-88 10am I called Linda. . . .

Linda stated she goes on late lunch almost everyday. Linda went to Bonanza for lunch to see Dave. Linda went to bank first on her lunch break. Dave paid for Linda's lunch. Linda had only salad and iced tea. Dave shared his ribeye and baked potato with her. Linda drove her car to Bonanza."

It appeared to Busch that Anderson was getting the brush-off from Linda Cox. She made excuses not to have lunch with him. Did he create this other personality of Dave Hendricks because of her? Busch wasn't sure what was going on. Anderson's writings switched from what seemed to be sexual fantasies with a police twist of "the clever cop gets the girl," but then got bizarre and turned to the dark side, as if a serial killer was stalking his next victim.

Anderson must have realized that Linda Cox would soon see through the Dave Hendricks ploy. What plans did he have in mind for the woman? He was constantly trying to arrange for her to meet a person that didn't exist, and that was during the week Cardenas's body was discovered. Did Anderson want to lure her somewhere? Was it sex or murder he had in mind for her? She did work at the same office. Had he planned to use her death to frame the bosses? Busch read further in the diary.

"Mon 6-27-88 6:30 pm I called Linda at home. She will see Dave tonight. Dave gets off duty today 7 am to 7 pm. Dave and his partner will eat dinner at Brinkers. Dave will be at Corvettes at 8 pm. Dave arrived at 7:45 pm. Linda arrived at 8:00 pm and she left at 9 pm. Linda walked up into Corvettes, but was too shy to stay inside to have a drink. Dave took her by the left arm and she pulled away."

Again, the writings switched. In the next paragraph he talked about her background, what church she attended, and what schools she went to. Anderson filled two pages, noting that Linda went to school with one of DeLaria's daughters.

"DeLaria's daughter," whispered Busch as he stopped reading. "That's the connection." Anderson's focal point turned back to a supervisor where he worked. Anderson hated DeLaria.

Busch noted a star drawn beside the next sentence in the diary.

"Linda lives with her parents and they are very protective of her."

"Tues 6-28-88 3 pm Dave went by Linda's house to talk to her. He asked if she wanted to go to St. Elizabeth Hospital for memorial service. She stated no because she just got home from Springfield and was having lunch."

Busch couldn't believe what he just read. Anderson is asking Linda Cox to go to Cardenas's memorial service, but is writing as though he is Dave Hendricks, the supercop.

"Tues 6-28-88 3:10 pm Dave went to St. Elizabeth Hospital for 3 pm memorial service. Dave stood at rear of room with two other plain clothes police officers. Towards the end of the service one of the officers asked Dave to sign the guest book. He did sign the book and listed he was with State of IL. Carolyn Tuft, reporter, was there and saw Dave when she left. Dave stood at back of room with two officers until all the *News-Democrat* reporters left the room."

Busch pushed his chair away from the desk and walked over to the file cabinet to get the Cardenas case file. Reading down the lead sheet he located a copy of the register book for friends and relatives of Audrey Cardenas at the memorial service. On the second to last line of the book was a signature Busch knew as soon as he saw it: "Dale Anderson State of IL."

Although Anderson signed his real name on the register, his diary maintained Dave Hendricks was at the memorial service. Again Anderson's behavior suggested he was more than just someone with a cop fetish. Busch thought it strange that in the eight pages of the diary which spanned June 25 to July 1, Anderson never wrote down Audrey Cardenas's name, even though he attended her funeral.

"Wed 6-29-88 8:30 am Dave sent flowers to Linda. A lady wrote up a note card to Linda. They should be delivered today at approx 9:30 am to 10 am. D A called Linda today. She stated she got the flowers. D A stated What flowers? Linda stated the blue silk flowers. D A stated Did Dave send you flowers? Dave had mentioned he might give you a present or flowers because he missed you at lunch. . . . I forgot to remind her, Cops are special and she must treat them different."

Busch felt that although the writings suggested Anderson could have a psychological problem, he did not believe Anderson was insane. There was too much thought process on Anderson's part. He was able to carry out everyday functions, use the legal system and others to his advantage, and cover his ass when he had to.

The next item of interest in the briefcase was the memorial service program on Audrey Cardenas, which Anderson must have taken while at the service. His intense interest about Cardenas bothered Busch, as did his attraction to the Cox woman. A timetable on all the events of 1988 could be the key to unlocking the mystery about Cardenas's death. Many of those times were in Anderson's notes and the Cardenas case file.

Apparently Linda Cox had not been interviewed by anyone during the Cardenas case or even in this investigation. She might have some insight into Anderson. Busch jotted down a note to speak with her later on; right now, he had more papers to read and copy for his meeting with the women from the Intelligence Unit on Monday.

* * *

Dennis Hatch reviewed the major case file from Commander Nonn. The unit had done a good job on the Lanman case, but from a prosecutor's perspective Hatch had only scratched the surface on trial preparation. Due to the amount of evidence collected, he would have to wait on the results from the crime lab. Other pretrial motions were sure to come in the Lanman case.

A rigorous believer in organizational charting of all phases of a case, Hatch set about outlining each. He had sixty to seventy witnesses that he planned to use during the trial. Hatch wanted to speak with each witness before the court date. This would take time, something he had little of, but he needed a clear picture of what had led up to the murders of the Lanmans. After listening to the witnesses, they were each placed in a given category. If they were witnesses that had made an observation from a location, Hatch would go to that location and interview them there to see for himself their vantage point. The people that had seen the blue Oldsmobile parked in the Lanman subdivision fell into that category.

Hatch visited many of them at their homes in the evening. He was willing to talk with anyone that had any involvement in the case. Neighbors and relatives of the victims and relatives of Anderson's were listed and interviewed during office hours when possible.

Hatch's persistence for details helped him separate accurate information on the case from some that he found to be lacking in substance. He charted out times given by all of Lanman's neighbors who had seen anything the day of the murders. The blue car was first noticed in the Villa Madero Subdivision being driven slowly down San Mateo Street at 2:00 P.M. by Martha Mayberry. Martha called her daughter, Janice Conder, who lived across from her on Tampico Street, to alert her about the strange car. Janice wrote down the license plate number of the blue Oldsmobile, watched the man get out and walk over to Chula Vista Street. The man returned and drove away around 4:45 P.M.

Anderson's daughter put the time when her father arrived home that day at 5:00 P.M., since she had just watched "The Bill Cosby Show." Hatch would need to prove that the distance between the Lanman house to Anderson's house could be driven in fifteen minutes at that time of day. He called the lab to check with Busch about making test runs between the crime scene and Anderson's house.

"Can you take care of charting the time and distance, maybe we can show the routes on maps?"

"Yeah, I'll cover that and I'll get a state plane lined up for this week. I'm going to take aerial photos of Villa Madero to use in trial."

Busch hung up the phone and returned to reading papers from one of Anderson's brief-cases. A small sheet of paper from a notepad caught his attention. There was a description of a person and a license plate number on the paper, a license plate number Busch was familiar with. It belonged to Inspector Dee Heil.

It wasn't until he found this that it dawned on Busch what Anderson meant when he met them for the first time. He said he had seen Heil, but didn't know him. He'd probably watched him work the crime scene on Cardenas.

The paper with Heil's description was only the first of many papers that suggested Anderson had an extreme interest in the Cardenas case. Opening the next box of papers took Busch back into June of 1988. Using Anderson's notes, police reports, and witnesses' statements, he pieced together what Anderson was doing before and after Cardenas came to town.

Anderson's work record with the Department of Public Aid was less than flattering. His first three years with the State were uneventful. In 1986, he requested a hardship transfer from the office location in East St. Louis to the Belleville office. The request was refused. Anderson became upset and threatened the woman supervisor in her office when she denied his transfer. He warned her that his relatives would seek revenge because she was placing a hardship on his family. The police were called to the office to escort Anderson out. He was later reprimanded for his actions.

By October of 1987, Anderson was once again having problems with management. After receiving a reduction in his level of pay, he cautioned his supervisor, Maurice Vale, that his family might seek revenge. During a grievance proceeding with a union steward, Anderson demanded he wanted "a pound of flesh or a little finger and a firstborn child," from management.

At the predisciplinary meeting the following week, Anderson announced that he fell at the office two days prior and hit his head. The next day he was off work on sick time, when a dog owned by the woman supervisor, whom Anderson had threatened, was poisoned.

His work performance continued to drop while his insubordination and threatening nature increased. Discrepancies during interviews between Anderson and Public Aid applicants reflect his inability to complete his work assignments. Anderson blamed his supervisor for any shortcoming that occurred with a client where he was the caseworker. He'd take clients' case files out of the office, which was against department policy, and led to the confrontation on May 23, 1988.

Anderson filed charges with the Belleville Police Department against the three supervisors for Battery and Theft. On June 3, 1988, they were arrested, posted bond, and returned to work that day. An article written by Carolyn Tuft, covering the arrest of the Public Aid officials, appeared in the *News-Democrat* on June 4, 1988. The Public Aid Office became Anderson's battleground. His mannerisms and demeanor, although always considered odd, took a turn for the worse. Many of his coworkers became afraid of him. He disrupted the office with outbursts directed at management, posted newspaper clippings saying "employee kills boss over dispute."

Busch realized that the time frame on Anderson's hatred toward Vale, DeLaria, and Kroupa predated Cardenas's arrival in Belleville. This could be an important factor. With the three sources of information from 1988 assisting him, Busch followed Anderson's footsteps into June of 1988.


Several calls were placed to the *News-Democrat* by Anderson as an anonymous caller reporting illegal activities by three state employees at the IDPA in Belleville. On June 7, Tuft was enticed by phone calls from Anderson with a promise of a story on death threats against him.

Unable to locate him at first, she had left a note for him:

"Tues June 7, 4:10 p.m. Mr. Anderson, I was told by your office that you were not there today. I am very interested in this public aid case and need to talk to you immediately regarding threats made to your life. Please call me ASAP at 234-8420. Carolyn Tuft reporter *News-Democrat*."

Around 7:30 P.M. that evening, Tuft interviewed Anderson at his home, and the following day reported the gun incident to a friend at the Belleville Police Department. Little attention was given to the matter. Most officers who dealt with Anderson for any length of time considered him to be strange, but harmless. They viewed his complaints against his supervisors as a work-related problem by a disgruntled employee.

*Anderson must have been about ready to explode,* thought Busch, as he read through the notes. Anderson wasn't satisfied with the outcome of the arrest and charges of his supervisors, so the manipulative bastard contacted the FBI on June 8, 1988, in an attempt to involve the three bosses on federal charges, but got no satisfaction there.

Locked onto Anderson's thought processes during that time, Busch tracked the man on paper. Anderson knew that he would be suspended on June 10, 1988 for thirty days pending discharge. He had to discredit Vale, DeLaria, and Kroupa to keep his job. In a frenzy to do that, he drove to the south side of St. Clair County and staged a shooting scene. Placing spent shell casings alongside the road, a napkin with a speck of blood, and small pieces of broken glass, he drove back to Belleville. But calls placed to the *News-Democrat* office are ignored. Nobody would go with him to the shooting scene.

On June 9, 1988, Audrey Cardenas arrives in Belleville. Dale Anderson is suspended for thirty days pending discharge.

# Nineteen

The investigation into the Lanman case continued as Busch focused on key points for trial. He
mapped out the three routes Anderson could
have taken driving from the murder scene to his
house. One of the routes crossed railroad tracks
at the east end of Belleville. On the trial run,
Busch was delayed by a train and was still able
to complete the trip in under twelve minutes,
even driving the posted speed limit.

Laboratory reports of the analysis of evidence
collected at the Lanman house made their way
through the routing system. Busch received copies, and copies were sent to the prosecutor.
Hatch read the reports as they arrived, charting
exhibits and sub-exhibits numbering in the hundreds. Using his own cataloging system, he identified an exhibit and what forensic examination
was conducted on it. A key piece of evidence
emerged from the microscopy section at the Bureau of Forensic Sciences at Carbondale, Illinois.
Forensic Scientist Glen Schubert's report reflected

his examination of the bloody cloth impression on the bed skirting collected from the murder scene, and the comparison of that impression to the six cloth gloves collected at Anderson's house. Schubert found that the left glove collected from the suspect's home was consistent with the bloody impression on the bed skirting.

*This was the first strand of physical evidence that linked Anderson to the murder scene,* mused Hatch, reading the Schubert report. Anderson had overlooked the bloody glove impression. He had gotten rid of the bloody gloves he wore during the murders, but had forgotten that he had the same style gloves in his dresser at home. Hatch filed the report in a folder marked "Crime Scene & Lab Reports," and placed the folder in a box to the side of his desk.

Perplexed by the muddied waters of the 1988 investigation around Cardenas's death, Hatch sought to clear some of the myths in hopes of getting a better view into Anderson's motive in the Lanman murders. He expected to meet with some resistance venturing into the issue of the 1988 letter, dubbed the "Cardenas Letter," where the teenage friend of Anderson's daughter had written about Cardenas being at Anderson's home. The *News-Democrat* was pushing for the Cardenas case to be reopened, and the judicial system stood firm on the conviction of Rodney Woidtke.

The "Cardenas Letter" had resurrected itself at

the *News-Democrat* shortly after the Lanmans were slain. Hatch, armed with Grand Jury subpoenas for reluctant people holding information, collected data on the letter's destination from Anderson's house to the *News-Democrat*.

On Saturday, September 30, 1989, three days after the Lanmans died, the "Cardenas Letter" was delivered to the lobby of the *Belleville News-Democrat*. The identity of the person who left the letter was withheld. The newspaper invoked the First Amendment privilege of confidentiality between a reporter and news source.

Hatch learned that Anderson had visited the office of the *Belleville Journal*, another local newspaper, in July of 1989, and had given them a copy of the "Cardenas Letter." That was two months prior to the Lanman murders, he noted. Anderson had attempted to link his supervisors to Cardenas's death again. The *Belleville Journal* relayed the letter to the Belleville Police Department, which had known about the letter in 1988 and written Anderson off as a "wacko." Hatch wondered why the *News-Democrat* had missed out on the "Cardenas Letter" for almost a year, only to have it delivered to them by someone, whom they refused to identify. Anderson had been arrested on the evening of September 29 and put behind bars on Saturday the thirtieth, when the letter arrived. Had he made arrangements by phone from the jail to have the letter delivered?

* * *

Hatch, using a large two-by-three foot sheet of paper divided into four-inch blocks representing each day of the month, noted any activity related to the case. He drafted twenty sheets to list the events between 1988 and 1989. Hatch and Busch used the time line to identify and compile data to fill the large calendar. That scrutinized the month of June 1988.

"It's this time frame when Cardenas is in town and Anderson is trying to get the *News-Democrat* involved that makes you wonder," said Busch, studying the monthly chart Hatch had laid on the conference table. "On the sixth, Anderson filed a police report with Belleville P.D. about receiving death threats against him and his wife if he testified against his bosses. That's before Audrey came to town."

"I see that," said Hatch. "Dale made some early calls to the paper before Cardenas's body was found, something about being held by De-Laria, Vale, and Kroupa. Either on the twenty-second or twenty-third."

"Here's a page from Anderson's diary covering that time frame," said Busch, placing a copy on the table as he read it. "Anderson tells about someone calling the *News-Democrat* and telling them Audrey was seen Sunday or Monday, and gives two addresses, which will come back to his bosses. On the twenty-sixth, he calls them again

195

and the reporter tells him, 'Dale, why not simply call Belleville P.D. since the newspaper passes this info on to them?' "

"He wrote all that down," laughed Hatch, now reading the page. "He's also trying to give them a license number, but they won't take it. He's unbelievable."

Later that evening, Hatch ordered pizza while they listed additional information on the calendar. Using Anderson's diary, they cross-matched events to check the accuracy of the diary. The calls to the *News-Democrat* through the month of June were verified through police reports and statements. Anderson had snuck into the *News-Democrat* office after hours in June and had to be ordered to leave the building. His excuse for being there was to learn the name of the reporter who had written an article about him, even though all articles were bylined with the reporter's name. How Anderson got into the building past the locked doors was never determined. Security measures were increased in the building after that, and his photograph was posted at the newspaper office after Tuft's interview with him on the seventh of June.

During the original investigation into the Cardenas homicide, a detective was assigned the lead of interviewing Anderson, but that interview never happened. The initial lead was passed over after the detective was unable to locate Anderson, who was watching the investigators and monitoring their radio traffic.

The Cardenas case was relinquished to the Belleville Police Department on July 1, 1988, when the MCS disbanded with Rodney Woidtke as the prime suspect. On July 8, the Grand Jury indicted Woidtke.

By July of 1988, complaints on Anderson's actions were becoming a daily theme to the Belleville Police Department. On July 11, Anderson went to the home of Teresa Anglin, a nursing student in Belleville, whose child was a classmate of Anderson's son. After being allowed into her home, Anderson began to ask personal questions that frightened her. Anderson sensed that he had scared her and hinted at being with the police department.

"What agency are you with?" said the young woman.

"I'm a special investigator with the State of Illinois. I'm in plainclothes. I'm working on a big case," said Anderson with a cold stare. "In fact, I'm working on the Cardenas case."

The woman tried to avoid looking directly at him; the look on his face scared her. She walked into the adjoining room, but he followed her wherever she went. Returning to the living room, she sat on the couch; Anderson sat close to her and put his arm around her.

"We should have lunch together tomorrow," said Anderson.

"I don't think so; I can't. You better go."

"You should be careful leaving the hospital at night. Cardenas ran at night. Late!"

She tried to remain calm, but her legs wouldn't quit shaking. She jumped up from the couch and moved to the other side of the room. Anderson stood up and moved next to her; she moved away and told him that he must leave so she could run some errands. After she convinced him that she might have lunch with him sometime, Anderson left directions to his house and his phone number.

She filed a complaint with the Belleville Police Department. A citation for Disorderly Conduct was issued against Anderson. Four other citations were written by the Belleville Police Department against him for Impersonating a Police Officer and Disorderly Conduct charges dating back to June.

On June 3, Anderson had called the *News-Democrat* and identified himself to the news reporter as being Bill Miller, a police officer with the Belleville Police Department.

On June 7, he represented himself as a police officer to Carolyn Tuft and flourished a handgun during an interview at his home.

Anderson returned to visit Teresa Anglin on July 12. In his diary he writes of that visit:

"I knocked on Teresa Anglin's door. No one answered. I saw someone look out the sliding door blinds. I walked back to my blue car. I heard on my police radio she maybe called the police. The police mentioned my name and address on the radio. Police started to check the folder on me. I was 10-32 (man with gun). I had two revolvers and was dangerous.

"I went to Long John Silvers and ate lunch. I heard 2 or 3 police cars went to my house. I came home about 2 p.m. and found a business card on my front door by Det Mark Heffernan."

On the thirteenth of July at 3:56 P.M., Belleville officers received word that Anderson was at the emergency room at St. Elizabeth's Hospital complaining of a head injury. While at the hospital, Anderson heard on his police scanner that officers were en route to his location, but it was too late for him to escape; he was having X rays done on his head and couldn't get out of the building before the police arrived. After medical treatment was completed and he was released, officers handcuffed and transported him to the Belleville Police Department. His large black briefcase-type bag, two police badges, and portable police scanner were taken from him and logged on his property sheet. Inside the bag was a file on Audrey Cardenas.

During booking procedures, Anderson's personal property sheet was filled out listing his clothing and one hundred and twenty dollars in cash. On July 14, 1988, Detective Mike Boyne took him to an arraignment hearing in front of a judge, where bond was set at four hundred dollars. When Anderson heard what the bond was, he reached inside his underwear and pulled something from his crotch area. Detective Boyne grabbed Anderson by the wrist as the black object cleared his clothing. In the brief struggle, Anderson fell to the floor and claimed Boyne struck him. The black object retrieved was a coin purse from which Anderson removed four one hundred dollar bills and posted his bond.

Boyne, taking the coin purse, immediately arrested Anderson for failure to comply with not removing all personal property during booking. Anderson, now seated in a chair in the courtroom, glared at the detective.

"Detective Boyne, give me my wallet," said Anderson.

"Do you have anything else on you?" said Boyne.

"No, but if I had a gun, I would use it on you."

Anderson was charged with assault for his statement to the detective. He fell to the floor and was taken to the hospital for treatment and returned to a cell at the Belleville Police Department. Two days later, Anderson was back on the street, released on a recognizance bond.


Audrey's father, Joe Cardenas, frustrated with the police investigation into his daughter's death, arrived in Belleville on July 15 and sought clues to find his daughter's killer. He visited the scene of the murder and sat alone several nights in the darkness of the creek bed, hoping to get a feel for what had happened there. Staying at a local hotel in town, Joe Cardenas appealed to the public for clues into Audrey's death by publicizing a phone number where he could be reached.

He was plagued with numerous calls ranging from inquiries from the news media to people who had visions. On July 16, Anderson placed a call to the hotel, but Cardenas was out. Two additional calls were received from Anderson, who alleged to be a special investigator. On July 21, he placed a fourth call. During that conversation, he told the father of the deceased that six Belleville police officers are responsible for Audrey's murder. Unknown to Anderson, the conversation was being taped. He told of how the six drunken cops were involved in the murder.

An arrest warrant for false impersonation of a government official was issued from the State's Attorney's Office for Dale Anderson on July 21. Anderson was arrested at his home, and several weapons were seized by the Belleville Police Department. Bond was set at $7,500. On July 22, 1988, Anderson posted $750 cash and was released.


On July 27, Anderson called Bonds Robinson,

an agent with the Illinois Liquor Commission, who attended his church. Due to a flaw in the Robinsons' phone answering machine, the conversation was recorded. In that conversation, Anderson alleged that six Belleville police officers could be responsible for covering up the facts about Cardenas's death. He told the agent that Audrey Cardenas visited the three administrators from the Public Aid Office and wrote down that interview in her notebook. She was later kidnapped and murdered by them. Anderson claimed to have Cardenas's notebook, but needed to get immunity from prosecution before he could release it to the State's Attorney.

On the twenty-ninth of July, Anderson had his daughter's friend write two letters: the "Cardenas Letter" and the second letter about Tuft's interview with Anderson. Both letters were backdated to June 29, 1988.

Hatch wrote in the last bit of information to fill in the last day of July on the calendar. Anderson's activities showed that he was constantly plotting against the three administrators and was in the middle of a heated exchange with them when Cardenas came to town.

"What about this poisoning of the woman's dog in 1987?" said Busch. "That's not above Anderson, and he did have some articles on poisoning."

"The timing is right. He had an argument with his supervisor and threatened her. I wouldn't put it past Dale," said Hatch.

"I wonder what kind of poison it was?"

"Aldrin," said Hatch. "The woman had an autopsy done on the dog."

Hatch slid the autopsy report on the white collie across the table to Busch. Picking up the report, Busch read through the toxicology findings. Stomach contents revealed "Aldrin" present. Unfamiliar with the poison, he called a chemist at the state lab and found that Aldrin was a pesticide that was currently banned in the United States.

Returning to the table, Busch opened the folder he brought with him and removed the seven-page document, copied from Anderson's diary, and handed it to Hatch.

"I think you'll find page four amusing," he said. "Keep in mind that Anderson didn't have any way of knowing these papers would be seized."

"Let's see what you got," said Hatch, in a skeptical tone as he looked at the pages.

"Wed 8-17-88 . . . I went jogging on Sun 6-19-88 after dark to B.T.H.S. East (Belleville Township High School). We left her apt down Douglas to B st. and up to Rt 161 and to East H.S.

"I could not keep up with her on B st and she got out of my sight and around at the H.S.

ahead of me. When I arrived at H.S. I could not find her. I thought she was playing hide and seek with me.

"I was wearing shorts with pockets, a T-shirt and tennis shoes on the evening of 6-19-88. I had a 38, small flashlight and ammo wallet with 18 rounds.

"I walked back to the apt, cleaned up and changed clothes and waited for her. A.C. never came back to apt. I drive back to H.S. to look for her. I could not find her. I drove around looking for her thinking maybe she got hit by a car.

"I did not call Belleville P.D. to help me look for A.C. because I did not want to answer a lot of questions. I thought about calling my friend Deputy Ralph Owens, but figured he would make an official report if he helped me look for A.C."

Hatch tossed the papers on the table and shook his head. He looked at Busch and began making the sound of music heard on the "Twilight Zone."

"You have reached the outer realm of the Anderson Zone," said Hatch. "What is with this guy?"

"I have no idea. The pages are dated two months after her death, but he writes about the evening she was last seen alive. We can confirm Anderson did have the conversation with the person he writes about in September," said Busch.

"He keeps talking about being charged with obstruction of justice for withholding evidence on the Cardenas case."

"Yeah, he mentions several times throughout his writings that he has Cardenas's notebook and apartment key."

"Weren't Cardenas's keys found by her body?"

"There was a set there, and I believe that Heil opened her apartment with them."

Hatch appeared deep in thought for a moment, then said, "I'm going to have to keep the two cases separated as much as possible for trial. I don't want to have jurors dwelling on who killed Cardenas while they're trying to decide on the Lanman case."

Busch understood what the prosecutor meant. The important issue here was the Lanman case, but he could not help thinking about the unanswered questions on Cardenas. Already up to his ass in paper alligators from other murder cases pending, Busch thought, *What the hell, a few more alligators won't make any difference. I'm going to run out two more leads on Cardenas.*

The following morning, Busch checked with the Public Aid Office and learned that Linda Cox no longer worked there. He located her at another State Office within Belleville. He was curious about what Anderson's attraction to her was and what Linda Cox looked like. *Probably*

*not a blonde,* thought Busch. *Most women Anderson had contact with were dark-haired, except
for his wife, who was blonde.*

Busch waited at the front counter of the office
for Linda Cox. A shapely brunette with me-
dium-length hair walked up to the counter. After
a brief introduction, she related her encounters
with Dale Anderson. Busch sat across the desk
from her and listened.

Working the phone switchboard at the Public
Aid Office in Belleville during 1987, Linda Cox
had first heard about Dale Anderson through office gossip. Rumors about Anderson threatening
a female supervisor in the East St. Louis office
and then poisoning her dog were circulating at
the office, where Anderson had been transferred.

When she saw him for the first time she
thought, "That's him." He looked "shy and stupid." During the first few months Anderson was
in the office, she had little contact with him.
Other employees who worked closer to him complained about his strange behavior. Behind his
back, they made jokes. At one of the office
luncheons, workers brought in dishes of food
and trays of snacks. Anderson brought Tup-
perware containers, which he used to take por-
tions of the food home with him. Coworkers
feared him and few associated with him.

Linda, however, was not intimidated by Anderson. She tried to be friendly at first, since he
seemed to be the outcast of the office. She

would wave to him from time to time when he passed by the switchboard from his desk in the back of the building to interview clients in cubicles located up front.

Most workers would tell her they were going up front to interview clients so that she wouldn't forward their phone calls to the back of the building, but Anderson would tell her that he was interviewing a client and be gone for long periods of time. Phone messages for him mounted and she tried to handle the calls. His absence from his work area did not go unnoticed by the supervisors. An investigation into rumors that he was spending excessive time interviewing female clients was underway.

Linda felt that Anderson had taken advantage of her good nature and tried to use her to cover for him during his time spent with interviews. Irritated, and not wanting to get further involved, she spoke to him about it.

He looked at her, but didn't say anything. She felt good about confronting him, something others wouldn't attempt. She thought DeLaria might be a little harsh on him. Although she had heard that Anderson often became violently aggressive toward opposition, Linda had not seen that side of him.

Busch interrupted with a question. "What was Anderson's attitude with other women in the office?"

"Everyone was scared of him. You see, they

were around him more than I was, and I didn't have much dealing with him. I do remember one time when several coworkers and I were leaving the building for lunch when Anderson invited himself along. One of the female employees who was six months pregnant at the time was with us. Anderson was obsessed with her and kept trying to touch her stomach.

"At lunch, he started talking about different sexual positions she could use to have sex while she was pregnant. His crude remarks shocked and embarrassed everyone at the table. I asked him to change the subject. He did. He began talking about bondage and expressed his irritation at his wife for not wanting to watch it on TV. Well after that comment, we left to go back to work."

"How did Anderson treat you after that?"

"Oh, he was nice to me. In fact, during the summer, the business with the flowers happened," the brunette said, shaking her head.

"Let me guess," Busch said. "It was June of 1988, and Anderson wanted you to meet Dave Hendricks."

"Oh, you heard about that."

"No, I read about it, go ahead and tell me what happened," chuckled Busch. "I'm sorry for laughing, but I have a strange sense of humor that comes with the job."

He listened as she talked about her experience

with Anderson and his efforts to have her meet Dave Hendricks. On the morning of June 27, 1988, Anderson called her at work and talked about a friend of his, a special investigator with the State of Illinois, that she should meet. Anderson invited her to have lunch with them. She told him she might stop by since it was close to where she worked.

At lunchtime she went to Bonanza, only to find Anderson there. He told her Dave wasn't there yet, but offered to buy her lunch. She made an excuse that she had banking to do during her lunch hour and left.

That evening she had agreed to meet with Dave Hendricks in the lobby of the Ramada Inn. A divorcee for seven years, she decided to see what Hendricks looked like, just out of curiosity. Arriving early, she walked into the lobby. Standing inside the door, she was startled when she turned around and saw Dale Anderson beside her. He held a brown briefcase under his arm.

"Hi, Linda!" he said with a strange look on his face. "I just came out of the restaurant to see if you had shown up."

"Dale, what are you doing here?"

"I'm here with my wife and kids for dinner. They're in the restaurant," said Anderson, pointing to his left.

"I'll stop and say hello to your wife," smiled Linda.

"No, I think they already left to go shopping.

I'll check and see," said Anderson, setting the briefcase at Linda's feet.

He walked off toward the restaurant. Linda had a bad feeling something was going on, but didn't want to upset him. She sensed he was watching her, and didn't turn around to watch where he went.

"They already left, probably while I went upstairs to the lounge to see if Dave had arrived. They went shopping, but I think I'll stay here," Anderson said with a strange tone in his voice. "Dave isn't here yet, but he should be soon. He's investigating the Cardenas case. Do you know how Audrey died?"

"No, I don't think that has been clear in the paper yet," said Linda.

"She was strangled and raped."

"How do you know? I don't think they said all of that in the paper."

"Dave Hendricks told me, he's working on the case," said Anderson, now holding Linda's left arm.

"Maybe I better go," she said.

"Why don't we go upstairs to the lounge and have a drink while we wait for him?" His eyes glared at her.

"I don't think so. I'm going to just go ahead and leave," she said, pulling free of his grasp.

She walked out to her car which was parked near the front door. Anderson, briefcase tucked under his arm, followed her. Linda remained calm as she opened the car door and got inside. Backing out of the parking spot, she locked the door and waved goodbye. She drove straight home. She no longer wanted to meet Dave Hendricks.

"Was that the end of Dave Hendricks? Surely Anderson knows that you know what his game was," said Busch.

"No! Dale showed up at my parents' house the next day," said Linda.

"That would be June 28," said Busch, "the day after the evening at Ramada Inn."

"Yes. He knocked on the door and wanted to talk with me. I told him I was having lunch with my parents and couldn't talk with him."

"Did he ask you to go to Cardenas's funeral with him? That was the day of her funeral service, which he attended."

"No, I didn't know that," said Linda.

"Tell me about the silk flowers," smiled Busch.

"Those were sent to me at the office a day or two later. I played detective and called the florist. They described the person that sent them. It was Dale. When he called, I told him thanks for the flowers, but I had started dating someone and wasn't interested in meeting Dave Hendricks. I tried to be cool about it. I didn't want to make Dale mad; I was afraid of him. I just wanted him to leave me alone."

"Did he?"

"Dale got arrested a few weeks later for acting

like he was a police officer. He called me once after he was arrested and told me the police had some of his papers that had my name on them. If they talked to me about him, I shouldn't say anything about Dave Hendricks. I told him I have enough problems without adding more."


Busch found the interview interesting, especially about Anderson claiming to know the method of death: strangulation. Anderson was the only person that made reference to the neck area of the deceased, the area that reflected damage from animals. The pathologist who autopsied Audrey's body could not rule out two methods of death: strangulation or a stab wound to the victim's neck.

Anderson's diary had fragments of truth in it. The problem was: Which parts were factual? The second lead Busch wanted to follow up on was the directions given by Anderson in his diary about following Audrey from her apartment. Busch noted that Anderson wrote: "I could not keep up with her on B st. and she got out of my sight. . . ."

Busch checked the route. "B" street was the longest section of street from Audrey's apartment. It was 9/10 of a mile. *There's no way Anderson could have kept up with an avid runner like Audrey for a mile,* Busch thought. *Of the streets around the victim's apartment, Ander-*

*son said "B" street was the one he couldn't keep up with her on.*

The thing that didn't fit with the crime scene was in Anderson's writings. He wrote: "I was wearing shorts with pockets, a T-shirt and tennis shoes on the evening of 6-19-88."

The impressions that were left alongside Audrey's tennis shoe impressions at the creek appeared to be made by boots with Vibram soles, not another set of tennis shoes.

A pair of Vibram sole boots taken from a person interviewed early in the Cardenas investigation were submitted to the laboratory and examined, but were not the boots that made the impressions in the creek bed. The killer's boots were never located.

# Twenty

Randolph County is composed mostly of rural areas on the east side of the Mississippi River, far removed from the high crime rate of the other counties in Illinois. Many of the residents are part-time farmers or work within that rural setting. People still leave their doors unlocked at night, and children play outside after dark.

Hatch had spent the last two months taking the case home to study. At a table in his basement, with the TV playing in the background, he had compiled and noted events spanning the last two years. He had learned many things about the man he hoped to place on Death Row.

Hatch had his own theories about Anderson, some paralleling those held by Busch. Together they had traced Anderson back to the day he was born in Canton, Ohio, on Thanksgiving in 1951. For the most part, Anderson's childhood was uneventful. He had been raised by church-going, middle-class parents, who had little trouble with him as a child.

In high school, Anderson had few friends and was considered a loner. His grades were good, but he had no social life and never dated. A girl named Mary, whose father was a cop, went with Anderson to the high school prom, but did not date him after that.

In college, Anderson attended Illinois State University where he met and later married Linda. He made the dean's list all four years, but seemed angry with his social status and complained about being from "lower-class white trash."

He worked part-time at McDonald's restaurants. During two summer vacations, in 1971 and 1972, he got a job in the coal fields south of Belleville with his father as a driller's helper.

Anderson graduated from ISU with a Bachelor of Science degree in education in June of 1973 and taught school for a period. In 1977, he applied for the position as Special Agent with the Illinois State Police, but was rejected.

Hatch's theory about what contributed to Anderson's dark side started developing in college. His personality was not socially accepted by others, especially women. Hatch noted that Anderson's work history reflected his dangerous personality as early as 1977. After being refused entry into the State Police, Anderson took a job with an insurance agency in Belleville as a claims adjuster, but was terminated within three weeks for falsifying work assignments.

In 1978, while employed with another insurance company, he was terminated after four weeks due to complaints about his behavior. He was asking female employees of the company for dates.

During the month he worked there as a claims adjuster, his supervisor also received complaints from women clients. Anderson had visited their homes and made sexual advances toward them, suggested their claims would be dealt with quickly if they would have a relationship with him.

When confronted with the allegations, Anderson went into a verbal rage with his employer and the police were called to remove him from the building. Anderson claimed to be an undercover agent for the police, but would not say for which law enforcement agency. He did mention that he had posed as an insurance investigator with a company in connection with a homicide investigation where the owner of the company was murdered. Anderson gave the victim's name.

Hatch realized that the victim Anderson talked about was the owner of the insurance company in Belleville where he had worked for a month in 1977. The insurance company owner was killed in St. Louis, Missouri, but the details on that case were sketchy.

\* \* \*

The following month, Anderson lied his way into a correctional officer's position with the St. Clair County Sheriff's Department. On paper, he portrayed himself in a favorable light and was hired into the program which was backed by federal funds. Anderson was issued a weapon and badge and worked as a correctional officer for eighteen months, until the program rotated new people in and Anderson wasn't retained.

*The defendant's entire life after college had been based on lies,* concluded Hatch. Anderson had wrapped himself in a blanket of secrecy which shielded him from his own failures. His cloak-and-dagger image about everything helped cover fraudulent claims of being the "supercop." Anderson's desire to be accepted fueled his clandestine nature. Even murder was acceptable.

Anderson concealed that he worked for Public Aid from his parents for eight years. During that time, he claimed to have worked for the Illinois Bureau of Investigation as a Special Investigator. Not until the article in the *News-Democrat* about him having his supervisors arrested did they learn the truth.

For the prosecutor, the irritating thing about Anderson was the senselessness of the murders. To randomly select two victims, and to choose a pregnant woman and small child, left Hatch with no compassion for the defendant.

On the morning of March 28, 1990 the first

day of the Anderson trial, Busch backed his
squad car out of his driveway and fifty miles
later was in the rural area of Randolph County.
The rolling hills of farm fields, broken by small
patches of timber, was a welcome sight as he
drove toward Chester.

He appreciated a change of scenery from the
metro-east, where structures bore the symbols of
Black street gangs and city youths found violent
death on any corner. Busch spent most of his
time working East St. Louis, where the "junior
gangsters" fought and killed each other over
anything and everything. He gave them the title
of "junior gangsters" because most of those
killed never lived past their twenty-first birthday.

Past Red Bud, Illinois, the small town's popu-
lation dropped as low as two hundred and fifty.
Entering the outskirts of Chester, a town of
three thousand, Busch noticed a large sign saying hometown of "Popeye." Later he learned
that the cartoonist Elsie Segar, inventor of the
Popeye character, spent his earlier childhood in
Chester and used that experience to create the
seaworthy sailor.

Busch located the courthouse. The three-story
structure sat on the west side of town, on top
of the bluff overlooking the Mississippi River.
Inside, a large three-tier water fountain was cen-
tered within a spiraling staircase that rose up
through a forty-foot opening to the two floors
above. Climbing the twenty-eight gray marble

steps, Busch reached the second floor where a score of news media waited for the trial to begin.

Looking at the violet-colored walls and squinting, Busch opened the courtroom door and saw Hatch standing over boxes of evidence stacked against wooden dividers at the front of the spectators' seats.

"Damn, those violet walls out there will wake your ass up," said Busch, rubbing his eyes. "Hatch, that looks like some color *you* would pick out."

"Do me a favor," said Hatch, preoccupied with the evidence sheets that filled the folder in his hand. "Can you help Delaney get my first group of witnesses lined up?"

"Okay, who's on first?"

Hatch handed him the yellow legal pad. Busch glanced over it as he walked out of the courtroom into the hall, and noticed John Lanman was listed as the first person to testify. Seeing Pastor Santos standing by the stair rail outside the law library, he stopped to talk with him.

"Santos, how is it going?"

"I'm fine, how have you been?" said the large man, extending a handshake.

"How is John doing?"

"Better. I think he's worried about the trial and everything. He seemed quieter than usual on the drive here."

219

"According to this," said Busch, tapping on the pad, "John will be the first one on after Hatch does opening statements. Maybe things will ease up for him after he gets this trial behind him."

Busch entered the law library where the others were. Hatch walked briskly into the room and stood beside John.

"John, I need to talk with you before we get started." Then looking at each witness in the room, he stated, "The judge has ruled that we can not tell the jurors about Jolaine being pregnant. If someone slips and mentions that, there will be a mistrial. So don't say anything on that issue."

Hatch, who had children of his own, studied the drained man before him and wondered how he, himself, would handle such a tragic loss if it had been his family instead of Lanman's. He put his hand on John's shoulder.

"I'm going to put you on first. Are you going to be okay? I want to be up front with you so you'll know what to expect, okay? They're going to say you did this."

"I understand," said John in a soft voice.

"You can't have an outburst or say anything to the defendant. If you do, there will be a mistrial, so just answer the questions honestly."

"I'm alright. I won't say anything to the man," promised Lanman. "I've never seen this Anderson or talked to him."

"I spent fifteen hours with him," Busch said, now standing beside the victim's husband, "and believe me, you haven't missed anything."

Lanman looked at him after his comment and laughed, which made Busch feel good. It was the only time Busch had seen him laugh.


The spectator's section was filled quickly and news reporters filed into the front row. Outside the courtroom, TV cameramen and photographers waited in the halls to get a shot of Anderson, only to learn that Anderson was brought into court through a passageway that led downstairs directly to the jail.

The jurors walked out of the jury room and took their seats in the orange chairs inside the dark, wooden, waist-high panels that composed the jury box.

After a few additional spectators settled into the last open seats, the bailiff informed the judge everyone was seated and called the court to order. Circuit Judge Jerry Flynn, who was presiding over the trial, allowed the prosecutor to begin his opening statement to the jury.

Hatch, dressed in a dark suit, greeted the jurors while standing at the edge of the jury box. He began a slow walk down the length of the wooden panels, making eye contact with each juror as he spoke. He promised to detail the bizarre scheme by the defendant to frame his former bosses.

"First-degree murders were committed by this man, right here in this brown suit," said the prosecutor in a loud voice as he pointed his finger at Anderson, whose facial expression never wavered. "You are also going to hear that the two victims had nothing to do with this man. Nothing. They didn't know him." Hatch looked directly at a female jurist. "They weren't acquainted with him, they were in their home minding their own business when this man came in and killed them both."

Hatch's intent was to outline for the jury, as if on a paint by number canvas, Anderson's twisted plot seeking revenge against his bosses for demoting him, and his obsession with the murder of the *News-Democrat* intern, Audrey Cardenas. Later, Hatch would use witnesses to color that canvas, completing the final portrait of a vicious and cunning killer.

"Anderson had to do something to prove to everybody that his three supervisors, Kroupa, Vale, and DeLaria, were committing fraud at the public welfare office," continued Hatch. "Audrey Cardenas was going to expose this in an article and because of that, these three people went out and killed her so that she couldn't print the article."

Hatch quickened his pace in front of the jurors as he talked about the man charged in the 1988 murder. "They arrested a guy by the name

222

of Rodney Woidtke, a drifter that came through town, and for the next year he was found mentally unfit to stand trial. He was then found fit to stand trial. Some people didn't believe Rodney Woidtke did it. He was eventually convicted of First-Degree Murder of Audrey Cardenas at a trial."

Hatch knew the jurors would be confused with all the information he was giving them, and wasn't surprised by the puzzled looks on a few of their faces. The skilled prosecutor was confident that any facts they missed during his opening statements would be covered in details by upcoming witnesses. Moving on, he linked the dates of the Lanman murders to the case in 1988.

"Because on September 28, Woidtke is to be sentenced. Anderson is trying to pin it on Vale, DeLaria, and Kroupa, he's got to do something by the time that Woidtke is sentenced on the twenty-eighth. He's got to do it," said Hatch, pointing at Anderson. "The only way he can tell these people and prove to everybody that these three people are responsible for Audrey Cardenas, is to go in and beat two people to death, to do a brutal murder of two people and have it happen before the Rodney Woidtke case is disposed of." Hatch paused to let his words be absorbed. "He's got to do it then."

Setting up an easel and placing the aerial

photo of Lanman's neighborhood on it for the jury to see, Hatch said, "You are going to hear testimony from other neighbors as to their contact with Jolaine and Kenneth Lanman on that day."

The black-haired attorney for the State picked up a wooden pointer from the table and approached the large photo. "This view now is going to be looking from the railroad tracks closer to that neighborhood. Lanman's house is here," he said, giving everyone time to study the photograph. "Nixon's house is here, Sabastine Hope lives here, Janice Conder with her family here, and her mother Martha Mayberry in this house."

Hatch not only showed the house of the witnesses, but gave them in the order in which they would be testifying. Without the aid of any notes on times and locations, Hatch's memory led the jurors through the events on the day the Lanmans were murdered. He recited the contents of the note found under the bed and the license plate of the strange car seen near the murder scene. Raising his hands in an outward gesture, he asked the jurors, "Now, what is the connection here? What is this all about? Who are Vale, DeLaria, and Kroupa? Who is Audrey Cardenas? Why are these two people," asked the burly lawyer, pointing to the photo of Jolaine and Kenneth, "who have nothing to do with anything, lying dead underneath their bed?"

Walking over to the defense table where Anderson sat, Hatch paused, then again pointed a stiffened finger at the defendant and spoke with a sarcastic tone, "Well, what you are going to learn is that this man here had an obsession to get revenge on those three people. Those three people, Bob DeLaria, Charlotte Kroupa, and Maurice Vale were his bosses at Public Aid."

To simplify the case for the jurors, Hatch said, "Anderson had to do something to prove to everybody his supervisors killed Cardenas. In order to do that, he committed the Lanman killing and forced Jolaine Lanman to write a note incriminating his bosses on the day before another man was to be sentenced for the Cardenas murder."

Hatch's statement brought a snicker from the defense attorney, who had waited for the prosecutor to finish. Bement approached the twelve people who would decide his client's fate and, with an air of indifference, said, "Ladies and gentlemen of the jury. I will first tell you a little bit again about what the judge talked about in opening statements. The demonstration you saw here by Mr. Hatch is not evidence. Opening statement is designed to be kind of a road map to tell you where things are going."

Bement talked in a soft voice to the jury as he geared up to counter the information given

225

by the opposing attorney. "When you listen to the story of how the State plans to show that my client, Dale Anderson, did this, I think of fantastic stories," said Bement as he held his hands up, making little circles with them for the jury to see.

"Think of *The Wizard of Oz*. Think of *Star Wars*. Think of all kinds of other fantastic stories to explain things that are otherwise unexplainable," he said. "What the State is going to ask you to believe is that this complex scheme to kill two people, that Dale Anderson has no idea who they are, kills these two people because of some strange obsession with three of his coworkers."

Bement pointed out to the jurors what he felt were flaws in the State's case. Using the list of the witnesses against his client, he attempted to take the effectiveness out of the prosecutor's prior statement. "Now, the State is going to bring in dozens and dozens of witnesses. The reason that you are going to see all of these is because none of them are going to be able to show or be able to tell you that Dale Anderson, my client, murdered the Lanmans."

The defense attorney admitted to the jury that his client had done strange things at work, but pointed out that a person whose character is different from others doesn't make him a murderer. Bement cautioned the jurists to listen very closely to all the State's witnesses and to analyze what they were saying.

"Ladies and gentlemen, this is not 'Perry Mason,'" said Bement, hoping to dispel any expectation of dramatic fireworks by the defense in this case. "I am not Ben Matlock. I am not going to produce the murderer or more likely not unless something unusual happens. I am not going to have someone break down on the stand and tell me that they actually were the murderer. That makes it more difficult when you talk about real life."

Bement knew what evidence the State had through the disclosure rule. Using that knowledge, he addressed the jury, "You are not going to hear one single piece of physical evidence that ties Dale Anderson to ever being in the Lanman house. You are not going to find one hair of his at the Lanman house, nor one fiber from his clothing, nor one drop of blood from the Lanmans' on any of his clothes, or in his car," said Bement with an air of pride.

Both attorneys had summarized for the jury the path the trial would take. Next, the bailiff left the courtroom and returned with a slender, saddened man, who stood in front of the clerk of the court to be sworn in. The man identified himself as John Lanman, which brought a low murmur from the spectator's section at seeing the husband and father of the victims.

Hatch covered the relationship of the witness with the deceased.

"What was your wife's age?"

"She was thirty-four," said Lanman.

"And your son, Kenneth. How old was he?"

"He was three-and-a-half at the time," said the father, with his lip quivering.

"Did you see them that morning before you left?"

"Yes."

Hatch covered the events of the husband's day up to when he returned home and entered his son's room. "After you looked down and saw the stains on that carpet in your son's bedroom, what did you do?"

"I turned back around and I looked into the master bedroom. The bed sat up against this wall like this and I noticed a blanket at the bottom of the bed. The first time I walked in, the piles of laundry were still on the floor, so I didn't really think too much about it, but when I turned around and I saw the blanket or the comforter along the side of the bed, I walked over and when I pulled it back, that is when I saw my wife."

"Okay. When you saw the clothes and reached down, do you recall what part of her body you grabbed?"

"I grabbed one of her wrists and pulled her out," said the husband.

"Could you demonstrate to the jury how you

did that?"

Lanman stood up and indicated how he reached out and under, while he talked. "Well, she was under the bed and I bent down and think I pulled back this way to see if she was okay."

"And what is the first thing you saw when you pulled her back?"

"I saw the scissors sticking out of her neck," said Lanman, closing his eyes to hold back the tears.

"Anything else that you remember?" asked Hatch.

"The face was bloody."

"What was the next thing you did?"

"After finding her, I became very concerned about my child, and I started to look further under that same bed to see if he was there," said the father, remembering once when Kenneth had hidden under the bed when they had played games. "I walked around to the end of the bed and looked underneath, and I found Kenneth under the end of the bed."

"How far was he underneath the bed?"

"Not very far."

"How did you get him out from under the bed?"

"I dragged his ankles and pulled him out. The only thing that I remember about him was that his face was covered with blood." Lanman wiped tears from his eyes as he sat in the witness chair.

Hatch retrieved a package from the boxes of evidence stacked behind him. He handed it to Lanman and said, "I am going to show you People's Exhibit 208. Can you tell us what that is?"

"That was Kenneth's teddy bear," said Lanman, looking at the blue and white patchwork bear stained with patches of reddish-brown.

"Is that in the same condition as you last saw it?"

"No," replied the father of the slain child.

Hatch knew that it would get more sentiment from the jury if he left the child's bloody doll out on the table for the jurists to see, but being a father himself, he chose to place the teddy bear with the black button eyes back in the evidence bag.

Hatch pulled another item from a sealed bag for the grieving man to identify. Lanman rubbed his forehead and tried to maintain his composure, then bowed his head and wept. Jurors and spectators sat silent while he attempted to regain his thoughts.

Anderson looked bored while he waited for the man to speak. When John began to talk, Anderson started taking notes.

"That's Kenneth's baby blanket. He used to carry that all over with him."

The items collected from the murder scene, many being emotionally draining for the witness, were viewed and identified as belonging to the household. Hatch wanted to cover any area that might be used by the defense as a point of attack. The witness was handed a package and asked to identify the item.

"Do you recognize what that is?" said Hatch.

"It is a pair of scissors," said Lanman. "We had a pair similar to that in the house."

"By that, with the black handle?"

"Uh-huh."

"Do you know where that was kept?"

"It was kept in the kitchen by the freezer in a drawer."

The husband's activity on the day of the murders was covered by the attorney for the State. By using that trial strategy, Hatch had presented to the jury an alibi for the husband and left little for Anderson's attorney to challenge.

In the law library, others who hadn't testified yet chatted across the long table as they waited for their turn to take the stand. Busch, his square-toed cowboy boots planted on the corner of the table, relaxed while he watched the people at the other end.

"I guess you are used to all this," came a woman's voice from the end of the table. "You seem bored."

Busch replied, "No, as a matter of fact I'm looking forward to the chance of getting up in

231

front of an entire courtroom of people and trying not to make a complete fool of myself."

There was a flicker of concern on Vicki Sartory's face before she realized that the investigator was kidding her. She smiled a nervous smile. "That sounds real encouraging."

Busch laughed and removed his feet from the table. "It was a joke, I'll probably be on the stand for a few days."

"My daughter, Brooke, has to testify, too," said the proud mother. "She saw the car and got the plate. I don't know what they want me for."

Her eleven-year-old daughter, walking around the room, her blue eyes scanning the tall shelves of law books, turned around to look at them.

"Your daughter is a very important witness in this case," said Busch as the girl sat beside her mother. "Are you scared, Brooke?"

"Uh-huh. I don't know those people. I don't want to go in there. He's in there!"

"You don't have to be afraid. Nobody will hurt you. When you go to school and have a new class you didn't know the other people, but after you're there it's not so bad."

"I don't want to look at him."

"Well, don't look at him. Just look at your dad, he'll be in there with you. Look toward the back of the court where your dad is."

Busch wondered what kind of thoughts were going through the young girl's mind. She was surrounded by adults who were all strangers, and she probably sensed their nervousness about going into the courtroom. Soon she would have to go into a room with the man who killed her neighbors. There would be rows and rows of people looking at her and she would be asked questions. With all that going on, could she remember the license plate number and be able to tell it to the jury? Hatch would be counting on her to do that.

Brooke was the fifth person to take the stand. Hatch talked softly to her as if she was one of his own children. He asked her what she did when she came home from school the day her neighbors were murdered.

"I went into the family room and watched TV."

Moving to the aerial photo, Hatch showed Brooke the location of her house in the large photograph that stood as tall as the pretty girl. He had her put a yellow tack where her house was. With quick steps she walked by the jury box under the watchful eyes of everyone and took the stand.

She brushed her long blond hair to the sides as she looked around. Her eyes caught his. She had forgotten and looked at the bad man. She tried to keep from crying, but he scared her.

"Did you notice anything out in the street at

that time?" asked Hatch as he stepped close to the stand to block her view of Anderson, who seemed amused at frightening the child.

"There was a car," said the shaking witness.

"What color was the car?"

"Blue."

Hatch handed her a blue tack to place in the photo where she had seen the car the day of the murders and again stood between her and the defendant to shield her from Anderson's relentless, piercing eyes. Brooke looked at the floor as she walked to the easel and placed the tack into the photo.

"Now, a blue tack has been placed across from your house," said Hatch, as he pointed to the aerial photo of the neighborhood. "Is that about where that car was?"

"Uh-huh," replied Brooke.

"Did you go outside later to look or see the car?"

"Well, I rode my bike outside."

"And did you notice anything about the car at the time."

"Well, could you be more specific?" said the girl.

The response to his question from the eleven year old took Hatch by surprise, but he grinned anyway and continued with his inquiry. "I mean, did you see the license plate number?"

"Uh-huh."

"And what was the license plate number?"

said the prosecutor, holding his breath for her response.

"234 166," she said.

Hatch breathed a sigh of relief. She had identified Anderson's car.

On cross-examination, Bement touched lightly on the eleven year old's testimony and attacked her memory of that day.

"Do you recall what you watched on TV when you first came home?" asked the defense attorney.

" 'Duck Tales,' " replied the girl.

"Do you recall if the police officers were wearing uniforms, or were they wearing suits when you talked to them?"

"Some of them were wearing uniforms and some were wearing suits."

Hoping to show a flaw in the witness's memory, Bement asked her to tell the court what the first officer who spoke with her was wearing.

"A uniform," said the girl with tears running down her face.

Bement finished his questioning. She had identified the first officer that spoke with her: Deputy Kelly Oliver in a brown police uniform.

At the end of the first day of trial, the State had put on eight people, including Jill Hindricks and Janice Conder. The order of the witnesses was of great importance to Hatch. He would spoon-feed jurors with bits of information, too much at one time would not be consumed and would fall to the wayside. He had given them enough to think about until the next morning.

# Twenty-one

After the first day of trial, Busch registered in the same hotel Hatch was staying at, and left the hotel phone number with his wife, Linda, if she needed to contact him.

At six o'clock that evening, Busch knocked on Hatch's door to see if he wanted to join him for supper.

"Hatchman, you want to get some vittles?" asked Busch.

"Yeah, sit down a moment. I want to run this past you, see what you think," Hatch said while seated at the small circular table covered with papers.

Busch pulled the long-barrel .44 magnum from his waistband and set it on the chair, then removed his coat and placed it on the chair over the gun.

"Expecting trouble?" laughed Hatch.

"No. I never leave home without it," joked Busch. "That's my traveling gun."

"I've planned to have you testify several times,

237

but I don't want to give the jury too much at one time. I don't want them to miss anything."

"I noticed that you have the two witnesses who saw Anderson in the neighborhood and on his visits to other houses for sale testifying at different times," said Busch, leaning back in the chair.

"Yeah, I wanted to give the jury two chances at the same information, show Anderson's pattern. . . ." Hatch stopped talking to answer the knock at the door and was surprised to find his wife standing there.

Monica had arranged with a relative to watch the children so she could spend the night in Chester and catch the second day of the trial.

"Hi, Buschman. How is Hatch doing on the trial?" she said, lifting up his coat from the chair to sit down. "Oh, my, whose gun is this?"

"That's mine. I'll move it for you," said Busch.

"You carry that big thing around with you all the time?"

Busch grinned when he thought of the double meaning of her question.

"That's kind of personal, lady," he said, sticking the long-barrel revolver in his waistband. His comment earned him a shaken finger as the phone rang.

Hatch answered it and handed the telephone to Busch. "It's your wife. Now you're in trouble."

"I've trained her too well; she can track me better than most investigators," quipped Busch.

During their conversation, his wife could hear a laughing woman's voice in the background. "You told me you would call and let me know if you were spending the night," she said, "but it sounds like you're having a good time." She hung up the phone.

"Can you believe this?" said Busch, looking at the Hatches. "She thinks I've got party girls here. Must have heard Monica laughing."

"That's funny," said Monica. "But you should call her back. I know I'd be mad as hell if I was in her place."

"Yeah, it's got me in stitches," replied Busch with a smile, "and I'll probably get real stitches when I get home." Shortly, he called his wife back, and the tall blonde found humor in the situation.

The three went to eat at a Pizza Hut.


Thursday morning, Hatch started the second day of the trial with John Lanman's current boss. He had called the Lanman house and spoke with Jolaine the afternoon that she was murdered.

"What time did you call?" asked Hatch.

"3:45 P.M."

"And how do you know that you called at that time?"

"I had the office look up our past phone bills and found the bill for that date itemizing that call at that time," said the employer.

"When you called that number, did you talk to anyone?"

"I talked to Mrs. Lanman."

"And how do you know that?"

"She identified herself as Mrs. Lanman, and she also indicated that she had typed the cover letter for the resume."

"Did you notice anything unusual about the way she talked or anything like that?" asked the prosecutor.

"No. The conversation was very cordial. She seemed to be, you know, upbeat that someone was calling their residence with a job opportunity for her husband."

"How long did you talk to her?"

"According to the phone bill for two minutes," said the man, looking at the phone receipt.

Hatch walked back to his table and picked up two enlarged photographs taken at the crime scene. They showed a phone sitting on a desk in the kitchen of the Lanman home.

"I'm going to show you what's been marked People's Exhibits 93 and 94. Could you take a look, please, and tell us what is depicted in those photographs?"

"It's the back of an envelope with my work and home phone numbers and my name on it."

"Is it spelled correctly?"

"Yes."

"That's all I have," said Hatch, referring to questions for Lanman's employer."

Bement rose from the defense table with a burst of energy as he pursued the time element of the call received by the victim. He argued that there were conflicting times with the State's witnesses that put his client arriving in the area around two o'clock in the afternoon and leaving around four o'clock. The phone conversation at 3:45 P.M. didn't make sense, the defense contended.

Hatch smiled at Anderson while Bement argued the point. The prosecutor had already arranged his next witnesses to cover that topic.

The jury heard from Martha Mayberry, a sixty-eight-year-old neighbor of the Lanmans. She had first seen Anderson's car drive into the neighborhood the day of the murders. She had called her daughter, Janice Conder, and they watched Anderson walk toward the victims' house.

Cheryl Scott told of Anderson's visit to her house the week before the murders, posing as a home buyer.

Maurice Vale was the twentieth person to take the stand and the longest witness of the day.

Vale reflected Anderson's poor work performance and told of his fear of the unruly employee.


Friday morning the beginning of the trial was
delayed while Bement and Hatch argued over a
point of law in front of the judge.

An hour later, the trial started. Hatch called
the twenty-first witness, who looked serious as
he sat in front of the jury.

"Would you state your name?" said Hatch.

"Alva W. Busch," replied the bearded man
with the receding hairline.

"And for whom do you work?"

"The Illinois State Police."

Hatch continued to draw out Busch's qualifi-
cations, covering the hundreds of homicide cases
involving stabbings, shootings, and mutilations.

"How big of an area do you or have you
worked in for the last thirteen years?"

"I cover a ten-county area."

"I would at this time offer Mr. Busch as an
expert as a crime scene investigator," Hatch said
to the judge.

"You may voir dire him if you wish," stated
Judge Flynn to Defense Attorney Bement.

"No. I have no objection to that," replied Bement.

"Let me explain to the jury the acceptance of
a person as an expert," said the judge. "The

Court will accept Mr. Busch as an expert in the area of crime scene investigation. I would caution the jury that merely because this witness is able to give his opinion does not in any way interfere with the jury's responsibility to weigh his testimony the same as any other witness. You still have the right to accept or reject what he testifies to, even in the area of his expertise. You may continue."

The jury listened as the prosecutor had Busch describe and identify items from the murder scene to the jurors.

"People's Exhibit 218. Would you take a look at that and tell us what that is?"

"That's the rope which I removed from around her neck," said Busch, holding the item for the jury to see.

"It appears that there is some white tape around two ends of the rope. Can you tell us how that got there?"

"Yes. I put it there. Instead of trying to untie this and destroy the knot, what I did was take a section of tape and tape around where I was going to cut and then cut through the tape so the people in the laboratory would know that this was my cut and not someone else's. It left the knot still intact."

"So then, if you were to remove that, two ends of the rope would come together and form the complete length that you found when you took it off?"

"Yes."

"Was it tight around her neck? Could you reach in and grab the rope, or how loose was it around her neck?" asked Hatch.

"It was loose," said Busch. "You could put your fingers between the back of her neck and the bow, and, if you pulled it toward the front, you could put your fingers between the front of her throat and the rope. It wasn't tight on her neck."

Hatch then questioned the investigator about the examination of the bodies at the funeral home.

"After I washed her up, I fingerprinted and palmprinted her."

"By washing her up, what do you mean?"

"Well, after I removed the clothing, I was going to photograph the wounds; so, I washed the body first."

As Busch vividly described the trauma to the bodies and talked about the injuries, Anderson sat with a tranquil look on his face. He ran the finger and thumb of his right hand up and down the edge of the defense table as he listened to Busch.

"After you removed the clothes and washed up the bodies, what did you observe about Jolaine's body after you removed the scissors, the rope, and the shirt from around her neck?" asked Hatch.

"Multiple stab wounds in the neck area and in

the chest, and injuries to the back of the head."

"How many wounds did you observe in the neck?"

"Eight to ten," said Busch from memory.

"And as you moved down the body, did you observe anything else other than her neck?"

"Yeah. She had three to four stab wounds in the chest."

"And what did you observe to the back of the head?"

"She had several injuries to the back of the head."

"What type of injuries?"

"I would say blunt trauma. They were approximately an inch and a half long and were irregular, the edges weren't smooth and kind of torn."

Handing the witness photographs that depicted what he had just described, Hatch moved on with the direct examination. Busch identified forty close-up photographs he took of the injuries.

"Without showing those to the jury, could you describe what is depicted? What types of injuries did you observe on Kenneth?"

"There were eight to ten stab wounds in the neck region. There was a grouping of stab wounds right below the neck to the top part of the chest and then another almost circular pattern of wounds to the center of the chest," said Busch as he looked at Anderson, who methodically rubbed the edge of the table and acted bored.

"And to the back of his head?" asked the prosecutor in a disgusted tone.

"It appeared to be blunt trauma."

"Was there any injury to the back?"

"He had what appeared to be bruising in the regions of the back of his shoulders which ran almost shoulder to shoulder, and from the back of his head down to about just below his shoulder blades," said Busch to the jury.

The court recessed for twenty minutes in the middle of the afternoon. The break was well received. Busch had been on the witness stand all morning and as well as a good portion of the afternoon. Driven by the desire for a soda, he found that all the soda machines in the lounge had long since been emptied by the large crowd of spectators.

"I noticed there's a bar near here, within walking distance," said Busch to Nester. "I'm walking over. Do you want to go?"

"Yeah, I'll go," said Nester. "Don't you have to go back on?"

"We've got time. You worry too much."

Hatch put on the next witness, a detective from the Belleville Police Department, who discussed the facts about the Cardenas case.

Then Busch took the stand for the third time. He described washing the bodies and examining the wounds matter-of-factly, and said that he has seen anything you could think to do to a human being.

On his cross-examination Bement had demonstrated that none of Anderson's fingerprints were found at the scene. Hatch's redirect covered the thoroughness of the evidence processing.

"Mr. Busch, when you go to a crime scene, you don't get big old chimney sweep dust and go through every room, do you?"

"No," said Busch.

"You don't put this black dust on every speck of wall, every piece of counter, paint that house black, do you?"

"No."

"Why not?"

"I don't like to waste my time when I'm working a crime scene. I try to put some thought process into where it is most effective to obtain fingerprints."

"What types of areas are you talking about?"

"Well, you try to visualize what occurred and where a person would place their hands to gain entry, to gain access, and some of the objects they probably came in contact with while inside the residence."

"Now, you talked about some shades in the

child's room. Those the ones that you checked?"

"Yes," said Busch. Then, he explained the areas of the house from which he had lifted fingerprints.

"Earlier you talked about other footprints. On People's Exhibit 256A," said Hatch, handing Busch the large section of paper that Kenneth had finger painted the morning of his death, "you talked about the footprint on the back of that exhibit."

"That is correct," replied Busch.

"And whose did that come back to match?" asked Hatch.

"A Deputy from St. Clair County."

Hatch had established that there were no phantom shoeprints left at the crime scene, no fingerprints.


Hatch's Friday evening didn't signal a rest for the prosecutor over the weekend. The judge had ruled at the close of the day that the State would have to subdivide all of its future exhibits; Bement had won his motion to suppress some of the items seized inside Anderson's briefcase.

After the ruling, Hatch elicited the help of Nester, Busch, and Delaney to itemize and retag over eight hundred items. Saturday afternoon found them away from their families working among the piles of evidence in the law library. By Monday morning, the State's retagged evidence exhibits sat in boxes on the floor of the courtroom behind the prosecutor's table.

The trial resumed promptly at nine o'clock that Monday morning. Hatch drew from the piles of documents that sat marked as evidence. The "Kroupa Letter," which Busch had found in one of Anderson's briefcases, would soon be shown to the next witness.

"Would you state your name, please?" asked Hatch.

"Charlotte Kroupa," replied the middle-aged woman.

Hatch continued his line of questioning and established that Kroupa worked at the Public Aid Office and had worked there for twenty-nine years. She verified that she had been one of Anderson's supervisors and did own a car with the license plate number of "CPK 15." Hatch asked her if Anderson had ever threatened her.

"October or so when we were talking with Mr. Anderson about the poor quality of his work intake, he was upset by that and he told me that his family didn't like what we were doing to him and he had friends that would take care of that, and I felt that was an overt threat to me," said the dark-haired lady in a stern tone.

"Mrs. Kroupa, had you ever talked to Audrey Cardenas?" inquired Hatch.

"No."

"Did you know Audrey Cardenas?"

"No."

"Did you ever tell anyone that you were a witness to the murder of Audrey Cardenas in June of 1988?" quizzed the prosecutor. He got a look of disbelief from the witness.

"No."

"Did you ever tell anyone that Maurice Vale and Robert DeLaria were bragging about the murder of Audrey Cardenas?"

"No."

Increasing his voice and the stern look on his face, Hatch asked, "Did you ever tell anyone that Maurice Vale and Robert DeLaria threatened to murder you?"

"No. I never told anybody that," she said, again looking at the attorney as if he'd lost his mind.

Picking up the document from the table and returning to the witness, Hatch handed her the letter. "I am going to show you what has been marked People's Exhibit 1039. Would you read that to yourself, please?"

The jury watched as she read the letter. Her face went white for a brief moment when she figured out what the letter was designed for and became visibly upset. Her reaction to the document was exactly what Hatch wanted the jurors to see.

"I didn't write this," she said, her voice a little shaky.

"This is not your handwriting?" asked Hatch,

holding the letter in his hand.

"Of course not," she said bitterly. "That is not my handwriting. I recognize it, but it is not mine."

Hatch moved on and covered the fact that Kroupa had submitted a standard of her handwriting. Her testimony had several punches that weakened the defense's case. It eliminated her as the author of the "Kroupa Letter" and helped explain to the jury why the investigators were in Anderson's house for so long; it took Kroupa five hours to complete the handwriting standard under ideal conditions.

Bement, during cross-examination, fought to salvage points for his client.

"Were you aware of the fact that some clients had complained to Mr. Anderson about Mr. Vale and Mr. DeLaria?" asked Bement.

"No," Kroupa said, shaking her head.

"Do you recall him telling you that in the early part of May of 1988?"

"Do I recall Mr. Anderson telling me that clients had complained about Mr. DeLaria or Mr. Vale?" repeated the witness, to make sure she had understood the question.

"Yes, ma'am," said the defense attorney.

"No."

Bement walked closer to the woman and placed his hand on his forehead. "Do you recall during this meeting in Mr. Vale's office that Mr.

Vale asked to open the briefcase to look at the statements that Dale had from clients complaining about Mr. Vale?"

"No. That is not correct. That is not what happened during that meeting," said Kroupa. "I was there."

"Mr. Vale grabbed the briefcase while in the office, and Mr. Anderson then fell while in the room?" suggested Bement.

"That is totally incorrect. It is preposterous and didn't happen."

"Now," smiled Bement. "You were aggravated with Mr. Anderson when you were arrested by the Belleville Police Department, isn't that right?"

"I was more embarrassed and humiliated than I was aggravated," she said.

Bement switched his line of questioning to where she parked her car, suggesting that anyone could have obtained her license plate number.

"So, the Public Aid Office runs from Main Street, the block all the way to Washington, the street behind it?" said Bement.

"That is correct."

"You have a parking spot right in front of the building on Washington, and that spot has a large sign that has your name on it?"

"Yes, it does," admitted Kroupa.

"Mr. Vale, until he retired, also had a similar spot with a sign?"

"Yes."

"That is all I have, Judge," said Bement.

State witnesses during the day testified to Anderson's filing of over eighty grievances against the Department of Public Aid in the last three years before being terminated. Anderson's request for a "pound of flesh, little finger or their firstborn child" was brought out by the union steward.

Documents examiner, William Storer, took the stand near the end of the fourth day of trial. Hatch placed the "note" from the murder scene, sealed in plastic, on the defense table. Anderson seemed drawn to it like a magnet, closely scrutinizing every word on the paper with a glimmer of approval. Bement pushed it away from his client back toward the prosecutor.

"How long have you been a document examiner?" asked Hatch.

"About thirty years," replied Storer.

Laying a foundation for the court, Hatch pressed the witness for his credentials. Storer had started out as an apprentice in questioned document work in 1958. He worked ten years for the St. Louis Police Department as their examiner before retiring and going into private practice. For the last twenty years, he had done contractual work for the St. Louis County Prosecutor's Office and the St. Louis Police Department.

"How many examinations have you done or

completed between questioned documents and known documents?"

"Well, it would have to be in the thousands," said Storer.

"Have you testified in other states?"

"I have testified in the State and Federal courts of Missouri, Illinois, Iowa, Arkansas, Kansas, and Kentucky."

"Have you been qualified as an expert in all of those states?"

"Yes."

Hatch quizzed the examiner about what he would look for in general and then went for the specifics of the letter found under the bed at the Lanman house.

"In this case, we would also look at the construction, at the way the *t*s are crossed, and the general construction of the *s*s with the terminal endings. The capital letter *W* being much taller than what ordinarily are tall letters, like the *L*s."

"Anything else?"

"There was one difference," said Storer. "The questioned writing on the note was more tremulous. It was more awkwardly written than the very smooth, very controlled known handwriting of Mrs. Lanman."

"So, based upon your observations and based upon your experience, do you have an opinion as to who wrote the note in People's Exhibit 199D?"

"Yes, sir."

"And who was that?" asked Hatch, turning to look at Anderson.

"Mrs. Lanman," said the handwriting expert.

Filing through papers on the table top, the prosecutor turned back to the witness. "Now, Mr. Storer, did you prepare any photographs which would help you in explaining your conclusion to the jury?"

"I did. I have made enough duplicate copies so there is one set for each two jurors, one for the court, and one for each attorney."

The two-part photographs of the note and known sections of Jolaine's handwriting were passed out.

"Now, Mr. Storer, did you observe anything about the orange tablet that was also given to you with the note?"

"I examined the surface of the folder in a darkened room at the laboratory with a low-angle lighting, and that kind of procedure will sometimes reveal indented writing impressions in a document. For instance, if one document is laying on another when the top document is written, the pen pressure sometimes will leave an indentation in the document below. My examination disclosed that there were the indentations of words from the note on the folder."

"Did you find anything else about the positions of the rest of that note? Did it flow the same way?" asked Hatch.

"It did not," replied Storer. "As the note was

being written, the paper was shifted slightly from one sentence to another. There is no question that this note was laying on top of this folder when the note was written."

"Did you observe where those specks were in relation to the note or the ink?" the prosecutor asked, referring to the specks of blood on the note.

"The little red dots or specks were scattered again throughout the note. Only in one area did one of these red specks intersect or come in contact with the writing and was in the . . . one can hardly see it with the naked eye, but it is in the downstroke in the word 'woman' or the *n* in 'woman' in the questioned note, and the red speck was on top of the ink."

"And do you have an opinion based upon that as to what was written first or what happened first?"

"Well, the writing came first and then the red speck came after," stated the expert.

Bement didn't belabor the handwriting expert. He pointed out the fact that the note wasn't written by his client and moved to excuse the witness.

In the next week of trial, State witnesses covered Anderson's work history at the Public Aid Office and the SWAT Team's entry into Anderson's home. Busch returned to testify three times during the week. The briefcases, weapons, surgical gloves, section of cord, and Anderson's collection of articles on Audrey Cardenas surfaced.

Forensic Serologist Debora Depczynski from the Metro-East Laboratory testified that the small crust of dried blood collected from the front seat of Anderson's blue car could have come from either of the Lanmans or from Anderson himself. Both Anderson and the Lanmans had the same blood type in the ABO system. With the limited sample, she was unable to conduct further testing.

Bement hammered the petite serologist on cross-examination. "So, the bottom line here is you're not able to test to a scientific certainty that it wasn't Dale's blood?" snapped Bement.

"Exclusively? No," replied the serologist.

Hatch countered with his next forensic witness, Microscopist Glen Schubert. Schubert delivered a crushing blow to the defense with his analysis. He had compared the cloth gloves seized from Anderson's house to the bloody fabric impressions on the bed skirting. He demonstrated to the jurors using the gloves and skirting.

"In my opinion, this could have been from a glove like this. I found one glove to be consistent

257

with this area of the fabric impression."

Focusing the jury's attention on the bloody area on the beige bed skirting, Forensic Scientist Schubert said, "In my opinion, the blood was probably on the glove, and it was pressed against the skirting."

Bement argued with the scientist during cross-examination about the gloves and the impression, pointing out that the gloves found at Anderson's home were only the same brand as the ones that made the impression. He finally had Schubert admit, "I cannot say these two gloves made these two impressions."

Pathologist Raj Nanduri revealed to jurors her pathological findings. "Jolaine Lanman was hit several times in the back of the head, fracturing her skull and causing massive internal bleeding," said the forensic doctor. "She had been stabbed ten times in the neck, three times in the chest which pierced the heart, and once in the abdomen."

Dr. Nanduri stated the child's injuries: "Kenneth Lanman also was struck on the back of the head and his left ear was almost torn off. He had twenty-seven stab and puncture wounds, ten in the neck, and the rest to his chest." Nanduri pointed out to the jury the shallow puncture wounds to the child's chest: "These are found in cases where someone wants to inflict pain or fear. The damage to the boy's bead could have been caused by someone stomping on the skull." She reported that both victims were alive when the wounds were inflicted.

Linda Anderson was the last person to testify on the eighth day of trial. She told of being afraid to leave the house after Dale suggested that she and the children should remain inside. Hatch kept his examination of Linda Anderson brief, but planned to use her again if the defendant took the stand. Hatch then rested the State's case against Dale Anderson.

Bement was to call the first witness on his client's behalf. The big question — would the defendant testify?

# Twenty-two

The afternoon of April 10, Bement, on his client's behalf, called Paul Anderson to the witness stand. He established that the nine-year-old boy was the son of the defendant and had been removed from the house by detectives the morning that the search warrant was served. Bement spoke slowly and softly to the young child.

"Did they ask you questions at the Sheriff's Office?"

"Yes," said the blond-haired fourth grader, looking around the room.

"What kind of things did they ask you?" said the man in the suit.

"Like . . . I don't remember," said Paul, watching his father write on the notepad.

"After you left the Sheriff's Office, where did you go?"

"My mom came and then we went over to my grandpa's and grandma's house."

When the defense attorney asked how long the boy stayed at his grandparents' house, Anderson stopped writing, took off his glasses, and wiped his eyes.

"About three weeks," responded the defendant's son to the question.

"When you were at the Sheriff's Department, did you have your clothes on?"

"I had my pajamas on."

Bement moved back to the defense table and patted his client on the shoulder to show support for him. "That is all the questions I have, Judge."


Hatch didn't want to cross-examine the young boy, but Anderson was trying to use his son to seek compassion from the jury. Dale probably would also call his daughter, who was older than Paul, because she was not as easily swayed as her little brother.

"Now, Paul," said Hatch, "Back at that time on that Wednesday, were you going to school?"

"Yeah."

"When you woke up the next morning, did you go to school?"

"No, they told me not to."

"Who told you not to?" asked the prosecutor.

"My dad."

"And did he tell you why you shouldn't go to school?"

"He just said there were some people outside and that he didn't want me to go outside or use the phone."

"Did you ever ask your dad if you could call

a friend or anything like that?" asked Hatch.

"Well, I didn't because I knew nobody would be at home. They would be at school," said the fourth grader. His response brought laughter from the spectators.

When the courtroom quieted, Hatch continued, "Were you scared at any time?"

"A little. I was scared because I didn't know what was going on."

Anderson smiled at his son when he walked past the defense table. Paul took a seat beside his mother in the back of the courtroom. Dale turned and scanned the room looking for his wife. Bement called her to testify, and she willingly answered the questions until the defense attorney went too far.

"In general, you are familiar with police coming into the house and Dale being arrested and all of those kinds of things, is that right?"

Bement received a brief "Yes" from Linda Anderson.

"After that, did your job then terminate?"

"Yes," answered Mrs. Anderson.

"And where are you employed?" asked the defense attorney. Dale waited for the answer with pen in hand.

"I would rather not answer that," said Linda, looking at her husband. "I don't want him to know."

Bement sprang to his feet. "Judge, I would ask that the Court instruct the witness to answer the question."

262

Judge Flynn raised his hands and motioned to the attorneys, "Would counsel approach the bench?"

A heated exchange ensued between the attorneys out of the hearing of the jury and off the court record. The judge listened as both presented their side of the issue. He motioned to the lawyers to retake their seats and then proceeded with the trial.

"I am not going to require the witness to answer that question," said Judge Flynn.

Bement's facial expression tightened as he continued, "Other than your present employment, do you and your family have any other source of income?"

"Through Dale. He receives Social Security."

"Is that disability payments?" asked Bement, making the point that his client was injured at work during a fall.

"Yes," said Anderson's wife, unsure why he asked.

When Hatch was allowed to cross-examine Linda, he knew that he would have to bring out Dale's secretive side at home. Linda Anderson only knew what Dale had told her and that was all lies.

"How did you know about the disability?" asked Hatch.

"Well, I saw the paperwork and all, and the checks; so, I knew he was getting disability," responded Linda.

"But you had no indication of why he was getting disability?"

"Well, he said job stress and . . . I don't know," she said.

Hatch switched his questioning to the events of the twenty-eighth of September. "Were you feeling all right?"

"I would have gone to work," replied Linda. "I didn't miss one day the whole time I was there."

"In fact, that was the first day you ever missed?"

"Yes, it was."

Again, the prosecutor moved to another topic with the witness to keep the defense on their toes. Referring to the defendant, Hatch asked, "At any time, did he make a reference to his supervisors in regard to any of his work?"

"All the time," said Linda Anderson.

"Did he ever say anything to you regarding whether or not Kroupa, DeLaria, and Vale should be held accountable or somehow be implicated in any of his actions with court, his discharge, or any of that?"

"It was all their fault, according to him," she said to the jury.


While waiting for the next defense witness to be called, Hatch noticed that Anderson and Bement appeared to be having words at the defense table. Anderson leaned close to Bement, his face flushed and looking angry. Bement was slowly shaking his

264

head from side to side. Anderson then sat straight up in the chair looking content. The judge instructed the defense counsel to call his next witness.

Bement rose slowly from the table and stood in front of the jury. "Dale Anderson," said Bement with an air of disapproval. Anderson smiled as if he had won the lottery, and approached the clerk with hand raised to be sworn in. Having Anderson take the stand came as a great shock to the jury, as well as many of the spectators. Jolaine's parents were among the people seated in the back of the courtroom.

Anderson's decision to testify had been anticipated by the prosecutor and was welcomed. Anderson had outsmarted himself. Hatch asked Nester and Delaney to take notes on Anderson's testimony so that he could concentrate on his examination of the witness. Later, when Hatch was given the opportunity to cross-examine Anderson, he would show the defendant that he was playing in the big leagues; this time, there would be no defenseless child or pregnant woman for Anderson to manhandle.

"Would you state your name, please?" said Bement to the witness.

"My name is Dale Richard Anderson."

"How old are you?"

"Thirty-eight years old."

"What is your educational background?" asked Bement.

"My wife Linda and I graduated from Belleville

High School in 1969. Both of us attended Illinois State University, and we both graduated in June of 1973 with Bachelor's degrees. Both of the degrees are basically in education."

By the end of the day, the jurors had heard how the defendant had worked his way through college, then held jobs as an insurance adjuster, a jailer, and a Public Aid employee with the State. Anderson portrayed himself as a solid citizen, a church-going family man.

When the doors of the courthouse opened the next morning, lines of people filled the lobby and snaked up the twin spiral staircases to the second floor. A portion of the crowd waited in the hallways outside the courtroom, while the overflow of curious onlookers gravitated into the lounge. Relatives of the victims and Anderson's parents were allowed to have the first choice of seats in the spectator's section. Again, the first row was reserved for the news reporters. The remaining purple chairs were open to the general public.

While the jurors waited in the jury room, Anderson was brought through the tunnel from the jail, and entered the courtroom to the right of the spectator's section. Out of sight of the jury, Anderson stopped and stood in front of the spectators and news reporters. His hands shackled with handcuffs and his bulging folder tucked under his arm, Anderson stared at many of the female spectators until they looked away. This seemed to fuel his ego. He was in control. They were afraid of him. Their reaction brought his lips above his double-dimpled chin into a tight smirk. Hatch watched as he amused himself with the crowd.

When the jurors came in, Anderson turned and took his seat at the defense table. Judge Flynn entered and the second day of Anderson's testimony began.

"You understand that you are still under oath?" said the judge to the defendant seated in the witness chair.

"Yes, sir," responded Anderson.

"Yesterday," said Bement, "you were telling us before we left about the incident surrounding the arrest of your supervisors at Public Aid. If I understand you correctly, there was no finalization of the charges?"

"I don't recall just how that worked out. We did not have a jury trial like we're having here today."

Bement trudged through the details of Anderson's having been placed on home assignment, his termination, and the grievance filed with the Illinois Civil Service Commission. He asked about Anderson's daily routine.

"My activities were pretty limited because I was considered one hundred percent disabled due to the injuries I received at work," claimed Anderson.

"Dale, we have heard a lot of testimony in the State's case regarding the lady by the name of

Audrey Cardenas," said Bement. "Do you know who she is?"

"Yes, I do," replied Anderson, his eyes scanning the jurors. "She was a reporter with the *News-Democrat* newspaper."

"Did you ever meet Audrey Cardenas?"

"Yes, I did. In June of 1988."

"How many contacts then did you have with this Audrey Cardenas?"

"I think there were about two."

"Did you give the opinion to anyone, as best you can recall, stating that you knew who was involved in the murder, and whether or not it had anything to do with your three supervisors?"

"There was a lot of speculation on who may have been involved. There was a lot of talk about perhaps people from the Public Aid Office could have been involved," replied the witness in a nasal-toned voice.

"Do you know Rodney Woidtke?"

"I know who he is. Like I say, he was also highly publicized in the papers about the case."

"Did you have any personal contact with him?"

"He had stopped by the Public Aid Office in Belleville, I believe, in May or June of '88."

"Have you ever identified yourself, since the summer of 1988 through today, as being an investigator for the murder of Audrey Cardenas?"

"No," stated the defendant. "It should be pretty clear to my relatives and friends that I have been working at the Public Aid Office since 1980. I know there have been some people who expressed different opinions, but they are not correct."

Hatch placed his elbow on top of the table and rested his chin in his hand. He thought about the lie that Anderson had just told. Anderson, for the last eight years, had had his own parents convinced that he was working as a Special Agent with the State of Illinois.

The next subject brought up by the defense was the identification of the two women who had had their homes for sale.

"In 1989, do you recall looking for a house, another house to buy?"

"No," said the witness.

"Is there any reason that you would have been to Cheryl Scott's house, or Jill Hindrichs's house, or anybody's house on the east side of Belleville to look at a house for the purpose of buying a house?"

"No," said Anderson. "I suspect what probably happened, the fact that my picture has been in the paper a number of times and the police came out to see them, all excited about working on a case, and they said we have a picture here—look at this picture—have you ever seen this man? Do you think this man has been to your house? I think that's the reason they probably made the statement they did."

Bement had not wanted Anderson to testify and had pleaded with his client to avoid the challenge of trying to explain away all the issues the prosecutor had raised. Anderson refused to heed his warning, and, like a small boat in heavy seas, was beginning to flounder. Anderson was already laboring with his responses in front of the jury. What would he do when the real storm of Hatch's cross-examination struck? Continuing with his direct examination, Bement allowed Anderson to address the issue of the letter written by his daughter's friend.

"You were present when she testified about a letter that she had written on your behalf regarding Audrey Cardenas," said Bement. "Do you recall that testimony?"

"Yes, I do," said Anderson, smiling.

"And what were the circumstances surrounding that?"

"That was back in 1988, and this was after the time when Audrey Cardenas had stopped by the house, and she was interested in the matter because, like I say, it was highly publicized."

"Go on," coaxed Bement. "What else happened there?"

"So, she said she was interested in writing a statement because she was aware of Miss Cardenas being at the house. I said 'Write a statement if you wish and write it in your own words.' "

"The time that she wrote the letter, was that after the murder of Miss Cardenas?"

"Yes. This was after."

"And she then testified that you wrote the letter and she copied it. Can you tell the jury how it actually happened?"

Shifting in the chair, Anderson looked at the jurors as he talked. "I had jotted down some notes about the occurrence and I had her write it in her own words, what she remembered happening. And, since that time, the police have talked to her a number of times. She's about my daughter's age. She is scared to death about this whole thing and really doesn't want to be involved in it, and I don't blame her for not wanting to be involved in it."

"Would counsel approach the bench?" instructed the judge. He then spoke to the jury, "We are going to take approximately a ten- or fifteen-minute break and I would ask the members of the jury if they would please retire to the jury room?"

The jurors entered the purple-carpeted jury room located off the front of the courtroom and waited for the legal rankling between the attorneys to subside in the judge's chambers.

When the trial resumed, the defense touched on the location of the Lanman house, the plates on Dale's blue Oldsmobile, and his client's activities on the day of the murders. Bement's next questions focused on those killings.

"Dale, did you kill Jolaine and Kenneth Lanman?"

"No, I did not," came the reply. "I had to talk about this for months now. I have tried to explain to these officers how did they think I could kill a little boy when I've got a son not much older than this little boy that got killed?"

"You have been asked that question by the police on several occasions, right?"

"Yes, sir," admitted Anderson. "Linda and I talked to the police about it. We tried to cooperate with them as much as we could. We tried to do everything we could to prove we were telling the truth, and we are not involved in this case. In fact, we have got the police polygraph tests that prove that Linda and I are telling the truth."

"I'm going to object, your Honor," said Hatch, rising from his seat. He was angered with Anderson's constant attempt to shield himself with his wife's good deeds. Anderson had never taken a polygraph examination, but he knew that Linda had passed her examination. He tried to trick the jurors into believing that he, too, had passed.

"Sustained," ruled the judge.

"And ask the jury to be instructed to disregard that remark," demanded the prosecutor.

"The jury is instructed to disregard the witness's last comment," said Judge Flynn, casting a look of disapproval toward Anderson. "That is totally improper."

"I am sorry, your Honor," apologized Anderson.

"Wait for the next question," instructed the judge.

"Dale, we have heard some testimony of a note being found at the scene of this crime; you have seen that note and members of the jury have seen

272

that note. Do you know what I am talking about?" asked Bement, with crossed arms.

"Yes, I have seen a copy of it."

"Did you write that note?"

"No, I did not."

"Did you, at any time, instruct or ask Jolaine Lanman to write that note?"

"No," said Anderson.

Bement felt a little more comfortable about Dale's responses to the questions so far. The briefcases were the next wave of exhibits that could sink his client. Anderson was riding out the questions and gaining more confidence the longer he was on the stand.

"Dale, the first question I know the jury wants to know is why do you have so many briefcases?"

"Well, after a period of years, you can accumulate some briefcases."

"Now, Dale, when they were opened earlier, there were many things in there other than Public Aid forms. Do you use these for other things other than keeping your work forms in?" asked Anderson's attorney.

"Since that time, I don't keep the Public Aid forms in there anymore."

Anderson told the jury he bought equipment consisting of handcuffs, blackjacks, and holsters while he was working at the Sheriff's Department, and that he used the briefcases to keep the dangerous items out of the hands of his curious children.

"You have also been shown through this trial, and the jury has been shown, that you have in

273

many of your briefcases a pair of latex rubber gloves," said Bement. "Can you explain to the jury what you know about that?"

"There has been a lot of discussion about some rubber gloves that the police found at my home," remarked Anderson. "Apparently, Al Busch or some of the officers put a couple of them in my briefcase."

"Then those gloves were not in the briefcases?" inquired the defense attorney.

"To my knowledge, they were not in the briefcases. We had them in a bag, I think, in a bedroom on a chair. In fact, there were some other things Al Busch showed us that were in the briefcases; but, these items were not kept in the briefcases," said Anderson. "I assume when Al Busch was collecting stuff out of the house, he just dumped it all in the briefcases and brought it down."

Bement released the witness to be cross-examined by the prosecutor.

# Twenty-three

"Now, Dale," said Hatch, pausing, "you talked about your education back when you went to college. What kind of courses did you take?"

"I majored in sociology and minored in history, and Linda and I got Illinois teaching certificates."

"I am not talking about Linda," said Hatch, again irritated with Anderson's use of his wife as a shield. "I am just talking about you. You have a four-year degree, is that right?"

"Yes. A Bachelor's."

"Did you ever make the dean's list?"

"I made the dean's list most of the time. Me and Linda both did."

Skipping to another line of questioning, the prosecutor didn't let the defendant get comfortable with one subject before changing directions.

"Now, when you worked in the jail, you would not carry a gun on your side, is that correct?" asked Hatch.

"That's correct," said Anderson. "When you work back in the jail itself, you don't take a firearm in there."

Hatch picked up the pace of the questioning, "And you don't carry blackjacks or any type of weapon like that with you either, isn't that true?"

Anderson's cold eyes fixed on the prosecutor standing only inches from his face. "The policy changed. When I first started there, they did have blackjacks back in the booking area."

Hatch knew how his fellow jailers rated Anderson when he worked as a correctional officer. They saw him as an intelligent person, but lacking in common sense. On one occasion, Anderson had locked one of the correctional officers, along with a maintenance man, in an area with twenty angry prisoners. Another time, while working inside the jail, he had an inmate hold the keys to the cell block so he could demonstrate agility exercises used to grade police officers.

"Did you ever work in Alton?" Hatch asked, addressing Anderson's work history.

"Yes. I think I did work there for a short time."

"You think you did?" snapped the prosecutor, irritated with the witness's lack of certainty in the answer.

"In 1977 or '78," replied Anderson.

"And why did you leave that insurance company?"

"It turned out to be a longer drive than I had anticipated was one of the reasons," said Anderson, almost grinning.

"Leaving them was because of the drive?" asked Hatch.

"That was mostly the reason."

"There weren't any problems at work?"

"I wasn't really satisfied or happy there," Anderson said, sensing the pressure of the prosecutor's question.

"Why not?"

"It just didn't seem like the kind of job that I was interested in at the time."

Hatch, aware that Anderson had prepared himself to answer questions about the problems at the insurance company, headed the questioning in yet another direction. Anderson had given him an opening into an area that was the basis of the case.

"You wanted to be a policeman, didn't you?"

"Yes, sir," said Anderson. "That is correct."

"Did you ever apply to any other police agencies other than the St. Clair County Sheriff's Department?"

"Yes, I did."

"And what was that?"

"I think I applied at the Belleville City Police Department."

"Now, wait a minute," said the prosecutor. "We are with this 'think' stuff again. Did you or didn't you?"

"It is a long time ago," complained Anderson.

"I know," said Hatch. "Everything has been a long time. We are all older, and we kind of remember some things, and we don't remember everything, but sooner or later, we know whether or not we went in and applied and put an application into a place of employment. Did you go there and put in your application?"

"I believe I did, yes."

"Did you get that job?"

"No. They said they had a restriction on wearing eyeglasses."

"Did you apply to any other police organizations?"

"I think I applied with the Fairview Heights City Police."

"Here we go with the 'think,' " shouted Hatch. "Did you or didn't you get a job with them?"

"No," Anderson said angrily. "They said you couldn't wear eyeglasses."

"What about the State Police, DCI, Department of Criminal Investigation? Did you ever apply to them?"

"Yes, I did."

"What year?"

"It was around 1977 or 1978."

"Did you get accepted by them?"

"I was on their waiting list," said Anderson with pride. "But I never got called to accept the position."

"You never got hired by the State Police, did you?"

"No," admitted the defendant.

"Now, when you talk about being a Deputy Sheriff, I mean, your basic duties at that time were just to operate in the jail, right?"

"As a booking officer or corrections officer," said Anderson, trying to protect the title.

"You worked in the jail, right? You never went out on patrol?"

"No, I didn't handle patrols. I didn't investigate crimes. I didn't do crime scene work like Al Busch does. I wasn't required to make arrests or handle investigations or do any type of patrol work."

"Did you want to do that kind of patrol work?" asked Hatch.

"I had expressed an interest in it when I was there," admitted the defendant.

"You thought you were qualified for that, didn't you?"

"Yes," said Anderson in a cold tone.

Hatch again changed topics to keep Anderson off guard. His questions were light and easy at first, but grew intense as Anderson tried to cover his tracks.

"Okay," said Hatch, "how often did you talk to Audrey Cardenas?"

"I believe it was only on two occasions."

"And do you remember when that was?"

"1988," said Anderson.

Standing with crossed arms, rocking back and forth on his feet, Hatch responded like a school-teacher. "A lot of days in 1988. Do you remember when you talked to her?"

"It was the summertime, in June of '88."

"Thirty days in June," stated Hatch. "Early June, late June? Can you give me a date?"

"Judge," interrupted Bement, "this has been asked and answered. He said he couldn't give a date."

"I will sustain the objection," said Flynn.

"And where was this that you talked to her?" asked Hatch, gesturing with raised hands to empha-size the question.

"She came out to the house."

"What was the nature of that conversation?" in-quired Hatch, referring to the alleged meeting in

Anderson's driveway.

"She asked me if she could get some additional information about an article that Carolyn Tuft had published in the *News-Democrat* a week or two prior to that time."

"She just came up to your house? Did she phone you before that or just appeared at your doorstep?"

"She just came out to the house," said Anderson.

"How did she get there?"

"I believe she drove."

"What did she drive?"

"I believe she had a pickup truck, kind of a small pickup truck."

"Did you take down the license plate of that truck?" asked Hatch, waiting to jump into another area with the defendant.

"No."

"You take down a lot of license plates, don't you?" asked Hatch, his voice suggestive.

"It was a common practice to jot down license plate numbers because sometimes you would have Public Aid clients that might own a vehicle and not be reporting that to the Public Aid Office," replied Anderson, attempting to explain away what he knew was coming next.

"Why would you write down Maurice Vale's, Bob DeLaria's, or Charlotte Kroupa's license plate?"

"Because of the dispute we were involved with," he lashed back.

"What has taking down their license plates got to do with the dispute?"

"There were occasions where they were . . . I saw a car driving by my house and discovered it was them driving by my house on several different occasions."

Hatch wanted to get into the forensic arena with Anderson and show the jurors how knowledgeable the defendant was in that area. The prosecutor would rely on Anderson's ego to draw him into the open. Hatch was certain that Anderson would try to use allegations of police brutality during the cross-examination. He directed his questions toward the Friday that the officers spent at Anderson's house.

"Well, the officers were making it pretty clear I didn't really have any rights the day they were at my house," claimed Anderson, with his face flushed.

"How did they do that?"

"They were acting about as unfriendly as you can get."

"What else did they do?"

"They were physically abusive," explained Anderson, telling the jurors how the officers forced him down in a chair.

"I know you are explaining, but sometimes words won't do it," said Hatch. "Show us how they physically abused you on that day."

"I would rather not, to tell the truth."

"And you don't want to show these ladies and gentlemen of the jury what these people did to you?"

"This was an unpleasant experience, Mr. Hatch," said Anderson, looking to his attorney for assistance.

"Judge, I am going to object," said Bement. "He is arguing." Bement pointed to Hatch. "He's explained."

The prosecutor let Anderson elaborate on the physical abuse he had received. Dale claimed to have been pushed down in the chair twenty to thirty times during the fifteen hours the officers were in his home.

"Did they touch you at any other time or any other place on your body?"

"There were times when they were stepping on my toes," said Anderson.

"Who?"

"Dave Nester, Al Busch."

"What kind of shoes did they have on?"

"Regular shoes. Similar to what you are wearing."

"Did you ever tell these officers to leave your house?"

"Yes, I did."

"Who did you first tell to leave your house?"

"I believe it was Al Busch."

"And when was that?" asked Hatch.

"It was either morning or afternoon."

"Did you ever go with Al Busch out to the garage and help him and say, 'I will help you search. Go ahead and look at what you want.'?"

"Some officer took me out in the garage."

Hatch challenged him with the fact that there were people outside and he could have called out for help. He had received a call from his wife and could have had her send help. Anderson told the jury that he was too afraid to risk that.

Hatch directed the defendant's attention to the evening of the murders.

"You testified you went out and drove your car around and then came home?"

"That is correct. That was between 5:00 P.M. and 6:00 P.M."

"It is still light then. Still summer, correct? You have the cardboard up by the time your wife gets home, right?"

"No. That is not true. The cardboard was not up."

"So, she is lying about that?" said Hatch in a loud voice.

"Because of the fact my wife had to leave her job when I got arrested, this is really destroying and upsetting her, and I believe this is the reason she made that comment and . . ." Anderson started to cry.

"So, she is lying?" repeated Hatch.

"Yes, she is," said Anderson, placing his finger under his glasses to wipe away tears. "You have to keep in mind she's mostly been a part-time elementary teacher during the years we were married. It meant everything to her working with these kids. It just tore her up when she had to leave that job."

"Why did she have to leave that job?"

"Because I was arrested," said Anderson.

"Not because of anything she did, right?"

"It was nothing she did," admitted Anderson, crying out loud.

Not swayed by the waterworks from behind Anderson's glasses, Hatch continued, "So the reason that she is lying or talking that way now is because she is upset with the fact that she lost her job?"

"My wife has been through hell these last six months."

"Because of what?"

"Because I got arrested in September of '89. It's turned our lives upside down."

"This whole incident has turned quite a few lives upside down, hasn't it?" countered the prosecutor.

"It's destroyed our marriage and our family," said Anderson, looking at the jury with reddened eyes.

"And what is the cause of this destruction?"

"Because I was arrested in September."

"Just because of your arrest?"

"All of the events that have gone along with that, with the arrest, and the police being out to the house to see her since, on occasion, and taking hair samples—having to pull hair out of their heads for the hair samples to compare on these tests," said Anderson.

Hatch had been waiting for Anderson to open the door to the forensic world, which he had finally just done. He smiled as he walked toward the witness. Leaning close to him, Hatch said, "Were you familiar with those types of testing based upon your training?"

"I haven't had any training on the kind of things Al Busch was talking about, like hair samples and things."

"So, you don't have any knowledge or any training or any indication about the collection of evidence at a crime scene?" Hatch spoke to Anderson in an inquisitive manner.

"I would have to say no," replied Anderson.

"What about fingerprints?"

284

"I wouldn't have the first idea how to collect a fingerprint."

"What about ballistics?"

"I believe the way it is done on ballistics, they sometimes fire a weapon into a tank of water or some other type of container to recover the slug and then they would put it under a microscope."

"Where did you come about with that knowledge?"

"I think we saw it on TV."

"So, you are saying you have no background information on the collection of blood, hairs, fibers, fingerprints, any of that?" asked Hatch.

"No, sir. I have never had any experience doing any of that."

"If you are at a point where we can break?" asked Judge Flynn. Then, addressing the jury, "There are some matters that I need to take up with the attorneys once again back in chambers. Some of you may be wondering about the schedule the rest of this week. Friday is a court holiday. It is Good Friday. We will not be holding court Friday."

After the session in chambers, Judge Flynn recalled the witness to the stand. "Sir, do you understand that you are still under oath?"

"Yes, sir," responded Anderson in a cheerful voice.

Hatch continued his questions about the inconsistencies of Anderson's versions of what happened and that of other witnesses. The defendant explained or denied issues while the prosecutor drew from him bits of information for the jurors to hear.

Referring to Anderson's attraction to Teresa Anglin, Hatch handed the witness an item. "Can you tell us what that is?"

"This is a newspaper," said Anderson. "This is some information showing a list of divorces granted in St. Clair County."

"And did you make a note on one of those divorces?"

"Yes, I did."

"And who was that?"

"One Teresa Anglin," said Anderson in a low tone.

"In fact," said Hatch, pointing to the article, "you had put a little star or X by that, right?"

"Yes."

"And the same thing on the other one," said Hatch, handing the witness a second newspaper clipping. "You put that there, didn't you, that red arrow?"

"I am not positive, but probably."

"When you marked your articles that you kept, you put arrows pointing to significant parts, didn't you?"

"Yes."

"When you went to that house, Anglin's house, what did you have with you?"

"I don't know," said Anderson, frowning.

"It is around noontime or so that you went there?" said Hatch.

"It could have been."

"Not carrying anything with you. Just go up to the door, right?"

"I don't remember," said the defendant.

"Can you tell us what these are?" asked Hatch, sliding two exhibit-marked documents toward the witness.

"It is some information written down."

"What is the date on that?" inquired the attorney as Anderson glanced again at the exhibits.

"One is July 11 of '88 and one is July 12 of '88," smiled Anderson. "Yes. This helps me out. On July 12, I had a radio in the car with me."

"What did you have it programmed for?"

"Fire departments, police departments, and the weather channel."

"What kind of police departments?"

"I had the Belleville Police Department on there."

"Did you hear anything about your name being on that scanner on the twelfth?"

"Yes," said Anderson. "Why don't you let me take another look at that note and I can give you specific information?

"I made a notation on July 12 of '88," said Anderson, reading from the exhibit. "But, after I had stopped by Miss Anglin's house and left, I heard some information on the police radio about me. 'Dale Anderson, he is 1032.' "

"What does that mean?"

"1032 means a man that is carrying a gun," said Anderson.

"So, you knew the police lingo?"

"That is right."

Hatch brought out that Anderson carried around the portable scanner to stay a step ahead of the police. Anderson's theory of corruption in the Public Aid Office and his belief that a city alderman was involved with the trio of supervisors were the next items on Hatch's cross-examination. Hatch was surprised at the defendant's allegations.

Referring to the political person that Anderson had accused of wrongdoing, Hatch asked, "And what did he do when he got the office?"

"He came down on June 6 and had a meeting with Vale at the Public Aid Office," said Anderson.

"Could you hear what they were saying?"

"Yes. It was right around the middle part of the day and I remember there was another caseworker I work with, Mayotis Dean. She and I were out there. We heard Vale talking about them being arrested. Something about wanting more money to take care of the problem that Mr. Vale had with the arrest charges."

"So you picked up on that, didn't you?" asked Hatch.

"Yeah. That is highly irregular. I said to Mayotis, 'That's awfully strange that Vale would be having that kind of meeting.' "

"And you made notes of that, too?"

"Yes, I did."

"Now, this Mayotis Dean, we haven't heard too much about her with Public Aid workers. Whatever happened to her?" inquired Hatch.

"She is now deceased," said Anderson matter-of-factly.

"And how did she die?"

"I believe she died sometime in 1989."

"I didn't say when did she die, I said how did she die?" explained Hatch.

"I'm not sure what you mean, how did she die?"

said the witness, needing some time to think.

"What was the cause of death?" asked Hatch, turning and walking toward the pile of State exhibits on the table.

"I believe it was supposed to be a heart attack," replied Anderson, stopping the prosecutor in mid-stride with his statement.

"Supposed to be!" said Hatch, turning slowly to face the witness. "What do you believe happened?"

Anderson had a worried look on his face. After a moment, he looked back at Hatch. "I'm not sure what you mean."

"You said it was supposed to be a heart attack," said Hatch, moving closer to Anderson. "Do you believe it was a heart attack?"

"I have reason to believe she might have been poisoned," said Anderson, bringing murmurs from the courtroom spectators.

"Poisoned! By who?"

"Someone at the Public Aid Office."

"Like who?"

"Some of the other Public Aid employees."

"Like who?" demanded Hatch.

"Possibly some of the supervisors she worked with," said Anderson.

"Like who?" shouted Hatch.

"Like Mr. DeLaria."

"Why?"

"Mr. DeLaria was her supervisor."

"Now, what made you believe that she was poisoned?"

"She said on occasion prior to her death that she thought people were tampering with her food or

289

drink at the office. Putting something in it.".

"And what did you think of that?" asked the prosecutor, remembering Anderson was the prime suspect with the supervisor's dog being poisoned.

"I thought that was pretty unusual."

"What did you do about it?"

"I told her to be careful about what she eats or drinks at the office."

Hatch removed an item from the table and handed it to Anderson and asked him to identify it. Anderson admitted that the news article was a death notice on Mayotis Dean which he had cut out of the newspaper on April 7, 1989; and a few days later, he had talked to a female employee at work about the possibility that Mayotis may have been poisoned.

The jury heard that Anderson had written a letter to Mayotis's husband, who was a police officer, claiming to have information about the poisoning of his wife. Two weeks later, the defendant mailed a second letter to the deceased woman's spouse.


The four light brown leather briefcases, the ones called assassination kits by the news media, were placed on top of the prosecutor's table. Anderson watched with interest as Hatch arranged them for his next series of questions.

"There are numbers on these," said Hatch, as he walked away from the items. "One, two, three, and four. Why is that?"

"Well, the briefcases looked very similar so it helps if you put a number on them to tell which is which."

Juggling a bag of empty brass shell casings in his hand, which he had just removed from one of the briefcases, Hatch looked at Anderson and waited for an answer to an unasked question.

"We were also shooting at some cans," said Anderson. "I noticed the exhibit was an old bag with the empty brass I had with some tissues in there, and I had cut my finger on one of the cans and used some of the paper for that."

"That is how that blood got on there, huh?"

"I noticed that was one of the exhibits you had," said Anderson, looking nervous.

"You wanted to explain that, did you?" grinned the prosecutor.

"I figured you would want an explanation."

"Why all these handkerchiefs with the little rubber bands on them?" asked Hatch, removing several from the briefcases and tossing them on the witness stand.

"No special reason. You use a handkerchief for . . . you know."

"For what?"

"For your nose," answered Anderson.

"Can you use cloth like this to clean up? Clean up one of these?" asked Hatch, removing a blackjack, a knife, and a metal bar from the briefcase.

"I can see what you're trying to say," stated Anderson, showing some anger. "You are trying to make something here. What you're trying to do is give the jury a false impression about some of these guns and knives that are in the house."

"Tell me the right impression," demanded Hatch.

Anderson regained his composure and turned to

the jury to speak. "There is no law against people owning guns, ammunition, or knives."

"Now, my question is, if you used a rag like a handkerchief to clean up a knife," said Hatch, rubbing the blade of the hunting knife with the white handkerchief, "what would you have to do with the handkerchief?"

"I see your point. Throw it away."

"Now," said Hatch, "let's talk about these. Have you worn rubber gloves before?"

"I've used a pair to clean out the guttering."

Anderson was asked to stand up and demonstrate how he would wear the gloves, which he gladly did for the jurors. He explained that his wife keeps several pairs of latex gloves in the house and used them for the kids where she worked if they had a bloody nose. Hatch pointed out when the defendant removed the gloves he inverted them, which if they were bloody, would contain the blood inside the glove.

Anderson reasoned that he had all the knives in the briefcases because, as some people collect different items, he collected knives. Hatch opened the briefcases and removed the next exhibits.

"Now, let's see what we got here," he said sarcastically. "Can you tell us what these are?"

"I believe this is a piece of cord off my daughter's curtain that broke, and we purchased some more cord to replace it."

"What about the other one?"

"It is a piece of clothesline rope; it looks like it broke."

"What happened?"

"It just wore out. It's the type of curtain you open and close with a drawstring, and the drawstring wore out and broke. So, we purchased a package of cord to replace it, and we hadn't gotten around to doing that yet, and I think you even have the package of cord as one of your exhibits."

"And this is the replacement cord?"

"No. I think one of those pieces is the one that broke off."

"But, there is no break in this rope, is there?"

"No," said Anderson.

"It broke off. So then after it broke off, both of them, you then decided to tie both ends into knots?"

"Yeah, if you don't, it can unravel."

"So that explains that, doesn't it?" said Hatch.

"Yeah, you are making a big deal out of a piece of old rope, an old cord."

"Well, there is a piece of rope that we are trying to explain here, Mr. Anderson."

"Yes, I know there's a piece of rope involved in this case."


Everything Anderson had said when Bement questioned him, Hatch had proven otherwise with witnesses. Hatch explained how Anderson made copies of a letter with the Illinois State Emblem and Governor Jim Thompson's signature at the bottom, then put what he wanted in the middle. Anderson was pretty slick on that, but Hatch caught it. Hatch's next question went back to 1988, again meaning that there was something he wanted the jury to notice.

293

"Back in August of 1988, did you see a news program about a murder in California concerning someone who had been in jail for a time period?" asked the prosecutor.

"Yes, I think so," said Anderson. "It was a TV program about some type of criminal case."

"Did you take some notes?"

"I believe I took some notes on that."

"Is the name on that Martha Delarosia?" asked Hatch, shaking a page from Anderson's diary. "You wrote that down on there and that had to do with a murder?"

"Yes."

"A man who got charged here, this man was arrested for it. He was investigated in the murder and while he was investigated, there was another murder, right?"

"That is correct."

"Kind of like what happened in the Woidtke case. There had been a murder. He was arrested, and while he was in jail, there is another murder," said Hatch.

"Well, Judge, I'm going to object," said Bement. "That is argumentative, and it is not quite the way things happened anyway."

"I will overrule the objection," ruled Judge Flynn.

"That's the same thing that happened in the Woidtke case, isn't it?" Hatch said, demanding a response from the witness.

"I would have to say no on that, considering the number of crimes that occur in this country every year," said the ex-schoolteacher.

294

"Wait a minute!" said Hatch. "In this case, you took notes. This man is arrested, while he was in jail . . . you have on here he was in jail, another woman is murdered, correct?"

"That is correct."

"Audrey Cardenas was killed. Rodney Woidtke was arrested, was in jail. While he was in jail, the Lanmans were murdered, were they not?" outlined the prosecutor.

"Yes, I see your point," said Anderson.

Hatch continued to do things to grate on Anderson's nerves. He wanted the jury to see Anderson's temper when things didn't go his way.

"Now, we heard some testimony about this pipe," said Hatch, rolling the heavy bar taken from Anderson's briefcase, across the table. "Where did this come from?"

"If I'm not mistaken, that came out of the trunk of my car. It is a handle to my car jack."

"Or it is real close to it," replied Hatch, again rolling the pipe on the table.

"It is the one you keep rattling around on the table when you show it to the jury," said Anderson.

"By rattle, you mean this," said Hatch, as he rolled the bar again to show the defendant he wasn't impressed with his whiny complaint.

Hatch pointed out that Anderson's car was a large Oldsmobile, and that the pipe would not be used for that style of jack. Anderson explained that the bar went to a jack for a car they had years prior.

Hatch pulled out a stack of newspaper articles collected from Anderson's home. He separated them into two piles on the table as Anderson watched. He took the first batch and walked to the witness and began reading off the titles of each article where the red arrows pointed: "Woidtke Undergoes Evaluation," "Transient Charged In Killing," "Woidtke Found Unfit To Be Tried On Charges," "Uneasy About Woidtke," "Woidtke Is Indicted," "Defendant's Inability To Stand Trial," "Cardenas Father To Return Home Though Killer Is Still On The Loose."

"Now, did you at any time go to any religious service in memory of Audrey Cardenas?" asked Hatch.

"Yes, I did. There was a funeral service for Audrey Cardenas in June of '88."

"And you signed the register there, didn't you?"

"I don't recall," smiled Anderson.

"Do you remember getting a program?" asked Hatch, removing one from Anderson's diary.

"Yes. These programs were given out to people that attended the church service. This was held in a chapel."

Returning to the table and gathering the remaining pile of papers, Hatch asked, "Now, you testified yesterday that you had no knowledge of any forensic type evidence, correct?"

"I recall saying I don't have any experience with that type of work," grinned Anderson.

"Well, you said the only knowledge you had is what you saw on television."

"I know sometimes I read stuff in magazines, books, or newspapers about some of these things," claimed the defendant, when he saw what the prosecutor was holding.

"You remembered that last night, didn't you?"

"I think after we talked, I got to thinking about it."

"You got back and thought about it all night, didn't you?" said Hatch, now grinning at Anderson.

"Well, after dinner, I got to thinking and I read over some police reports about this."

"Well," said Hatch, "let's look at People's Exhibit 602 group. Can you tell me what the heading is on that?"

"Illinois State Police Crime Laboratory," replied Anderson.

"In fact, you had a folder with articles on the State crime laboratory, didn't you?"

"Yes. It seemed of interest at the time."

Hatch tossed the exhibits on the table as he read the titles: "New Forensic Laboratory Opens Doors For Business," "Crime Laboratory To Open In Fairview Heights," "Laser Helps New Laboratory Perform Work For The Police."

"Do you recall the paragraph, 'Although the laser beam could cause blindness if viewed by the naked eye, it would enable law enforcement officials to see worlds of evidence in fingerprints that previously they were unable to get.' Do you remember that?"

"No, I don't," said the witness.

"Do you remember the paragraph," asked Hatch, " '. . . the services include blood identification, chemical analysis, crime scene processing, document examination, fiber impression, fiber identification. . . .' Do you remember reading that?"

"I probably did at the time," said Anderson, looking bored with the attorney.

" 'Crime Laboratory Follows Up On Clues,' "

said Hatch, reading the title and continuing. " 'If criminal blood is left at the crime scene, identification of certain enzyme characteristics can tell police whether it could have come from a particular suspect.' Remember reading that?"

"Only vaguely. It has been so many years back."

Hatch read on, describing the titles of articles saved by the defendant. " 'Alert Technicians Find Culprit At Crime Scene,' 'Fingerprints On Computer Can Solve Old Cases.' When did you save that article?" asked the prosecutor.

"It is dated in 1988," said Anderson.

"What is the date?"

"July 3, 1988," replied Anderson.

# Twenty-four

The last part of Thursday's cross-examination of the defendant resumed after a short break. Hatch again tossed a newspaper article on the witness stand for the accused to see. " 'Suit Alleges Police Harassment,' " quoted Hatch. "That is the suit you filed, right?"

"Let me get closer to it," Anderson said. "Yes."

The jurors were then told about the federal lawsuit Anderson filed in July of 1989 against the Belleville Police Department and the City of Belleville.

"September 12, 1989, fifteen days before the killings of the Lanmans," said Hatch. "Your attorney was ordered withdrawn from that. He asked for a motion to withdraw and it was granted, right?"

"Yes, that was in September of '89," said Anderson.

Hatch stressed the next point during his cross-examination of the witness. He ran his fingers through his hair in aggravation at the evasive answers from Anderson. "That there is People's Exhibit 847. Can you tell us what that is?"

"I can't read it that far away," said Anderson.

Holding the folder closer to the witness, Hatch waited for a moment and stared at him. "Did you take great pains to make sure that you didn't leave fingerprints on them?"

"I don't know if I did or not," snapped Anderson.

Anderson was beginning to display a temper. Hatch's tactics of rapidly changing the line of questioning before Anderson could think anything through was starting to wear on the defendant. Again Hatch struck out of nowhere with a damaging flurry of questions. "Do you recognize that?" asked Hatch, handing Anderson the exhibit.

"It says, 'Identification card for Dale Anderson, FBI,' and I remember what this was. We sometimes have Halloween costume parties with our church and, as I recall, that one year that had been the character I had used at the Halloween party."

The entire spectator's section erupted in laughter, while the judge and jury tried to refrain from any signs of amusement. Hatch lashed back, "You like to impersonate people not only on Halloween, though, didn't you?"

"No," replied Anderson, still looking at the FBI identification, taken from his wall safe.

"How about those?" asked Hatch, handing Anderson other items.

"These are Public Aid business cards, got the name Mr. Vale, Mr. DeLaria on the cards."

"Both of those and this identification were found in your safe. Is there some reason why you would want to keep a Halloween identification card in your safe?"

"Not especially."

"We are going to go ahead and break for the day," said Judge Flynn. "As I indicated to the members of the jury yesterday, we will not be having court tomorrow, so the next day that you are due back in then will be next Monday."

Hatch, after having been away from home for most of the last three weeks, was anxious to return to Belleville and his family. Late Thursday night, he came home and found his wife and kids asleep in their rooms. Opening a can of beer on the couch, he flipped through TV channels to catch a late movie on TV.

Friday morning he showered and loaded suitcases into the car for the trip to North Carolina, where Monica's relatives were holding a family reunion. Although it was a fourteen-hour drive, he was happy to be with his family, away from the pressures that accompany a lengthy trial.

Saturday night, Hatch caught a flight back to Illinois to make preparations for the final leg of the trial. Easter Sunday found him back in Chester.

As for Busch, his caseload meant another holiday spent away from his family. He had worked that weekend, including a murder investigation on Good Friday: a young St. Clair County man had been brutally killed in a garage during a party. The body had been placed in a weighted canvas bag and dumped into a creek in the southeastern corner of the county.

Busch spent two days at the creek conducting search efforts with a group of divers attempting to recover the victim's body from the swift and dangerous waters. After many dives, volunteer divers located the body.

Busch, who only went to church two times a year (Easter and Christmas), kept his promise to attend the Easter Service with his family. Because he'd had little sleep after logging twenty-three hours of overtime, he sat through the hour-long sermon fighting to keep his eyes open.

Early Monday morning, Busch drove to Chester and met with Hatch in the law library.

"Well, Counselor," said Busch, looking at Hatch, "did Anderson kick your ass while I was gone?"

"No," laughed Hatch, "but Dale doesn't like you anymore."

"Stop it, or you'll have me in tears," growled Busch. "I heard Anderson was like Niagara Falls on the stand."

"Yeah, real tears," said Hatch. "I'll probably finish with Dale this morning and call you for rebuttal."

"Is there a motion to exclude witnesses?" said Busch. He wanted to sit in on Anderson's testimony.

"No, you can go in if you want."

Busch summoned the bailiff and asked that a seat be reserved for him to watch Anderson testify when the trial resumed. He sat in a chair next to the extra deputy who was assigned to guard Anderson. From his vantage point from the middle of the room, Busch could watch the jury and the people in the gallery.

Anderson came into the courtroom via the door near the gallery, where he stopped to survey the room. At first he looked hard at the spectators, but then shifted his head toward the side until he saw the inspector. His facial expression changed. He had a look of concern.

*Anderson is still up to his intimidation tactics,* thought Busch, as he returned a cold stare. *Old Anderson better save some of that tough-guy routine for when he gets to the prison. There he'll need it. Even some of the worst prisoners in Menard don't take kindly to a child killer.*

Jurors were seated in their orange chairs, and the bailiff called the court to order. Anderson, having been previously sworn in, retook the stand. Hatch asked, "Back on September 7, 1989, do you recall getting a letter?"

"I don't remember specifically," said Anderson, but then admitted that he probably had received several.

"It is a letter addressed to you: 'Dear Mr. Anderson: Your request for a continuance is granted. The hearing will be convened on Tuesday, December 5, 1989 at 9:30 A.M. No further continuances will be granted.' "

"That is what it says," agreed the witness, referring to the letter from the Civil Service Board.

"And you wanted to explain to the hearing officer about Kroupa, Vale, and DeLaria, didn't you? You were trying to get a lot of evidence on them, weren't you?"

"I was collecting some information."

"I'm not talking about information. I'm talking about evidence. You were trying to collect some evidence against them."

"I guess you could consider some of that evidence."

Hatch pivoted and fired off the next question. "Why did you save that?" he said, holding an article dated May 14, 1989: "Unexplained Deaths Puzzle Miami Authorities."

"I'm not sure why that is in there."

"Didn't you also keep this in a file with Mayotis Dean, and make a notation that this is possibly the same thing that happened to her?"

"I'm checking it," said Anderson, as he read. "This is an article where some people had died and it was considered a homicide case, but there were no signs of trauma or violence to the body."

"Why did you save that?"

"Due to the fact some of the things that Mrs. Dean had told me about the Public Aid Office," said Anderson.

"As a matter of fact, it's shortly after she died, that's when you saved that article."

"Yes. I believe she passed away in April of '89."


Hatch picked up a small slender blackjack from the table and slapped it in the palm of his hand as he walked toward Anderson. "We have seen these blackjacks throughout these briefcases. Why do you keep this one in your safe?"

"Another thing occurred to me when we were talking about these blackjacks," said Anderson, as he watched the prosecutor slip a hand through the leather strap.

"Okay," said Hatch, willing to allow the witness to expound on his thoughts, "go ahead."

"When I was reading off the autopsy report, it said the cause of death was from a pair of scissors. It didn't say anything in there about the victim having been hit with guns or stabbed with knives."

"Hit with a gun," repeated the prosecutor. "Blunt trauma."

"Yeah. Talked about blunt trauma. If you look at those blackjacks closely, if those had hit anyone, there'd have been a lot of blood on them."

"Blood. How do you get blood off things?"

"You would never get the blood off that kind of material," said Anderson with confidence.

"How do you know that?" Hatch shot back.

"Just from past experience."

"What past experience?"

"Just from general knowledge."

Hatch came at Anderson from a different slant, "You talked about that you started thinking about the wounds?"

"Yeah," growled Anderson. "I was reading the autopsy report and it said the cause of death was a pair of scissors, and then when Doctor Nanduri gets up there and says the cause of death would be any number of items: knives, guns, clubs. I thought that was kind of—"

"So," injected Hatch, "you are disputing her expertise?"

"Well, it seemed odd that when she did the autopsy, she didn't know any possible suspect might have guns, clubs, and knives, so she said the cause of death was a pair of scissors. But then when she gets up to testify and she knows that Mr. Hatch has briefcases with guns, blackjacks, and knives, she said yeah, all of those could be the cause of death, too."

"And she is part of the conspiracy, too, here, isn't she, Dale?"

"I'm just saying it wasn't in the autopsy report."

"And you're saying that Busch planted this stuff, Nanduri is lying, all of these people are lying and they are pointing the finger at you?" yelled the prosecutor. "Your own wife testified against you. Is she part of the conspiracy, too?"

"My wife is very upset and angry."

"Last week you were bawling like a baby up here. How come you are not crying about that now?"

"I have cried about as much as I can cry about it."

"We had all of these witnesses come in and testify against you and you are as cool as a cucumber. Why?"

Anderson turned to the jury to explain how witnesses were wrong about him.

"I will show you People's Exhibit 141. Who is that?" asked Hatch, giving Anderson the eight-by-ten photos.

"That is Mrs. Lanman."

"What condition is she in?"

"It looks like it was taken after she died," said Anderson, with no hint of emotion.

"What do you notice in the picture?" asked

Hatch.

"I notice a pair of scissors and some blood."

"Ever seen that picture before?"

"I don't think so."

"Do they repulse you?"

"They look pretty terrible," said the witness, his facial expression never changing.

Hatch continued with the photographs, asking Anderson what each depicted. "I would assume that it is a picture from the autopsy of her."

"Pretty observant, aren't you?" said Hatch. "Have you ever seen wounds like that before?"

"I don't think so."

"You also had a pair of scissors in this one case, too, didn't you?"

"I believe there was a stapler, a pair of scissors, a staple puller, and a bottle of 'whiteout' in the desk in the living room," claimed Anderson.

"So, this is again more stuff that Busch or somebody planted in this case?"

"I don't know if it is all that important, you know, whether Busch was trying to plant it, or just toss it in and bring it down to his office," said Anderson, turning to look at Busch, who was seated nearby. "I don't know if 'plant' would be the right word."

"If someone was going to stab somebody with a scissors," said the prosecutor, laying the murder weapon in front of the witness, "how do you think it would have been done?"

"I wouldn't think scissors would make a very good weapon. They are not really designed like a knife."

Busch had waited most of the morning for Hatch to get to the ID card of the Spanish boy in Anderson's safe. He listened with interest when the topic arose.

"Now," said Hatch, placing the three-by-five inch laminated card on the table portion of the witness stand. "Tell us who this is?"

"This is an ID card on a Jorge Cardenas," said Anderson in a matter-of-fact tone.

"Where did you get that?" inquired the prosecutor.

"I believe this was with some of the information that was turned over to the State's Attorney's Office. It was with some other papers that I gave some information about."

"Where did you get the card?"

"I would need the papers to help answer that," said Anderson.

"Did this guy give it to you?"

"As I said, I probably need the papers to reflect on it."

"What kind of papers are we looking for? What is on the papers?"

"Well, we could ask Al Busch about that," replied Anderson.

"I am asking you about it," said Hatch. "What is on the papers?"

"I would need more information to answer that question."

"You can't tell us one bit of information about where this came from?"

"With Mr. Busch's help, I could do so."

Busch looked at Anderson after that statement. *What the fuck is he talking about?* thought Busch. He had no idea what papers he was referring to. Busch wished he knew how and why Anderson had the ID card. The answer might clear up the issues on Cardenas.

Hatch wanted answers to the question, too. He continued his examination. "Did you get it in '88? Did you get it in '89? Did you find it somewhere or did you take it from somebody?"

Anderson again looked across the courtroom at Busch. Busch's face was cold and hard when he looked back.

"As I said, I would probably need Mr. Busch's help to answer the question," said Anderson.

Hatch dropped the line of questioning, knowing that Anderson would not give in to the question, but noted that it was the only question that Anderson couldn't explain.

Bement, on redirect examination of his client, went over some of the critical things, trying to downplay them. "Well, there has been some indication that you are not happy with your supervisors; that you told some other people that they were involved in the Cardenas murder. Why is that so hard to believe? Tell the jury why that is not the way it happened," said Bement.

"It is silly to think somebody would kill a woman and a little boy over an argument from two or three years ago. It is silly," said Anderson.

"You didn't kill the Lanmans to get back at your supervisors, did you?"

309

"No, I didn't."

"You have also testified that this whole circus that we have been involved with for the last month and since September of '89 has adversely affected not only you, but your family. And what effect has that had?"

"This thing has just torn us apart. I mean, my kid has been teased at school. My wife had to leave her job because I got arrested."

"Dale, if you ever expected to have to defend why you had these in here on a murder charge, would you have done things differently, in regard to storing these items?" asked Bement, tapping on the four briefcases.

"Yeah. I would have probably thrown them all in the trash can."


Anderson left the witness stand, and Hatch called Maurice Vale as a rebuttal witness for the State. The jury listened while Vale testified about Anderson's temper.

Busch took the stand and was asked about his treatment of Anderson during the fifteen hours inside the house. His partner, Dee Heil, was also there with them and verified Busch's statements.

Hatch called Karen Anderson as his next witness. He then established that she had originally told police her dad was home at 3:25 P.M. But, after the police talked to Karen's friend and got back with Karen, she recanted her story. This was very important, because she got home from school about 3:15 P.M. She did her homework on the couch in the living room, and that happened to be against the inside wall of the garage. She heard no sounds coming from the garage. Never heard the garage door open, never heard the car start and leave. As far as she was concerned, he wasn't home.

Anderson had told her on the phone to stick to her story, but after the police told Karen that her friend, who was there, said Anderson pulled up when she was leaving, Karen remembered he wasn't home. When Karen finished testifying, she looked at her father. Her eyes watered as she passed the jury box.

Hatch called Linda Anderson to the stand. Linda, who sat in the gallery while her husband testified, had been shaking her head from side to side during his statements. She seemed determined to set the record straight about what really happened.

"Mrs. Anderson," said Hatch to his last witness, "at any time during your marriage to Dale Anderson did he ever go to a Halloween party dressed as an FBI Agent?"

"No, he didn't," said Linda.

"Have you ever baked a cake or done anything for a gift for Maurice Vale, Robert DeLaria, or Charlotte Kroupa?"

"No, I never did."

"At any time have you sent any Christmas cards to Maurice Vale, Charlotte Kroupa, or Bob DeLaria?"

"No," responded Linda, looking at her husband.

"Now, there has been some talk about some brief-

311

cases," said Hatch. "I draw your attention to the table in the middle of the courtroom, and to the four brown briefcases. Do you recall when those were purchased by your husband?"

"Yes, I do. They were during the time that I worked at the day-care. They were purchased within the last two years."

"Were those briefcases around when your husband worked at the St. Clair County Sheriff's Office?"

"No," said Linda, "because that would have been eleven years ago or more."

"When you were in the house the morning the police came in, at any time did you see any of the officers being abusive, either physically or orally, with anybody in that house?"

"No. They were very professional."

"I am going to draw your attention to People's Exhibit 1047, being a pair of latex gloves. At any time did you use any latex gloves that were in your house for work in regards to treating of children?"

"Never did. I don't have any need for those gloves. We never even used them at the day-care."

"Did you ever use those briefcases?" asked the prosecutor.

"No, sir. I didn't even know the combination. I never even opened them."

Hatch had completed his rebuttal.


Judge Flynn spoke to the jury. "What I am going to do then is go ahead and break for the day. Those of you who are taking notes, would you kindly put them back into the folders, and the bailiff will pick them up."

The judge's voice was firm as he gave instructions to the jury. "I want to reiterate what I have said to you on so many occasions before, and that is that you are not to speak with anyone, including each other, concerning the evidence that you have heard during the course of the trial. As I have indicated, I anticipate that you'll begin your deliberations tomorrow, and I promise that you will have all the time that you might want to discuss the case among yourselves, after it is given to you for deliberations. So we will see you then tomorrow morning by 9:00 A.M. in the jury room."

# Twenty-five

On the morning of April 19, 1990, Hatch shuffled papers on the prosecution table as the jury waited to hear the State's closing argument. Standing in front of the twelve jurors, he made eye contact with each person as he spoke.

"Ladies and gentlemen, it has been awhile since I have talked to you. You have seen a lot of me talking to people up there but as I sat there just a few minutes ago, everything started racing through my mind. Somehow I feel like I have to go through every little thing and try to relive with you what we have heard from this witness stand.

"Why are we here? What is the reason that you people have been sitting in those chairs listening for four weeks, to all this evidence?" He pointed a finger at the defendant. "Because this man right here killed two people. A woman and her child. We don't have to prove why he killed these people. We don't have to do that.

"We have a man sitting here charged with two counts of First-Degree Murder. Why? Let's look at him for a minute. He came up on this witness stand and told you something about his past. He used to work for an insurance company, and it just so happened everytime he went to work for somebody, he moved on within a month or two months. He wanted to be a police officer in the worst way. He applied to the Belleville Police Department. He applied to the Fairview Heights Police Department and the State Police and all of those people turned him down.

"This is no dummy sitting here. This is not a stupid man. This is a very smart man. Graduated from college, made the dean's list. He got good grades. He did a fine job at the Public Aid for a number of years, but this man is also a cold and calculating man. And when he got turned down, he thought he was something better."

Hatch raised his voice as he talked about Anderson's time spent on the witness stand. "He comes up with reasons and you saw him testify, he had an answer. He can explain everything. This is the big innocent man that we are supposed to believe. Did you ever see him scream 'I didn't do it, I didn't do it, I didn't do it!'?" asked Hatch. "No. Very cold, very calculated," stated the prosecutor.

Hatch, hoping to put the final strokes of paint on the portrait of the monster, took the jury back to June of 1988 to show the state's theory of the cunning mind of Dale Anderson:

"On June 9, 1988, Anderson staged a shooting scene hoping to draw the *Belleville News-Democrat* back into an issue with the supervisor. He called the newspaper office several times, but the incident with Carolyn Tuft, on June 7, had convinced the reporter and the newspaper that Anderson's credibility was shaky at best, and they backed away from any dealings with him. Anderson was upset when the newspaper wouldn't listen to him. He returned to the scene he had manufactured and retrieved the spent shell casings and the napkin with the drop of blood and placed those in the briefcase.

"On the tenth of June, Anderson's disruptive activity at work forced the supervisor to place him on home assignment. Anderson used the time to seek revenge against his bosses. He contacted the FBI, and they were told about the corruption at the Public Aid Office, but they didn't believe him. The newspaper would not listen to him. Anderson had to do something. His hatred for Vale, DeLaria, and Kroupa had festered inside him. They were the reason why he had problems.

"Audrey Cardenas disappeared on June 19. Two days before Cardenas's body was discovered, Anderson called the newspapers and told them he had information about the abduction of the intern and gave the two license plate numbers belonging to the trio. When nobody responded, Anderson made a second call and claimed that Audrey was seen at Vale's and Kroupa's. Nothing happened. Cardenas's body was found on June 26. Other Public Aid employees were told by Anderson that the dead girl had visited the trio. With all the clues left to point the blame at the supervisors, Anderson waited. On the eighth of July, the Belleville Police Department took over the investigation. Anderson became angry. He must get the blame for the in-

316

tern's death focused back to the trio, so in July he used his daughter's friend to write the letter that Audrey had been threatened by the supervisors. That should do it. Again, nobody paid any attention to Anderson or the letter.

"In the months that followed, all the attention of the Cardenas murder went to Woidtke. Anderson made statements claiming Woidtke had visited the Public Aid Office, but no connection was made. Anderson decided to kill Kroupa. He wrote the letter that he planned to have her copy. It would happen in December. The letter was dated December 11, 1988. Anderson's legal problems landed him in the county jail and kept him from following through with his plot to kill Kroupa.

"By fall he was running out of time. The Civil Service Board would not grant him another continuance, and Rodney Woidtke would be sentenced toward the end of September. Anderson wrote out the note he planned to have the victim write, and on September 27, 1989, put that deadly plan into effect. He killed at random."

Hatch's voice grew louder as he talked to the jury about Dale Anderson. He accused the pale defendant of being a coward. "When nobody would listen to him, he reacted with violence. Why not kill the supervisors?" shouted Hatch, leaning close to Anderson's face as he spoke. "Because he's not man enough. He picked on people who wouldn't suspect him. Someone he could control, like a woman and a three-year-old boy."

Moving quickly to the briefcase on the table, Hatch pulled the metal bar out and slammed it on the folders. The heavy bar made a loud noise that startled everyone. Hatch continued to hit on the folders as he talked. "He hit them one-two-three times," said the prosecutor, who then threw down the bar and picked up the scissors, stabbing the pile of papers with the black-handled murder weapon. "He poked and he stabbed the scissors, the knife, or something twenty-seven times into the three-year-old baby . . ." demonstrated Hatch, his voice tense with emotion.

If they didn't have the picture by now, they would never see it. Hatch took his seat and waited for Bement to begin the defense's closing argument.

Bement wasted no time in attacking the State's case.

"You may recall that when I talked to you several weeks ago in our opening statements, I told you at that time that you were going to hear a fascinating story. You were going to hear dozens and dozens of witnesses come in to testify. The purpose for that quite simply is that the State, without throwing in the kitchen sink, doesn't have sufficient evidence to find that Dale Anderson murdered Jolaine and Kenneth Lanman," said the defense attorney.

"Why do you think we heard over a day's worth of testimony from neighbors testify about how strange Dale is? Why do they put all of this evidence about what happened at the scene on first and then fill up the next three weeks with red herrings for evidence? So many missing pieces in this case. We are going to see through my argument how that just is not a logical way to show that these murders were committed by Dale Anderson."

Bement argued that the State's witnesses were not exact on their times and that they had serious problems with changing their stories. He spoke of his client's misfortune for being different from most people, and blamed poor investigative skill for Anderson's arrest. "We have a case here where there is absolutely no physical evidence. The Major Case Squad, using their tunnel vision, finding a person they think probably was involved here, excluding all other possibilities. Doesn't that cause you some concern?

"As you sit here," said Bement, "you promised me during the voir dire (to seek the truth), do you remember when we had all of you sitting there and brought you in two at a time, I asked you specifically throughout the State's case and even through this stage, that you wouldn't make up your mind. I am expecting that all of you are keeping your promise as you sit here; that Dale Anderson is an innocent man. I am going to hold you to that promise that, as of this time, he is still innocent.

"We know a lot of other things. We have learned more about Dale Anderson and his life than probably any of us ever want to know. We know that he has been married for sixteen years to Linda. He has two children, thirteen-year-old daughter Karen and a nine-year-old son Paul. He's lived in Belleville his whole life. He is not on trial here to determine whether or not he was a bad employee. He is not on trial for the Audrey Cardenas murder. I think the State's spent more time showing he is involved in that murder than he was involved in this murder. Why did they do that? They can't prove this murder. Mr. Hatch stood here making him out to be a cold, bold-faced liar. He lies about a lot of things. Does that mean he is a murderer?

"Dale was generally mild-mannered. He was not a violent type of guy. And we are asked to believe a story that in September of 1989 he picks, at random, a house. He doesn't even know who lived in the house, knocks on the door, goes in and brutally kills two people to get back at his supervisors, who he hasn't had any contact with in over a year. Does that follow anything you know about Dale's personality or about what you know from your everyday experiences? No, it doesn't," said Bement. "He is a civil servant. He is a clerk. That is what he does. To make the quantum leap into the next plane that he now is a man doing vicious murders doesn't work."

Bement turned his sights toward John Lanman to create some doubt in the jurors' minds. He pointed out inconsistencies in the husband's testimony. "It's not any more proper for me to say Lanman killed his wife and child as it is for you to say Dale Anderson killed them. So I am not going to suggest that," said the defense attorney.

Hatch's face went taut when Bement used that ploy at the end of the closing statement. The prosecutor was angry now. Bement had gone too far. Hatch waited for his turn to answer the defense's allegations. This was Hatch's last chance with the jury. He rose to his feet and walked briskly to the easels located at the front of the courtroom. He placed the bloody photos of the victims on the easels, which brought gasps from the gallery and some of the female jurors' eyes teared.

"It's outrageous to accuse John Lanman of doing this to his wife and child. It is inhuman to say, 'What did you do first, what did you do next?' and expect him to remember after walking into a scene like this," said Hatch with disgust as he moved toward the defendant. Hatch extended his arm toward Anderson and waved his finger only an inch from the accused's face, who was moving his head from side to side. "His attorney is doing the same thing. He is pushing things off on someone else. But you hold him accountable," said Hatch. "Tell him he's guilty of murder, *not once but twice.*"

After the judge gave them instructions, they moved into the jury room to begin deliberations.

The foreman of the jury was a Randolph country resident named Dennis Lively. A forty-year-old heavy machinery operator, he never expected to be sitting on the jury in the most sensational murder trial in county history. But, after dutifully listening to four weeks of testimony, he was determined to do his civic duty.

Lively sat down at the long table and waited for everyone to be seated. The attitude in the room was similar to that of a funeral home. All were serious. Looking down the table at the seven women and four men, he realized that only one of the other men had ever been on a jury before. *What should he do as jury foreman?* wondered Lively. They were looking at him for guidance, and he felt like he was about to burst. Maybe he should say something to get the ball rolling.

"Well, we need to talk about this. It is a very serious matter," he said to the other jurors. "Why don't we just say what's on our mind. We can start here," he pointed to the man beside him, "and just go around the table."

Everyone seemed in agreement, and around the table the discussion traveled. Some jurors had little to say; others were more talkative as their turn came. Suddenly it struck Lively that some sounded as though they were uncertain.

Two women jurors were having problems. They now realized the gravity of the situation and what it would mean to find the defendant guilty. They would be asked to sentence a man to death. It wasn't that they doubted the guilt of the accused, but rather the consequence of finding Anderson guilty.

*No one except God could look in his heart and know this was not just an emotional decision,* thought Lively as he pondered the issue. He was a very logical person and did have compassion for criminals and other human beings. He was not sure if at some future point Anderson was executed, whether he would feel some degree of guilt, but the thought didn't bother him now.

Lively had no legal background, but he had listed in his mind ten points that were relative to the case and were the basis of his decision:

*(1) Alibi.* Anderson's alibi about being in the ga-

rage was shaky at best. Why would you pull your car in the garage to clean the garage? He had no support for this. Even his own daughter said she could not hear him in there, and she was right next to the garage. No support for his trip downtown checking tire dealers.

*(2) Motive.* There was absolutely no doubt about this one. The trio was hated by Anderson. In his mind they had ruined his life. The facts are documented and proven. The death letter at the scene tied Anderson to the motive.

*(3) Physical Evidence.* Three people positively ID'd the car and tag number half a block from Lanman's house. Janice Conder identified Anderson. Six people observed the car coming and going, 2:45 P.M. to 4:45 P.M. Anderson's experience with the Sheriff's Department and his files on forensic science showed why there wasn't more physical evidence. He had thirty-six hours to clean up.

*(4) Emotional State of Defendant.* Was he capable of doing this hideous crime? Yes. He seemed very calculating. He had looked at the pictures of Jolaine from the crime scene with the scissors still in her neck and other pictures without any emotion. Anderson had a problem. He had tunnel vision. All he could see was the trio and that he had to get them. He probably hadn't thrown away or destroyed more of the circumstantial evidence because he thought he was so slick and covered up so well that he wouldn't even be a suspect.

*(5) MO (Modus Operandi, method of operation).* Two women who were selling their house nailed him on this one. Jill Hindrichs described Anderson but

could not positively ID him. She also saw him walk a block back to his blue car. Cheryl Scott did positively ID him. She could very well have been a victim herself. She also observed him walking back a block or so to his car.

*(6) Circumstantial Evidence.* This could be a tough one if it were not for the overwhelming amount. The briefcases. Linda swore that they were less than two years old. Anderson had claimed he hadn't even been in them for years, but they contained very recent files and notes.

*(7) Physical State of the Defendant.* Was Anderson strong enough to overpower Jolaine and drag her around by the rope around her neck? Yes. The guy was big enough at that time and in perfect health.

*(8) Weapons.* These were very definitely in his possession at the time of his arrest. The blackjacks, knives, and the steel bar, and he had thirty-six hours to clean up.

*(9) The Victims.* He went in, scoped-out the place and who was there . . . a defenseless young woman(120-130 pounds) and a young boy sleeping. It was easy to catch her off guard. There was no connection between him and the victims.

*(10) Support From Family, Friends, Coworkers.* His own wife and daughter were scared to death of him and were friendly witnesses for the prosecution. Where were Anderson's character witnesses? The prosecution had over sixty different witnesses testifying what a lazy, manipulative, angry, lying, secretive, calculating, and insensitive individual this was, who always wanted to be a policeman.

* * *

Lively asked for a vote around the table. Each juror had to declare what choice they made by saying it out loud. The foreman listened in silence.

# Twenty-six

While the jury deliberated, Hatch busied himself preparing for the death penalty phase of the trial. Seated in the law library in the courthouse, he flipped through his notes and waited for the jurors to reach a decision.

Hatch was optimistic that Anderson would be found guilty, however past experience had taught him to guard against too much rose-colored enthusiasm when dealing with the viewpoints of twelve different people. He had seen it happen before. All it would take is for one of those twelve to vote not guilty. What seemed like a sure thing could be lost.

It was quiet in the library. Hatch's thoughts drifted momentarily back to his early childhood, and he remembered the first time his father had taken him to his father's law office. He would sit in his father's high-back office chair and spin around, stopping only to play with pens on the desk.

Hatch's attention was drawn back to the task at hand when the bailiff entered the room and told him that the jury was returning. They had deliberated for only two hours. Hatch closed his briefcase and walked back to the courtroom. The jury was already seated and the news reporters and spectators had packed in to hear the verdict.

Judge Flynn asked, "Will the foreperson please rise?"

Lively stood up, facing the judge. He held the folded paper that contained Anderson's fate in his hand.

"Sir, has the jury reached a verdict?" asked the judge.

"Yes," said Lively.

"Would you please hand it to the bailiff and you can have your seat."

Anderson watched as the paper was passed to Judge Flynn. He seemed sure of himself as he sat at the defense table. It appeared he was confident that he would be victorious.

Judge Flynn opened the paper and read aloud to the court. "We, the jury, find the defendant, Dale Anderson, guilty of First-Degree Murder of Jolaine Lanman. We, the jury, find the defendant, Dale Anderson, guilty of First-Degree Murder of Kenneth Lanman. Signed by the foreperson and the other members of the jury."

Anderson swallowed hard, looked down at the floor briefly, and showed no emotion. Linda Anderson squeezed her pastor's hand, who was seated beside her in the gallery.

Judge Flynn asked, "Does the defendant wish to have the jury polled?"

"Yes," replied Bement.

"Starting, if I might, with you," said the judge to

the jurist nearest to him, "and going down the row, my question to each of you is going to be the same. And that is are the verdicts that I just read your individual decision here in this case and, if it is, I want you to answer, 'Yes.' If it is not, please answer, 'No.'"

Anderson stared at each juror as they answered "Yes." Many of the female jurors would not look at the defendant. When Lively's turn came to respond, he looked directly at Anderson and gave his answer. He wanted Anderson to know that he was not intimidated by him.

"Let the record show that the Court has polled the jury, and each and every member of the jury has indicated that the verdict as read constitutes their judgment in the case," said Judge Flynn. "I am sure that you're all aware of the fact that we will be proceeding now into what I referred to originally as 'Stage Two,' and I intend to start that hearing at 9:00 A.M. tomorrow morning. Let the record show that the defendant is remanded to the custody of the Sheriff. Court adjourned."


Linda Anderson walked out into the hallway when the courtroom emptied. Jolaine's mother greeted her, and told Linda that there were no ill-feelings toward her for what her husband had done to the woman's daughter and grandson. Linda's eyes teared as they talked.

Hatch was swarmed by reporters and gave a brief statement. "I'm obviously pleased with the verdict. I think, based on the length of the deliberations, the jury listened to all the evidence and came to the proper conclusion," said the prosecutor as he headed for the stairs to leave.

Reporters, like pigeons, then flocked to Bement to gather any crumb of information. "This isn't over," stated the defense attorney. "There was such a large number of items brought in, an overwhelming show. It was tough to overcome that. I think the jury was overwhelmed by the number of witnesses who bashed Dale Anderson."

Busch had not been present for the festive occasion of hearing the jury find Anderson guilty. It was an event that he would have enjoyed, however he had been scheduled to be in court in St. Clair County that day. Where he had spent the better part of two days on the witness stand testifying in another case.

It wasn't until Busch returned home and caught the evening news that he learned that Anderson had been found guilty of the Lanman murders.

The following morning, Lively, along with the other eleven jurors, was present for the death penalty phase of the trial. Lively had had a rough night and hadn't slept well. The thought of deciding if a man should be executed weighed heavily on his mind. He kept thinking of Kenneth Lanman and how the child's life was cut short in such a brutal way.

Bement had put on a witness, a psychiatrist, who

practiced in a particular specialty. She had seen Anderson periodically since the summer of 1988, and had diagnosed him as being depressed, psychotic, manipulative, and paranoid.

After hearing her testify, Lively thought, *you don't have to be a doctor to figure that out.* Lively could see where Bement was going with this witness. He was using her to cast doubt on Anderson's sanity.

Hatch did an excellent job with his cross-examination of the psychiatrist. He pulled up a chair in front of her and put on a dramatic show of how someone could fake symptoms of mental disorders. Hatch brought out the little trick Anderson could do with a copier, producing the letters with letterheads from the Governor's office and the State Police. Then he showed the doctor what Anderson had done with her letters that she had sent him for CAT scans. Instead of receiving the negative result that the hospital had sent him . . . all of a sudden Anderson had letters stating that he had a mass in his head and lesions from a severe blow to the head that he allegedly received during the scuffle in Vale's office. That's how Anderson got one hundred percent disability. Anderson may have some problems, but he's not crazy. He continued to manipulate people to get what he wanted; he did that with the psychiatrist and everybody else.

Bement put Anderson's two children back on the

stand to remind everyone that if they voted for the death penalty, they would be executing the children's father. Bement brought Linda Anderson back on. She admitted that Anderson had provided for them. The amazing thing was that none of them had pleaded for mercy. His own family had no compassion for him. After Linda had finished testifying, Hatch had begun his closing argument and reminded the jurors about their duty, and being able to vote for the death penalty.

"In a proper case, can you sentence someone to death?" asked Hatch. "You are going to make a decision that is going to affect you in some ways for the rest of your life. It's going to affect that man for the rest of his life, and society for the rest of their lives, and the question is, 'Is this a proper case?' "

Lively and the others listened as the prosecutor touched on the meaning of the terms given in the instructions; aggravating circumstances of why a person should receive the death penalty.

"What are the aggravation factors that we have?" said Hatch, as he held up two fingers for the jurors to see. "He's killed two people. He has killed a person under twelve in a brutal and wanton way, and in a cold, calculated scheme. Premeditated. Going through Anderson's mind was someone he could get access to. Cheryl Scott, Jill Hindrichs, Jolaine and Kenneth Lanman."

The jury was warned by the prosecutor not to fall victim to the defense's argument that Dale Anderson was suffering from a mental illness and lacked any prior criminal record. He reflected on the seriousness of the case.

331

"This is our system that has to tell this man that what he did was the worst thing that you can do to anybody, and that is to kill somebody for no reason. Cold and premeditated!" shouted Hatch. "Not just once but twice, he took out his vengeance with a human life. Some of us could understand the brutality to Jolaine, but to Kenneth? That's the one that just grabs at you and you say, 'Why kill him?'

"Was he stomping on him? Did he have his knee on there and beat him? Then to turn him over and just stab him time and time again," said the prosecutor, as he neared the defense table where Anderson sat.

Hatch tapped on the defense table with his finger and then pointed at Anderson. "Tell this man that 'For what you did, you deserve to die. You don't respect life, anybody's life except your own,' " Hatch said. "He has no respect for anybody. He has manipulated his family, the Court, and everyone he has had contact with. He is a liar and he is a brutal, cold-blooded murderer. He does not deserve to live."


Bement knew that he would have to do something to sway at least one juror to save his client's life. *Just one, that's all it would take.* The State had put on a strong case and had left no stone unturned. Bement hoped to stir up some compassion in the jury.

"The last couple nights, I've tried to decide what am I going to say to you. I know that, at least in some part, it is on my shoulders whether someone is going to live or die. I have a real problem with that.

What is this whole society, death penalty about? I have to bear the burden. Is it my responsibility? In some part obviously it is.

"I don't envy you in any way that you have to make this decision. You have to do some serious soul searching here about what you want to do. The death penalty was designed to be a deterrent for other people to commit murder, but don't be fooled that this is a deterrent. The reason we have death penalty is to get even. Now, is getting even by killing somebody else, is that what our society should be doing? It is not a deterrent. We have just mad dog killers who do it because they love to do it and are certainly not going to deter them. And we have people who have some mental disorder and can't rationalize and reason the same way that you and I can. It is not going to deter that person either. The death penalty did not deter the murder of Jolaine and Kenneth Lanman.

"We know that before this incident that you found him guilty on, that Dale had not been a criminal. He didn't have any violence in the past. He had been a family man and treated his family decently. Until the last couple years, he had been a good worker, and he had been a regular person, like you, like your next-door neighbor, then something unfortunately did happen.

"If you find that Dale suffers from some mental or emotional disorder, that it impairs his ability to reason, to make decisions, that is another thing you can take into consideration. You heard the doctor testify about the way that Dale has a mental disorder; he's manipulative, psychotic, obsessive compulsive, and paranoid. Now, because of whatever is the matter with Dale, can you throw everything away and say his life needs to come to an end?

"When you go back in the jury room, think about what you are doing. You see, you have to unanimously agree that he should be given the death penalty. But only if one of you believes he should not, stand by your guns because if you can't agree, then he cannot be given the death penalty. Don't let this happen," said Bement.

The jury received the final instructions as to the elements of law on the death penalty from Judge Flynn.

"Under the law, the defendant shall be sentenced to death if you unanimously find that there are no mitigating factors sufficient to preclude imposition of a death sentence. If you are unable to find unanimously that there are mitigating factors sufficient to preclude imposition of the death sentence, the Court will impose a sentence of natural life imprisonment and no person serving a sentence of natural life imprisonment can be paroled or released, except for an order by the Governor for executive clemency.

"When you retire to the jury room, your foreperson will preside during your deliberation on your verdict. Your verdict should be in writing and signed by all of you including your foreperson. You may now retire to the jury room and begin your deliberation."

* * *

Back in the small room with the frosted windows, Lively faced the same eleven people with whom he had already spent four weeks. This would be the last time they would be together. He had come to know a little about each of his fellow jurors. Going into this deliberation, Lively figured that the one woman who had difficulty deciding Anderson's guilt during the first deliberation would cause a delay in the death phase. He was surprised that she voted in favor of the death penalty when it came her turn to vote. Two other women held out. The vote was 10-2. After a half hour passed, and they discussed almost every conceivable reason why Anderson should die, one of the two jurors that were holding out relinquished and voted with the others. One still opposed it.

As foreman, Lively tried to see where she stood on the vote and what issue she was having problems with. She seemed predisposed against the death penalty. A male juror, irritated with her attitude, asked her, "If Anderson butchered them in the courtroom in front of you, could you give him the death penalty?"

"I don't know," she said.

Lively stopped the heated argument between them and called for a vote. Again it was 11-1 in favor of executing Anderson. She was firm in her beliefs. Lively held a verdict sheet out to her, and asked if she could sign it knowing that it would mean that Anderson would not be executed. To the foreman's surprise, the woman grabbed the paper from his hand and scrawled her signature across the bottom. That was it. It was over. It had taken two and one half hours to finish.

With the jury seated, the bailiff called the court to order, and an uneasy quiet fell over the room.

"Will the foreman please rise," said Judge Flynn. "Sir, has the jury reached a verdict?"

Lively felt sick to his stomach as he rose to answer the judge. "I guess you could say that, Your Honor."

The verdict was read by the judge: "We, the jury, do not unanimously find that there are no mitigating factors sufficient to preclude the death sentence. The Court shall not sentence the defendant Dale Anderson to death. Signed by the foreperson and the other remaining members of the jury."

Anderson turned toward the prosecutor and smiled. Reporters crowded around the defense table to get Anderson's response to the verdict.

"There was a lot of evidence to show I was not guilty of this crime. I'm terribly upset that the jury has found me guilty. This basically has destroyed my life and my family's lives," said Anderson as he was led out of the court by deputies.

The swarming reporters and cameramen followed Anderson to the prisoner van outside to catch a final statement while he was being placed in additional shackles for transportation.

"I really don't think justice was done. I didn't kill Mrs. Lanman and her child," said Anderson. "I could look her husband in the eye and tell him I didn't kill them."

Reporters waited in the hallway to interview jurors. They got an array of statements from the people that sat in judgment:

"This trial will haunt me, and the decision that was made will too."

"Anderson was a genius. It wouldn't surprise me if he'd wiggle his way out somewhere. I think the murders were planned. It wasn't something where he suddenly lost his mind."

"This man is not insane. He's calculating and knew exactly what he was doing."

The newshawks swooped down on the jury foreman to get the identity of the lone juror who spared Anderson's life. Lively would not give her name. Although he didn't agree with her, he respected her for her courage. She had not compromised her position and stood alone for her beliefs. How lonely and embarrassed she must feel.

Reporters pressed him for a statement about what happened during the deliberation. It was obvious from their questions that the reporters had heard from other jurors, some of whom were not happy with the woman.

"She was very adamant," said Lively. "We sat there over two hours. We could've sat there for hours, but it wouldn't have done any good. She wouldn't budge.

"I'm very disappointed. Anderson is a cold-blooded, calculating killer. He had mental problems but not to the point he didn't know what he was doing. He knew."

Lively wanted to talk to the prosecutor. He looked around the crowded hallway and saw Hatch standing by the brass drinking fountain. He walked over and shook his hand.

"I'm sorry we let you down," said Lively.

"It's alright," said Hatch, shaking hands. "He still got life, and I know that's not your fault."

Lively felt good after he talked to Hatch. It seemed to take away some of the guilt about not getting the death penalty. As the two men talked, reporters converged on the prosecutor to get his reaction to the verdict.

"What Dale probably thinks is, 'I beat the system a little bit,' " said Hatch. "That's my biggest disappointment."

Then grinning at the reporters, Hatch said, "But he's going to be in for the rest of his life, and he knows why he's in prison for the rest of his life."